THE CUT

ALSO BY WIL MARA

The Draft

Wave

THE CUT

Wil Mara

Thomas Dunne Books
St. Martin's Press ≋ New York

This is a work of fiction. All of the characters, organizations, and events portrayed in this novel are either products of the author's imagination or are used fictitiously.

THOMAS DUNNE BOOKS.
An imprint of St. Martin's Press.

THE CUT. Copyright © 2007 by Wil Mara. All rights reserved. Printed in the United States of America. No part of this book may be used or reproduced in any manner whatsoever without written permission except in the case of brief quotations embodied in critical articles or reviews. For information, address St. Martin's Press, 175 Fifth Avenue, New York, N.Y. 10010.

www.thomasdunnebooks.com
www.stmartins.com

Library of Congress Cataloging-in-Publication Data

Mara, Wil.
    The cut / Wil Mara. —1st ed.
        p. cm.
    ISBN-13: 978-0-312-35930-0
    ISBN-10: 0-312-35930-6
    1. Football stories.   I. Title.
PS3613.A725C88   2007
813'54—dc22   2007023710

First Edition: October 2007

10   9   8   7   6   5   4   3   2   1

For Tracey

ACKNOWLEDGMENTS

The Cut would not exist if not for the overwhelming time, talents, energy, and generosity of so many people. First, my beloved wife and three children, who motivate me to reach ever higher. Then my editor, Pete Wolverton, and my agent, Tony Seidl, who are football fanatics in their own right. Kudos also to Katie Gilligan, Pete's assistant; a tireless worker and a wonderful person.

The number of friends who patiently answered countless questions, reviewed portions of the text, or helped in other vital ways is staggering. I don't even know where to begin, so I'll just list them alphabetically—Zennie Abraham, Ernie Accorsi, Walter Anaruk, Walter "Butch" Bartlett, Gil Brandt, Mo Carthon, Bill Chachkes, John Clayton (the best there is), Craig Ellenport, Chris Florie, Leslie Hammond (my gratitude is boundless), Jon Harris, Matt Israel, David Kaye, Pat Kirwan, Marv Levy, Milt Love, Warren Murphy, Bill

Parcells, Bill Polian, Keyshawn Johnson, Chris Redmond, Tim Ryan, Brian Taylor, Frank Winters, Lisa Zimmerman, and Mark Zimmerman.

I would also like to thank the good media folks who helped promote *The Draft* and generally get the word out about this series. I am grateful to all of you.

And finally, a heartfelt sentiment for Peter Snell, who was always supportive of me and my writing. He passed away, suddenly and tragically, just a few weeks before the '07 draft. He was one of the most beautiful souls I have ever known. I miss you, old friend.

AUTHOR'S NOTE

This story exists in a kind of "alternate universe." It is a blend of fact and fiction, and the choice of where one element meets another has been made erratically. You may note, for example, that the great bulk of the plot unfolds on the grounds of the State University of New York in Albany. This is, in truth, where the New York Giants hold their annual training camp (unless they change the location before the book hits the shelves, and if that happens, we can't do anything about it). On the other hand, you'll also see that the New York Jets are said to have reached the last AFC Championship Game but lost to the Cincinnati Bengals. While this, too, might reflect reality at some point, it never happened at the time stated in the text. I simply made it up to serve the needs of the story.

Above all else, this is a work of fiction. It is best to take it from that angle before moving forward. There is some factuality, yes, but this isn't an almanac. Read it for the purpose for which it was intended—enjoyment. Football is, in my view, the greatest of all modern sports. If you're a fan, you should be able to draw great pleasure from this novel and those to follow. But if you're the type who nitpicks over every tiny detail, then I suggest you put the book down and go check the towels hanging on the bathroom rack because one of them might be crooked.

THE CUT

Barry Sturtz finally ran out of patience.

"T. J.'s numbers for the last two years have been *incredible,*" he said for the third time. "No one here can debate that. Last year alone—eighty-seven receptions for eleven hundred and forty-four yards and thirteen touchdowns. The best stats for any tight end in the *whole damn league!*" He pounded his fist on the burnished mahogany table to underscore the last three words.

"No one's denying his value, Barry," Palmer responded. "We all know he's one of the best at his position." Thirty-six-year-old Chet Palmer had been the Giants' general manager for the last three seasons. With his thinning hair, dark suit, and tortoiseshell glasses, he looked more like a corporate accountant.

"No, Chet," Sturtz corrected, almost out of breath, "he *is* the best at his position."

"Okay, okay," Palmer said, hands up defensively. He didn't have much of a stomach for confrontation. "But we have a contract already, and we expect him to honor it. He's got one year left. After that, we'll be happy to discuss a renegotiation." The third man in the conference room remained silent, as he had throughout most of the meeting.

Sturtz shook his head. "No, we're discussing it now. T. J. has put up the best stats of any tight end in the league for the last two seasons, and what has he been getting for it? *League minimum*—this year he'll make less than five hundred grand. Dinkins, meanwhile, will get two point seven million from the Cardinals, Schaefer will get two point one from Denver, and Barone will get one point eight in Miami. T. J. is performing better than *all of them.*"

"Barry," Palmer said calmly, as if his greatest concern during this exercise in organizational thievery was to remain civil, "we took him in the sixth round. We gave him sixth-round money and a sixth-round contract. He didn't have to take it, but he d—"

"*He's being ripped off!*" Sturtz screamed. An icy silence followed, during which the ticking of the wall clock became noticeably louder. Palmer seemed a little nervous now, whereas head coach Alan Gray continued to appear unaffected.

Of course Brookman was being ripped off. They both knew that. The whole team knew it. The team, the league, the sportswriters, the fans—anyone who knew the first thing about the business of professional football knew that T. J. Brookman was being grossly underpaid for his services. He was the best new tight end the game had seen in ages—amazing considering he was a nobody from a nowhere school out west. His statistics had been damn good there, but then most of his opponents had been a joke, barely a notch above high school talent. He did well at the combines, too, but he was still written off. That was what most scouts did to anyone who wasn't playing at the top schools in the top systems. In spite of decades of evidence to the contrary, the pros still turned their noses up at anyone who wasn't considered elite. When T. J. started shining in New York—beginning the second half of his rookie season when the starter went down with a broken leg—Gray was quick to take credit for the "find." "I knew he had something to offer," he told the media after Brookman's third game—eighty-eight yards, two touchdowns, and eleven key blocks against the Redskins. The fact that Gray had to be talked into drafting T. J. by the scout who had *actually* discovered him seemed to have slipped his mind.

Sturtz laid his hands flat on the table and leaned forward. "We're not asking for top money, even though T. J. is the league's top tight end. We're asking for an average of the three top salaries. That's more than reasonable. T. J.'s younger than those guys, so he'll be productive for a long time. He signed for nothing, he's played his heart out, he's lived for this team day and night. He deserves this, and you damn well know it."

Palmer said, "I'm sorry, Barry, we just can't do it. Not at this time."

Sturtz shot into an upright position, shaking his head and looking out the window at a perfect summer afternoon. He'd rather be anywhere else in the world than in here with these two bastards.

"Okay, then," he said, "I'm going to have to insist that he sit out until we get something done."

"Sit out? You mean a holdout?"

The shock in Palmer's voice was pleasing. "That's right."

"Camp is right around the corner. Be reasonable."

"I'm trying to be," Sturtz said quickly. "But I see no other way. I'm doing this with a clear conscience, believe me."

This wasn't completely true—Sturtz hated contract holdouts. While they did create leverage for a player, they usually accomplished little else, and the long-term damage was always considerable. Bruised egos, hurt feelings, seeds of mistrust, not to mention the time that the player missed practicing and learning the team's system. Also, the agent's reputation took a hit, as other teams would be wary of him—and his clients—in the future.

"Barry . . ."

"You've left me with no other option. You've backed me into a corner."

Alan Gray smiled as he ran a hand over his hair. It was short and neat, a bit longer than a military cut. It had once been dark brown, almost black. Now it was evolving into a pewtery silver. The face wasn't exactly handsome, but the features were strong and fully realized. His eyes were particularly striking, small and watchful, and they seemed to burn with a kind of sinister intensity.

"No," Gray said quietly as he spoke for the first time in almost a half hour. "No new contract. I need your kid on the field, in camp and practicing, in less than two weeks."

Sturtz laughed. "I'm sorry, Coach, but I'm afraid I'm going to have to insist that T. J. sit out until he gets a fair deal."

Sturtz was happy that Gray had finally jumped into the mix. He had wanted to address him directly from the start. In his view, this was the man who had the most to lose if T. J. didn't play.

"This team suffers without him," Sturtz went on. "Last season he was the most productive receiver you had." This was an incredible fact, but a fact nonetheless. The Giants' wide receivers had all been spectacular years ago, but they had drifted beyond their prime and were now in the twilight of their careers. Last season had been a comedy of errors—dropped balls, missed routes, easy interceptions. T. J. was the bright spot. The experts were saying he was their future, as well as the future of the tight end position—one that was becoming increasingly important in modern football.

Some even said T. J. Brookman was Alan Gray's only hope of keeping his job.

Gray pursed his lips and began nodding. "Yeah, maybe you're right," he said, rising to his feet. "Maybe we need to get this matter settled, and right quick, too."

"I couldn't agree more."

"As of this moment, consider your boy on the bench."

"Excuse me?"

"If he doesn't practice, he doesn't play," Gray told him. "That's my rule."

Sturtz studied Gray for a moment, then chuckled and tucked his hands into his pockets. "You're bluffing. You can't afford to do this. Your offense will crumble."

"I doubt that. We can always find someone else."

"There's no one else like T. J., and you know it."

"We'll have to alter the system a little bit, but . . ." Gray finished the sentence with a shrug.

"Okay," Sturtz said, a fine layer of perspiration breaking out across his brow, "then release him. Let us get a deal somewhere else."

Gray smiled, and in that smile Sturtz saw that he had already considered this option. The sonofabitch had huddled with Palmer and forged a tag-team strategy long before this meeting.

"Sure, that sounds good," Gray said. "But I doubt you'll find a team that'll give us what we want for him."

"And what would that be?"

"Oh . . . two first-round picks."

"That's absurd. No one in their right mind would . . ."

Sturtz trailed off, his mouth hanging open. *They know this. They know no one would agree to such a deal.* "You can't do this," he said angrily. "You can't. I won't permit it."

"Of course we can," Gray replied in a tone so casual he could've been discussing the weather. "Right, Chet?"

"According to the contract that T. J. signed, we have tremendous latitude in what we can request if we decide to put him on the trading block."

"I can't believe you're doing this," Sturtz said unsteadily. "After everything he's done for this team."

"We'll make him plenty expensive," Gray ploughed on. "Or we can keep him and just sit him. Since we're not paying him much, we can find some other guy. Yes, I believe we've got lots of options here."

Of all the ruthless scumbags Barry Sturtz had dealt with in his life, from the meeting rooms of zillion-dollar sports franchises to the ruthless Bronx neighborhood of his youth, these were the only two who had succeeded in making him feel physically ill.

"You're just trying to create leverage for yourselves," he countered, feeling like a dying animal on its back, flailing at its tormentors. "You know you're ripping him off. Everyone does." He gathered up his things and stuffed them into his shoulder bag. "And I'm still telling him to sit until he gets a new deal."

"Watch out, Barry," Chet Palmer warned. "You have your reputation to think about."

He was right, and Sturtz knew this. But today he just didn't feel like giving a damn. Not with these guys.

"You need T. J. here, playing," Sturtz told them. "Your own butt is on the line if he doesn't. Both of you, in fact."

"Don't bet on it," Gray replied.

"That's just what I'm going to do," Sturtz said as he opened the door and went out.

Alan Gray's office was large but not spacious, not like something on the top floor of a corporate skyscraper. And, like its occupant, it was cold and utilitarian, giving away nothing personal. A huge flat-screen TV hung on one wall with wires running to a DVD/VCR combo. There was a pile of game tapes stacked on a nearby file cabinet, each neatly labeled. A markerboard larger than the TV was attached to another wall, decorated with the X's and O's of some play that was still in development. The handsome walnut furniture had been chosen and delivered at the team's expense. Notably, there were no framed family photos, no indication that the man had a life outside of here. Anyone who bothered to read the bio that had been written up for the team's media guide knew that he had been married to a woman named Lorraine for thirty-three years, and that the couple had two daughters—Eleanor and Marilyn. Independent research by the curious revealed that Eleanor was in her second year of law school and Marilyn was a marketing major at Brown. The only time anyone had seen Lorraine in the flesh was during the first party the team threw after Gray's hiring, but that was only for the rest of the coaching staff and select front-office personnel.

Shortly after returning to his desk, Gray summoned two of his coaches—offensive coordinator Dale Greenwood and tight ends coach Jim O'Leary. He almost didn't need to bother, as word of the meeting with Sturtz spread like flu in a daycare center. In fact, it would be on *SportsCenter* by the following morning, courtesy of a loose-tongued member of the organization that the top brass had yet to identify.

The door was half open, but Greenwood, leading the way, still knocked.

"Come in," Gray said, reviewing some papers. "Take a seat."

Greenwood was a large figure with a round face, steel-rimmed glasses, silver hair with faint traces of its former black, and an easy smile framed by a light rosiness to his pudgy cheeks. Every article of clothing on his body was flawless, from his pressed khaki shorts and team polo shirt to the fresh white socks and out-of-the-box sneakers. Holding the shorts up was a brown leather belt, and attached to it were a cell phone, a pager, and a PDA. He was never without these devices.

O'Leary, who was Greenwood's subordinate as well as Gray's, was a bit more pedestrian. He also wore a collared shirt bearing the Giants' familiar blue-and-red logo in concert with khaki shorts and sneakers. It was not at all unusual to see a great percentage of a club's staff dressed almost identically, as if they all worked in the same fast-food restaurant. He had boyish features, spoke softly, and was notably good-natured as long as the boys under his tutelage were performing well. His neatly cut red hair was barely noticeable under the team cap that he wore every day, which protected his fair Irish skin from the brutal New Jersey sun.

The two men took their seats on the other side of the desk. Gray went on reading for a few seconds, then looked up and, without any transition, said, "You both need to know that I just told Barry Sturtz I was going to sit T. J. Brookman this season."

Dale Greenwood felt something die inside him. "He's the best guy I've got, Alan."

"I'm aware of that," Gray replied, "but Sturtz wants to renegotiate his contract. He wants more money."

Jim O'Leary said, "But T. J. *is* the best tight end in the league right now, Coach. We kind of figured he'd be asking for a new contract anyway."

"I think it's a bad idea for any team to continually give in to this kind of thing," Gray responded. "He signed a contract, and we expect him to stick to it. And if that means we get him cheap, then we get him cheap. We don't need to compromise. Besides, we're already neck-deep in cap problems."

Thanks to Chet Palmer's management blunders, was the unspoken sentiment that lingered between them.

"So what now?" Greenwood asked.

"Get some replacements in here, and fast."

"Replacements? For T. J.? No one plays like T. J."

Gray shrugged and picked up another piece of paper. "Then we'll have to make some changes to our system."

Dale Greenwood knew what this meant—*he* would have to make changes to *his* system. A system he had painstakingly created and nurtured over the many years of his career. A system known for its innovation and originality. Parts of it had been designed with Brookman in mind, based on his unique skills and abilities. It was more than just a collection of plays—it was his masterpiece. Having a guy like T. J. Brookman in your arsenal was a joy for any offensive coordinator, particularly considering the fact that this team refused to spend much on offense. A lucky "find" like Brookman was the only way to put a decent unit together in such a skewed environment.

"I know that'll be a pain," Gray said, "but I'm confident you guys can handle it."

Alan Gray had a defensive pedigree and, much to Greenwood's relief, had never interfered much with the way the offense was managed. As far as the offensive guys were concerned, Dale Greenwood was their head coach. Gray didn't get too involved, as his great love was keeping opponents from putting points on the board. Scoring them was something he left to others. But, as Dale Greenwood had also discovered, Gray was always willing to let the credit for the team's offensive achievements fall into his lap. He had done so in the bright glare of the media many, many times. Greenwood played the good sport and remained tight-lipped on these occasions, but many who knew him suspected his patience was wearing thin.

"There's no chance that Maxwell could fill the role, right?" O'Leary mumbled halfheartedly. Glenn Maxwell was the Giants' other tight end—as well as an occasional receiver, special teamer, and, in a pinch, both lineman and punter. He was serviceable at everything but an expert at nothing.

"No chance," Greenwood said. "He has to stay right where he is. He doesn't possess the kind of skills we need."

"That's what I figured."

"Look," Gray said, "the real bottom line is that we can't just give in to any of the Sturtzes in this business. If we cut this deal, agents for every other guy on the team will be marching in here the next day. It's time to move on. We need to find someone else, and someone cheap."

"Do you have anyone in mind?"

"No, I'll leave that up to you two. Let's get, say, three new guys on the field. Training camp is less than two weeks away. Send them what they need and tell them we're looking forward to having them."

"Sure, okay."

"Does Kenner know about this yet?" Greenwood couldn't help invoking the name of the team's current owner. Mostly he wanted to gauge Gray's reaction.

"I haven't said anything to him, but I'll call him later, although my guess is he'll be too busy with whatever he's got going on in Europe right now."

Dorland Kenner, the team's owner for the last five years, was the son of the previous owner, a billionaire entrepreneur who passed away at the age of ninety-six. Few people in the organization had even met him, but those who had came away with a favorable impression—smart, focused, decent. The problem was, he was so busy with the numerous other business interests he'd inherited after his father's death that he had no choice but to rely on Alan Gray and Chet Palmer to run the team.

"I'd like to maintain my moratorium on press interaction among the coaching staff about this," Gray went on. "No talking to anyone. Not about anything else, and not about this. They'll find out things from other people, but not from us, okay?"

"Yeah."

"Good. All right, get to it."

Everyone stood.

"This really is a big gamble," Greenwood said as he headed for the door.

"I know that," Gray replied, slapping him on the shoulder. "But I'm a gambling man, Dale."

At the same moment that Greenwood and O'Leary were exiting Gray's office, Barry Sturtz was turning onto the New Jersey Turnpike and heading south, away from Giants Stadium in the Meadowlands and toward Newark International Airport. He hated the Northeast, with its miles of traffic jams, oppressive legislation, and ludicrously high prices. When he finally had enough money to buy a home, he packed up and headed south to the Carolinas, where sales were booming and people from the Northeast were migrating en masse. He found a three-story farmhouse and twenty acres of untamed land for less than half the asking price of anything in the Garden State. He dumped another sixty thousand into renovation and ended up with a fully modernized castle.

He attached a Bluetooth headset to his ear and pressed a speed-dial button on his cell phone. It rang twice before Brookman picked up.

"T. J."

"Yo, what's up?"

"How are you?"

"Doing okay, how about yourself?"

"I've been better."

"Oh yeah? How'd it go?"

"Not good."

"No?" The kid sounded surprised. "What happened?"

Sturtz took a deep breath. "They don't want to renegotiate. They're digging in their heels."

"You're kidding."

"No, no kidding. And it gets worse."

"Worse?"

"I tried threatening them with a holdout. You know, like we discussed?"

"Yeah?"

"And they said they'd sit you."

Brookman's response was instantaneous. "*What?* Can they even do that?"

"Yeah, they can," Sturtz replied. "They can sit anyone they want to. They could sit the whole team if they felt like it."

"I can't do that. I'd lose a year of stats, a year of exposure."

"I know."

"And who wants to sit? I want to *play*."

"I figured you would."

"What about the contract? Does anything there help me?"

"Not really. It doesn't specify that you *have* to play, only that you have to make the team. Like I've told you before, since it was your rookie contract and you were a low draft pick, they had a lot of leverage. Unfortunately, your last agent gave in to everything they demanded." Sturtz tried to say this with as much objectivity as possible—he knew T. J.'s last agent, knew the guy was a bit of a lightweight, but he didn't like to say it in so many words. He derived little pleasure from bashing his contemporaries.

"Damn . . . I wish you'd been my agent then," T. J. said. He'd expressed this sentiment several times in the past.

"Yeah, me, too."

"I'm losing money every day."

"I know."

According to the amended 2006 Collective Bargaining Agreement, a team is allowed to fine a player who is voluntarily sitting out of training camp the maximum sum of $14,000 per day. Exact amounts varied per team, and the Giants had thus far made it clear that Brookman would be paying $3,500 per missed day for the first week, and another $3,500 per day would be added in each successive week. Thus, if he still wasn't in camp during the fourth and final week, he would be charged the full $14,000 for each day of absence. Furthermore, the team was allowed to charge him another $14,000, *plus one week's salary,* for each missed preseason game.

"I mean, I can afford it, but . . . it's going to be pretty rough. I hope to hell this works out."

"I know, and they know it, too. It's more leverage for them. That's the whole point of the fines in the first place."

"So what about being traded? Is that possible?"

"I suggested that, and they said they'd do just what I told you they would—make you too expensive. No one would pick you up. They're not going to give you away, T. J. They're going to want a fortune for you—and that's because they *don't* want you going to another club."

"So . . . they don't want me there, but they don't want to let me go?"

"No—they *do* want you there, but they don't want to pay you any more than they are now. That's really what it comes down to."

"That's crap."

"I know."

"These guys . . . oh, man. I can't believe it. I just can't believe they'd do this."

"Tell me about it."

"I've given them everything I have."

"I know. I don't like it, either."

Sturtz heard him exhale deeply, and it made him feel worse than he already did.

"So what do we have to do?" Brookman asked.

Sturtz turned onto southbound Exit 14. "Hang loose for a few days and see what happens. That's the most sensible option right now. Remember that you're one of the best tight ends in the league, maybe *the* best. The position has been changing and evolving, becoming more valuable, so our timing is pretty good. We have that going for us."

Whereas the duties of many positions had remained more or less static over the years, the tight end spot had unquestionably increased in importance, particularly over the last decade. Defenses were faster now, more nimble and, in a word, more brutal. Defensive schemes had also gotten more complex as coordinators became better at figuring out offensive formations and how to get to the quarterbacks. In the modern era of professional football, therefore, defenses were gaining the upper hand. It was no coincidence that many D-side wizards were being elevated to head-coaching positions over their O-side counterparts. Bill Belichick, Marvin Lewis, and Tony Dungy all had defensive pedigrees—and all went on to become successful head coaches. The Age of Defense, it seemed, had arrived.

In order to survive, therefore, the offense had to evolve as well. Quarterbacks had to rely more on running plays and short passes—passes that got the ball to receivers quickly, before the pocket inevitably collapsed and the quarterback found himself under a pile of linebackers. And with the advent of the quick-passing game came the increased value of the previously underused tight end. Because the tight end had to be a big man, he added blocking power. But because he could also catch the ball, he was able to confuse defenders, creating new matchups and one more person to watch out for. Tight ends became Renaissance guys, able to perform multiple tasks and fulfill many roles. They were suddenly moving around in the backfield, replacing fullbacks, and sometimes throwing a pass or two. They drew linebackers and safeties out of their zones, opening routes for primary and secondary receivers. When they were ignored, they provided a safety net for quarterbacks who found their intended receivers unavailable. And due to their size and toughness, they were often assigned the generally unpleasant chore of running routes over the middle—truly the Valley of Darkness in the National Football League. More teams ran double tight end sets; more teams viewed them as not just key blockers but extra receivers. They were getting four or five passes per game, for sixty or seventy yards. Some could run deep routes. A few found themselves scoring eight or ten touchdowns per year. In short, the tight end was becoming an offensive VIP, and his importance would only increase in the years ahead.

"Twenty years ago," Sturtz went on, "we wouldn't even be having this conversation. But now, I know a lot of teams can use you. Gray and Palmer know that, too. All of this might just be a bluff. I think it is, so we'll wait for them to blink."

"Okay," T. J. replied. "Damn. . . ."

"I know, this is bullshit. Let's see what happens. Meanwhile, keep yourself in shape, keep working out. Remember, these guys are animals, but we'll get 'em. Okay?"

For a moment Sturtz thought he'd lost the call. Then Brookman said, "Sure, okay."

"Trust me. Have I let you down yet?"

"No, you haven't. I know it's not your fault. It's just . . . I've given everything to these guys. Everything. I can't believe any of this." He sounded defeated now, tapped out.

"We'll figure something out. Just hang tight. I'm not letting these bastards beat us. They're out of their friggin' minds if they think I'm going to make it easy for them."

"Okay."

"Talk to you later."

Sturtz ended the call and put the earpiece back into his bag, which was sitting open on the passenger seat. As he slowed to a halt at the toll booth, he thought about Gray and Palmer again and muttered a few words that would've been unrepeatable in mixed company.

Jim O'Leary came into Dale Greenwood's office just as Barry Sturtz was boarding his flight back to North Carolina.

"I've got them," he said.

Greenwood, who had been sitting behind his desk working on the offensive itinerary for the first week of camp, looked up. "All right, let's see."

It was a simple sheet of white paper with a list of names. There were eleven in total, but eight had already been scratched out by O'Leary. Greenwood studied the other three for a few moments.

"Oh, sure, I know these guys. Good choices."

"Thanks."

Greenwood kept looking at the list while massaging his chin, then set the paper down and shook his head. "This is crazy, Jimmy. Just sheer lunacy."

O'Leary, who had never been a fan of internal politics—even after he became convinced this was one big reason why he hadn't climbed higher on the coaching ladder—simply shrugged.

Greenwood sighed. "All right. You'll make the calls?"

"Sure," O'Leary said. "I'll take care of it."

"Thanks."

2

Hamilton

Jermaine Hamilton hated golf. He was simply no good at it, could not "get" it. He'd tried hard enough during the past eleven years—bought a nice set of clubs, took lessons, and spent countless hours on the best courses in the Charlotte area. But he never really found his groove. Finally, late last year, he called it quits, shoving the expensive clubs somewhere in his attic and forgetting about them.

Now his agent, Matt Nolan, wanted him to take them back out.

"Come on," Nolan said over the phone earlier in the day, "it's for charity. No one's going to give a damn how good you are. Besides, you'll be with three other guys, and it'll be best ball." Hamilton gave a noncommittal grunt. "How about this?" Nolan went on. "I'll make sure Dilfer is in your group. I think I can arrange that." Aside from being a longtime journeyman quarterback in the league—and one of the few of that species who could claim he started, finished, and won a Super Bowl, which he did with the 2000 Baltimore Ravens—Trent Dilfer was also a superb golfer. He appeared at many charity events, where he usually ended up in the top of the field. "You can whiff at the ball all you want, and no one will notice," Nolan said. "They'll be watching Trent the whole time anyway. Whaddaya say?"

Hamilton said he'd think about it, then asked the question that Nolan knew was coming: "Anything else going on?" And Nolan, following the script the two of them had unintentionally created over the last two years, said, "No—sorry, pal. Nothing today."

That call came shortly after ten. Now, at one thirty, Hamilton was in the basement of his comfortable Georgian home. Built in 1999, it was a two-story brick house with a three-bay garage, hardwood floors, four full bathrooms, a swimming pool, and an extensive irrigation system. Hamilton and his wife got it for a steal at less than half a million from an investment banker who was tangled up in a securities scandal and needed some quick cash for his legal defense. Its value had skyrocketed since, and real estate agents were always calling to see if the present occupants were interested in giving it up.

For the first time since he moved in, Hamilton was thinking about it.

The basement had been finished by the banker. He'd covered the cinder blocks with Sheetrock and the cement floors with wool carpeting. He'd also divided it into four rooms—one large central chamber, two smaller ones, and a half bath. The main room became a kind of narcissistic temple, with plaques and trophies, a framed copy of the first check he ever received for seven figures, a set of clay poker chips bearing his initials in an absurdly ornate script, and an enormous painting of himself that followed the brooding, old-school style of gentlemen's clubs of the early twentieth century.

Hamilton didn't have a fraction of the ego the banker did, so when he recast the room to fit his own preferences, it was for an entirely different reason. He decided to make it a museum of sorts—not for his love of self, but for his love of the game of football, with only a modest nod toward his involvement in it. There were lighted glass cabinets with climate-controlled interiors, and the memorabilia ranged from worthless to priceless—ticket stubs from his earliest high school games, balls and jerseys signed by legends both living and gone. There were framed photos, posters, and letters, and shelves full of books and magazines. Inside a freestanding case was a square foot of aging sod—a small section of the field from Hamilton's best game as a pro. It was against the Saints, when he had twelve receptions for 164 yards and three touchdowns. The soiled cleats and jersey were also there, enveloped forever in the vacuum-packed aura of that magical afternoon. The grass was gnarled and colorless, the soil dry and flaking. Time had robbed it of all moisture. A good breeze would blow it to dust.

There was an unusual display in the southeast corner of the room, the one that many visitors noticed first—a single locker. It was little more than a tall wooden box with a shelf near the top, and another toward the bottom for sitting on. There were hooks on either side for hanging jerseys or street clothes and, under the seat, a small cabinet with a lock.

Hamilton kept it exactly as it had been during his tenure with the Panthers; it still had his nameplate screwed onto the upper shelf—"Hamilton 66." Although he had played for four different teams, his time in Carolina was his most cherished. They were his peak years both personally and professionally, the culmination of all his hopes and dreams from the moment he discovered the game as a toddler. He had never focused on anything else, never cared about anything else. All he wanted to do was play for a pro team, and he shaped his life around that goal so that all effort and energy was devoted to it. And when he reached that fabled land via the second round of the 1997 draft, he knew he was at the threshold of the happiest time of his life.

There was nothing—absolutely nothing—about being in the NFL that he didn't love. The shining moments on the field were givens; even the most indifferent player got a charge out of those. Same with the adoration from the fans and, of course, the big money that went with being a member of the athletic elite. But Jermaine loved the little stuff, too, the minutiae that the average pro overlooked—the quiet moments before a game, sitting alone in the locker room, hands together in prayer. He liked going to the team facility in the off-season and working out by himself, walking through the bowels of the stadium when no one was around, or helping the maintenance guys do little chores most people didn't even know about. He simply had to be *around* it, feel like he was a part of it. It was the only world in which he felt he belonged. Even when his father bought him his first football and warned that sports wasn't the easiest way to make a living, he knew he would do it. There was no scientific formula to it, no solid physical evidence he could hold in his hand. He just knew.

The one negative factor that he refused to acknowledge for

years was that the day would come when he'd have to let it all go. Of course he knew his career would end at some point, but that time seemed so ridiculously distant that it wasn't worth thinking about.

But time has a funny way of creeping up on people who don't pay attention to it, and while Jermaine Hamilton was living the dream, the years zoomed by. It seemed as though he had just signed his second four-year contract with the Panthers when, suddenly, he was being led into his coach's office, politely asked to take a seat, and told that the team was moving forward without him. True, his last two seasons hadn't been as productive as the first four, but he was still putting up good numbers, still contributing. He had plenty of gas left in the tank.

Several other teams thought so, too, and one of them signed him—the Dallas Cowboys. He spent two years there, the first of which was the inevitable I'll-show-'em campaign in which he returned to his earlier glory and earned an Offensive Player of the Year Award. That was at the age of twenty-eight, and he still wasn't feeling the early pull of his thirties. He felt young and fresh, as if he had an open road ahead of him. But the second year in Dallas wasn't anything close to the first, and the end of that season culminated in yet another roster move that left him unemployed.

He landed a one-year deal with the Rams the following March, started fourteen games, then pulled a hamstring. While it was only a minor injury, it gave St. Louis's rookie tight end an opportunity, and the kid made the most of it. With apologies, Hamilton was again shown the door.

He saw limited playing time during his six months with the Chargers—seven games, only two of which he started. He knew they would cut him, and he took it in stride. His injury had healed completely, and his performance during his few on-field appearances wasn't that bad. The bottom line, he felt, was that he was still reliable. He was an excellent blocker, rarely dropped passes, and had a remarkable playbook memory. But he was now fighting not just age but a reputation as a has-been, someone who had hit his peak and was on his way down. In the fiercely competitive National Football League, that was a roadblock few could circumvent. Perception was everything. In spite of Hamilton's efforts to get himself into flawless condition in the off-season, no one called for him the next year. For the first time since 1997, he watched five months of pro football from his living room.

At first he kept his spirits high by continuing his workout program, studying his old playbooks, and telling himself someone would call. Through the miracle of the NFL Sunday Ticket and digital video recorders, he built a library of every game played that year—and watched to see which teams might be able to use his services. Matt Nolan moved closer to sainthood when he fielded every call from his favorite client with characteristic patience and good cheer. *It looks like the Chiefs might need a second guy, Matt, give them a try*, or *Eckersley from the Patriots got hurt, so we should talk to them*. Nolan followed Hamilton's requests faithfully, and he couldn't help but admire the guy's determination.

But no one bit on the hook, and as the season drew to a close, Jermaine Hamilton began a downward spiral into the kind of depression from which many never return. Whereas before he was up every day at five thirty, jogging, now he slept until eight or nine. His carefully planned diet was cast aside in favor of comfort foods, most of which he had barely touched since being drafted—barbecued spare ribs, roast beef hash, lasagna, and piles of chocolate bars. He stopped accepting most visitors and phone calls, didn't shower some days. He was still friendly with fans, but he no longer made formal appearances.

This was when his basement museum was subconsciously promoted from hangout to refuge. From the moment the Super Bowl ended that year, he spent at least half of his waking hours down there—watching game tapes, staring into the glass cases, and thumbing through scrapbooks until the edges were filthy. There was a part of him that realized he was losing mental ground, knew it seemed like he was headed for a sanitarium. A stronger part of him knew this wouldn't happen. He wasn't the type to end up in a straitjacket and a padded cell. He simply couldn't let go of the world he loved, and this was the closest thing to it that was available to him. But it wasn't the same—he *had* to get back out there. That was where salvation was waiting. Once he got back on the field, he told himself, he'd be fine. Friends who were still lucky enough to be on other teams invited him to practices, just to be there. He always declined. Even his old Panthers coach offered to let him hang around. But he couldn't bear to watch without being a part of it.

Eventually his agent began looking for things for him to do, things that were somehow connected to the league without putting him anywhere near the field. That was where Nolan's charity golf tournament idea came from. It was a common kind of activity among retired pros—golf tournaments, broadcasting spots, commercials, product endorsements, collectibles shows—but Hamilton couldn't bring himself to pull the trigger on any of them. It would be a form of acceptance, a confirmation that he acknowledged the end of his playing days. It was the football equivalent of a rock band taking a gig in Vegas—the best days had come and gone, and now it was time to reflect and remember. He just couldn't do that yet.

There was another problem as well.

He sat on the couch in shorts and a crewneck and watched a tape of his third game with the Panthers. It was a 24–21 overtime win against the Cardinals in which he was responsible for a crucial two-point conversion in the closing seconds of regulation. Without it, they would've walked out of Sun Devil Stadium with a 19–21 loss and 1–2 record. It was the first time the team hung all its hopes on his shoulders, and he rose to the occasion. It also supercharged the team's confidence and led them to eight more victories in the following nine contests. They would make the playoffs that year but fall to the 49ers in the second round. Still, what an amazing ride that first season had been.

For the average NFL player, watching a game tape meant seeing a lot more than what was on the screen. Jermaine remembered conversations he'd had with guys in the huddle, jokes on the sideline, and the coach's halftime speech when they were behind. He remembered he ate sushi for lunch that day, then threw it all up shortly before taking the field. He also recalled some quick words of encouragement from a guy on the team he really never got to know that well, a defensive back named Charles Edwards. Edwards, normally quiet and distant from his teammates, clapped him on the shoulders and said, "Relax, rookie, you've been doing good." Although Hamilton exchanged only two or three more sentences with Edwards the rest of that season, he felt deeply saddened when the guy died the following March after his SUV slid off an icy road, sailed silently through the air for about fifty feet, then slammed into an oak tree, snapping his neck and killing him instantly.

Melanie came into the room. She was a small and strikingly beautiful woman of thirty-four, dressed in a tight black skirt that stopped well before the knees and a matching camisole that was stretched almost to the breaking point. A tiny corduroy jacket did little to hide her considerable cleavage, but then it wasn't supposed to. Dark stockings and three-inch heels rounded out the ensemble, plus a Prada handbag and a pair of diamond earrings.

"I'm going," she said simply.

Hamilton turned, took in his wife's formidable appearance, and muted the TV. "Please don't."

"I'm sorry, Jermaine."

Summoning all his strength, he said, "Where will you be?"

"Carly's."

He knew this was a lie—or, at the very least, a half-truth. Maybe she really was going to Carly's, but that would only be the start.

"And then?"

"I don't know. We'll see."

"Any chance you'll be back before I go to sleep?"

"Maybe."

He could do nothing but stare. They both did. His eyes were flooded with pain. Hers were colored more by frustration, anger, and—the part that hurt him the most—indifference.

"Mel, come on. I really don't—"

She put her hand up, a signal for him to stop. "We've had this discussion a thousand times. I'm not going to hang around this house for the rest of my life while you sit down here in this weird place of yours."

He got up. Although he was an enormous individual, there was nothing even remotely threatening in his body language.

"Mel, I'm going through a tough time right now. I need you, I need you to be here. You've got to understand."

"And what about me? You don't take me out, you don't talk to anybody . . . you don't shower!"

"It's not going to be like this forever, I swe—"

"I'm not spending the rest of my life taking care of an overgrown child!"

There it was, out in the open and drifting in between them like a specter. And that was what it'd been for the past year—a specter. A ghost. Something they hoped they were only imagining. But it wasn't imaginary anymore. It was as real as the concrete under the carpeting and the cinder blocks behind the walls. It explained so many other things, too—her sudden devotion to fitness, the renewed contact with some old friends, her new wardrobe. . . .

She *doesn't want me anymore, either.*

His wife took a deep breath. "I'm going. I'll be back later."

She turned and went out before he had a chance to reply. She pounded up the steps, the anger making her sound about five times heavier than she really was. He heard the front door slam shut and her black Jaguar XK convertible roar to life, tires screeching as it tore out of the driveway.

Then all was quiet again.

It was past dark when the phone rang. Hamilton happened to be in the kitchen, the first time he'd been out of the basement since the confrontation. He was making himself a sandwich.

The caller ID displayed Matt Nolan's number. *Not more golf crap.*

"Hey," Nolan said, sounding particularly bubbly.

"Hey."

"What's wrong?"

"Nothing."

Nolan knew it was a lie, but it didn't matter. "Well, I've got something that'll cheer you up."

"Yeah? What's that?" Before his agent answered, he added, "I'm not golfing."

Nolan chuckled. "Golf, gimme a break. No, my friend, you don't have to get out your clubs. That's for *retired* players."

Hamilton stopped spreading the mayonnaise on the torpedo roll. "What are you talking about?"

"You have to get something else out of storage—your pads."

Nolan told him why.

Hamilton thought perhaps he was still downstairs, asleep on the leather couch and dreaming. He wasn't.

His greatest wish in the world had been granted.

3

Reese

Corey Reese high-stepped his way through the agility trainer, turned swiftly, and went through it again. Then he took a breather. He was dressed in black satin shorts and a loose white T-shirt. His Nike sneakers were brand-new and would've retailed for over a hundred bucks if he'd paid for them—but thanks to a sweet endorsement deal made long ago, he'd have as many new pairs as he wanted for the rest of his life.

With his hands on his hips, he took a moment to survey his neighborhood. It was a collection of modern mansions, each spaced far enough apart so that getting to know the "folks next door" required considerable effort. He and his family had lived here for almost five years, and they still didn't know anyone. There were nearly a hundred homes in the development, but only four were visible from his current vantage point. One was owned by a guy who made his fortune on the Internet, although Reese didn't know the details. He had a dozen cars, all vintage. He was also apparently divorced, dated often, and had two young daughters. Reese couldn't tell the daughters from the girlfriends.

He drained the remaining contents of a Gatorade bottle and tossed it aside. Then he jogged in place for a few moments. A breeze whirled up and cooled him off. His own home, about a hundred yards away, was of an imposing size and suitable for a young millionaire, but architecturally uninteresting. It was little more than an enormous cube with a few interchangeable frills, cut from the same template as other houses in the area. But it was still beautiful in its opulence, and it served the needs of his family. It had central air and heating, a swimming pool with a flagstone patio, and a fully automated lighting system. It screamed wealth, which suited him just fine. Nothing was too luxurious for his wife and kids.

He checked his heart rate and blood pressure on the wrist monitor. Good enough—125 over 82. He got back in front of the trainer and made five more runs. When he stopped this time, it was to lean down and adjust the knee brace. He'd tried six different models before opting for the current one. It looked like a prop from *Star Trek,* but it seemed to be doing the job. It had a pivot-point design with an adjustable hinge. As he loosened the straps, he caught sight of the scars again. All the times he'd seen them, not to mention all the violence and brutality he'd seen in his years in the game, yet those deep lines still made him cringe. They would never disappear. And he knew what was behind them, what lay beneath that pliable husk of dark flesh. He'd done his homework on the injury and the surgery required to repair the damage. He knew exactly what was going on within this section of his body, and visualizing it sometimes made him feel light-headed.

It happened two years ago, in the second-to-last game of the season. His Titans were playing at home against the team that replaced them in the Lone Star State, the Houston Texans. It was an important game for Tennessee, as they were in the thick of the wild card race. The Texans, conversely, were in their first year with a new head coach and only managed six wins. But five of those six had been the five they'd just played, so they were on a roll. Knowing the postseason was beyond reach, Houston's coach wanted to see if they could at least go undefeated for the rest of the year. It would provide momentum into the following season, a sure sign they were getting better and had something to be proud of. It would also be a real feather in their cap to defeat a team that was, at least on paper, performing on a higher level. So, playoffs or not, Reese knew his opponents would be primed.

The first two quarters went well enough, with Reese getting the ball six times for forty-six yards and one touchdown. Then came the third quarter. They were ahead by nineteen points, so they switched to a ground game to chew up the clock. He was given a lot of blocking assignments, trying to create outside lanes for halfback Gregory Cope and fullback Jared Lemmon.

With three minutes to go before the fourth, quarterback Reggie Burton pitched out to Lemmon with Cope leading the way. Cope was a decent blocker for his size, but he couldn't punch the required holes by himself. Reese's job on this play was to soften up the line before Cope got there. He executed well, leveling Houston's defensive end and then stepping in front of their outside linebacker.

Reese wasn't sure what happened next until he saw the film later on. Houston's middle LB read the play and came charging in to plug the gap. This was Derrick Elgin, and Reese remembered Elgin screaming, "Left side! Left side!" He was considered the leader of Houston's defense, so the others followed him with the blind obedience of a flock of sparrows. Reese ended up in the middle of the melee, and somewhere in the mess he felt an explosion of heat in his right knee. He was no stranger to pain, but this was something more. He was immediately overcome with shock—not so much physical, but the mental astonishment that such tremendous agony could exist at all. He rattled off a string of expletives, then wormed his way out of the pile and fell again. He would remember the soft ground coming up to meet him—*whump!*—and then all other awareness was eclipsed by the crushing torment that radiated from his jumbled knee. Players on both teams stepped back; whistles blew. Corey thought he heard a collective gasp from the crowd, but that might have only been imagined. Familiar faces appeared— trainers, physicians, and head coach Jerry Wynn. They worked on him for a few minutes while the crowd held its breath. Everyone hoped he would follow the standard heroic script by getting to his feet and, with the aid of two smaller but fully grown men, hobble to the sidelines. That didn't happen. Instead, they lifted him delicately onto a stretcher, then onto the shuttle cart.

Fifty thousand fans erupted in deafening applause as one of their favorite players was driven into the tunnel and out of view.

Reese received the bad news from team physician Arnold Clark after the MRI. Clark was a conservative-looking older man with a wave of silver hair across his brow. He was tallish and thin, and he wore stylish tinted glasses. What Reese liked best about him was that he had a gentler manner than a lot of team docs he'd encountered.

Hovering over Reese in his elevated hospital bed, Clark put a hand on his shoulder and said, "It isn't good, son. I'm not going to give you any false hopes."

"What's wrong?" His voice was weak, like that of a small boy. "Isn't it just a bad sprain?"

"No, I'm afraid it's more than that." Clark smiled. Then he sat down on the knitted sheet, which reeked so strongly of disinfectant it was almost nauseating, and issued the grim news. The knee had been extensively damaged—medial and lateral menisci, anterior and posterior cruciates, fibular collateral, and the transverse. The cruciates were torn, and there was further damage to the cartilage and patellar surface of the femur. A few bone chips were also floating around. Reese didn't understand everything Clark was saying, but he had no trouble grasping this much—he was done playing football for a while.

Maybe forever.

"When, Doc?" Reese asked, fighting back tears. He knew Clark wouldn't mind if he cried; he was that kind of a guy. But years of conditioning in one of the last bastions of pure masculinity made it all but impossible. "When can I get back out there?"

"It's going to take some time. Time, hard work"—the doctor looked squarely at his patient—"and a bit of luck, too."

A chill settled over Reese's body like a breeze carrying a light snow. "But I *will* be back, right?"

"We'll see. Just be thankful it wasn't worse. I've seen players end up with crutches, canes, or wheelchairs for the rest of their lives.

There's very little chance of that happening here. With the right kind of care, you'll be able to walk again with no problem."

"But not play?" A tear finally streaked down his face.

Clark paused, then patted Reese's hand. "We'll see," he said again.

Jerry Wynn came by about an hour later. Corey sat up when he saw him and even managed a brave smile.

"Hey, Coach."

Wynn was one of the older head coaches in the league, so much so that his retirement was a point of constant speculation. He was one of the few members of the "old guard" who had managed to survive and adjust to the free-agency era. He had a certain gentleman's charm about him, the kind of guy players didn't resent even when he was yelling at them. Although he'd never said so in public, he was all about the *game*—and nothing else. He considered the peripheral stuff a necessary evil, but he paid it no more mind than was required.

"How are you?"

"Doing okay."

"Yeah? You sure about that?"

"Well, the doc says I'll have to wait and see. But I think I'll be all right in the long run."

Wynn leaned over and inspected the knee. "Looks . . . rough."

"Feels it, too."

"I'll bet."

Reese waited for the inevitable declarations. *If you don't recover from this, I promise the team will take care of you,* or, *We're all pulling for you,* etc.

Instead, Wynn turned to him, put a hand on his shoulder, and said, "I want you to know two things, Corey."

"What's that?"

"One, I'm very proud of you. You have been an invaluable member of my team, and one of the best tight ends I've ever seen."

A lump formed in Reese's throat. This hadn't happened since his last child was born. He felt foolish and hoped Wynn didn't notice when he swallowed it down. "What's the other?"

In a way that was so direct yet so gentle Corey Reese would never forget it, Hynn said, "There's more to life than this game."

Reese's eyes began to sting. Under no circumstances would he descend to tears in front of this man, but damned if maintaining his composure wasn't becoming a struggle.

"I'm not saying you won't be back," Wynn added, putting his hands up. "I'm not saying that, Corey. The knee is a very tricky thing. I've seen guys come back from knee injuries that were so bad we feared they might not even *walk* again. So I'm not telling you your career is over. I'm just saying. . . ." A fresh smile now. "If it does come to that, don't let it bring you all the way down. Do you understand? What I'm saying is this—don't let football be the full measure of who you are. None of us should do that, okay? There's more to life. *There's more to life than this game.*"

Reese's response was barely audible. "Sure, Coach. Thanks."

Then Wynn was gone, leaving him alone with his thoughts.

Jeanine and the kids came later that night. Corey did his best to appear cheerful, but his wife suspected the worst from the moment she entered the room. They'd known each other since seventh grade, so he couldn't hide much from her. He didn't want the kids to worry, though. They were too young for any of that, he decided— Corey Jr. was only eight, Lizzie five, and Brenda three. He wanted every day of their childhood to be magical, so this would remain a secret for now.

When Corey's mom arrived a half hour later, he had her take the kids down to the coffee shop. Then he told Jeanine everything. They held each other, and they both cried. It was, he would think later, one of the three worst episodes in his life—the death of his father a month before he was drafted, the death of his younger sister from leukemia when they were both teenagers, and this. He'd never felt so weak and helpless.

To his great surprise, it was also a moment of enlightenment. By the time he and Jeanine were in their freshman year of high school, he knew she would always be the love of his life. But he had no idea just how much he had come to depend on her, how much he needed her. Looking back on that day, he shuddered to think what the experience would've been without her. Some women would've bolted. There were so many players whose wives and fiancées and girlfriends seemed to build their affections on the promise of a good income and lavish lifestyle, and the moment trouble arrived they headed for the nearest exit. Jeanine wasn't like that at all. He'd always thought so, but now he had proof. They were facing a crisis, and she didn't step back—in fact, she stepped forward. After that night he knew he could never be apart from her. With her strength and support, he would defy the odds. He would astound Clark and the very laws of medicine. He would be back on that field, diving into the end zone and hotdogging in front of the cameras. He'd be on top again, leading the evolution of the tight end position. He *had* to—for his love of the game, his love of his fans, and his love of winning.

On a more practical level, he knew he'd fall into financial ruin if he didn't.

———————

He grew up in a mostly white, working-class neighborhood in northern California. His parents met on an assembly line and married within a year. They had four children, and although money was always tight, they managed. As one of the few African American kids in his class, he learned how to fit in and forge alliances, and so was rarely hassled for his color. His mother was a sensible sort who taught the values of home and family. His father was a quiet, dignified man who worked hard, mastered his trade, and made sure his children had the things they needed. Theirs was a steady and solid life. Perhaps the Reeses would never hold a seat on the New York Stock Exchange or a membership in a country club, but they would also never live on welfare or end up in a tenement in the middle of an urban war zone.

Once Corey realized he had the potential to play in the National Football League, he began to envision a grander life for all of them. He dared to dream of a life lacking the burdens of financial worry, where there were virtually no limits, no ceilings. He knew a little bit about his family's genealogy—knew, for example, that he and his siblings were the first on either side to attend college. He also knew that, should he puncture the tough membrane of the league, he would be the first in his line to make truly good money. If that happened, he thought, he would share his rewards with all of them. His parents could quit their jobs if they wished (his mother eventually did, but his father refused), and his brother and two sisters could go out and buy whatever the hell they damn well wanted. When he asked Jeanine to marry him, he was still in college. But he was also at the top of every prospective draft list. He told her their kids would never want for anything. She knew he meant it. He had never been egocentric; he loved sharing anything good that came his way. If he made a million dollars and spent most of it on friends and family, he was happy. The love and attention he received in return was all he seemed to require. It was this quality that had made him a favorite with the fans. He gave generously to charities, earned a reputation as a young man with a strong moral foundation, and was at his best when bathing in the glow of public adoration.

He was drafted high in the second round. The Ravens had given up their first-round pick in a trade the previous February. That meant Reese was actually their first pick. Their general manager, Jon Sabino, gave him a very fair three-year contract with a $2.7 million signing bonus, and the moment he got the first installment he went out and bought the house. Then he purchased two more homes—one for his mother and another for his brother, Donny. His sisters had both done well in their own careers and turned down his offer to pay off their mortgages, so he got them new cars instead.

On the field he was superb. Statistically he was among the top line tight ends in the league in his rookie year, his strengths being his quickness and vise-grip hands. He wasn't quite as good as a blocker, but it almost didn't matter—he was a reliable safety net for his quarterbacks. His ability to shake defenders was uncanny. He appeared to have a priceless gift: He could reduce the speed of a play in his mind to the point where he could "see" how it would develop. If it was unfolding properly, he would lure defenders away from the center of the action, weakening their chance of breaking it up. If, on the other hand, something went wrong, he could get open almost at will, giving his quarterback a new passing option.

His personal income grew parallel to his value both on and off the field. He was assailed with everything from endorsement offers to cameos on sitcoms. With this increased wealth came increased spending habits. The last time he'd really paid attention to his bankbook was at the beginning of his third year, when his accountant told him he had amassed a fortune of just over two and a half million dollars *after* taxes and all the gifts he had bestowed on his loved ones. (The accountant himself received a Cartier Pasha Seatimer the day he told Reese he was a bona fide multimillionaire).

He held back nothing from his children—whatever they wanted, they got. He and Jeanine were conscientious enough as parents to see that the three of them didn't morph into typical "rich brats," but Corey also wanted them to grow accustomed to high living and know nothing else. They would never feel the sting of wanting without having, the way he had as a youngster. All their wishes would come true.

At some point, in spite of warnings from the accountant, Reese's finances passed from black to red and headed into the treacherous land of mounting debt. Too many lavish gifts, too many trips to exotic locales in the best hotels, and too much ignored investment advice. The accountant hung in there, but he was exasperated. Reese chose not to listen to him. He was certain there would always be another payoff down the line, another endorsement or a bigger signing bonus. He was at the top of his game. He promised himself that, yes, someday he would dial down the spending and "get real," as he termed it. But it wasn't time for that yet—he was still in his twenties, living a life that most couldn't even conceive. He'd have plenty of time to play the miser later on.

The day he fell to the turf in LP Field he was under the zero-line to the tune of more than $1.7 million dollars, and his contract was ending at the conclusion of that season.

As his family's sole breadwinner, he knew he was in big trouble.

The surgeries went well, but, as Clark had predicted, the rehab was slow and torturous. Reese did everything he was supposed to do, and he maintained a positive attitude. His agent kept everyone in the league updated on his progress. Meanwhile, creditors came calling. The beleaguered accountant kept them at bay with minimal payments, but the last of the cash reserves were running out. There were suggestions of selling off nonessential items. Heartbroken, Reese resisted the idea. He changed his mind when the only other option was giving up the cars and the house. The wolves were closing in.

Standing on the edge of his property that breezy July afternoon, he realized his situation really wasn't uncommon. Moving trucks rolled through the development all the time; surely they weren't always bringing people *in*. He'd never suspected this lifestyle could be so transitory. Then he remembered some of the local stories he and Jeanine had heard through the years: the guy who got caught embezzling and lost everything, the couple who were running heroin and lost everything, the elderly couple who got scammed and lost everything. Being wealthy, he concluded, was a tightrope walk—and many fell off. Acquiring wealth was tough, but maintaining it was tougher.

He went through the agility trainer again, then spent a few minutes cutting corners in a four-cone drill. He was doing all right, and the knee felt fine. He wished some trainers could see him. At least someone in the media. He was ready for his triumphant return, he was sure. Even Dr. Clark had said his recovery was nothing short of amazing. Now all he needed was a team to join. *No problem. . . .*

He picked up the Gatorade bottle and jogged back to the house, entering through the sliding door on the porch. Corey Jr. was sitting on a stool in the kitchen, eating saltines with peanut butter and watching Nickelodeon. Jeanine was boiling the fat out of some chicken breasts in preparation for a barbecue. She wasn't smiling, Reese noticed. She didn't smile much anymore.

"Where are the other two?" he asked.

"Upstairs, playing and fighting."

Reese nodded. In happier times that would've been funny, but the money problems were like storm clouds that never cleared. They were always overhead, blocking out all warmth and sunshine.

"Can I show you something?" Jeanine asked, setting the stove to simmer and wiping her hands on a towel.

"Sure."

They went through the living room, which had a thirty-foot ceiling, and into the office, furnished with a small desk, some bookshelves, a computer and printer, and a cabinet with a lock. Jeanine opened the latter and took out the latest set of overdue notices. They had arrived earlier in the day, but she'd waited to show them to Corey so he wouldn't be distracted during his workout.

He read through them quickly. More penalties, more punishments. He was beginning to grow familiar with the names. The language was increasingly hostile, the underlying sentiments more threatening. Lawyers were now involved because no one felt there was any choice. The situation was drifting out of control, and the numbers were staggering—five and six figures. Numbers he had dismissed in the past were starting to become real. He had bought a car for an old friend that cost more than his parents' combined income for a year when he was a child. He thought nothing of it at the time. Now he thought of it in exactly this way.

"I'm going to talk to Freddie tomorrow," Reese said, hoping the thought of getting his agent involved would provide some comfort, some sense that things were happening. "I'll see if we can get something going." Little did either of them know his agent would be calling later that very evening, after he first spoke with the Giants.

"Are you sure you're ready to play again?" she asked. "I don't want you forcing it and ending up . . . you know, crippled." Tears broke free; she was unable to help that. Just the thought of it, and of everything else that was happening right now. . . .

He smiled and took her in his arms. "Come on, now. I'm ready. I can do it. Look, either I can or I can't. But I'm not going to sit around here and wonder about it. The only way I'm going to know is by trying." He lowered his voice and added, "And the only chance we have of getting out of this mess"—he held up the letters—"is by trying."

She nodded, but she clearly didn't like the idea. She had a feeling she would never know if he was being completely truthful or if he had decided to take the risk in order to keep their world intact. She knew he'd be willing to take that risk, even with the possibility of spending the rest of his life in a wheelchair, but she could not determine how great the risk really was. Truthfully, neither could he. All he knew for sure was that they had run out of alternatives.

He had sacrificed everything for this life. He would take any opportunity to hold on to it.

4

Foster

His mother sat, as she always did, in the rocking chair by the largest window in the living room. The oversized pages of her latest book hung over her legs as she ran her wise fingers over the Braille pimpling. Her face was a living catalog of expressions, revealing the emotions of each passage. Sometimes her lips moved, too, but silently.

Cleona Foster began losing her vision shortly after her sixty-second birthday. She developed headaches when she read—a favorite activity all her life—because she was suddenly having trouble seeing the text. Her primary care physician referred her to an ophthalmologist who misdiagnosed the condition, and by the time a second doctor realized she had cataracts, her vision was so cloudy that the damage was irreversible. As she had accepted so many other bad breaks in life, she accepted this one and began learning Braille while she could still detect bright light and a few hazy shapes. She also practiced getting around her small home on Caspian Avenue in Atlantic City. The last image her dying eyes ever registered was the soft-edged figure of her son, Daimon, coming into her bedroom on the afternoon of December 9, 2004, to kiss her on the cheek before leaving for work. She could barely detect his movement as he left. Then she took a short nap, and when she awoke, there was only darkness.

Daimon watched her from the doorway that separated the living room from the tiny kitchen. He watched her rock slowly back and forth, reading line after line, smiling at the happy parts and shaking her head at the sad ones. And he felt a familiar anger rumbling inside. It had been there so long that he couldn't remember the time when it wasn't. The unspeakable cruelty this woman had endured, the harshness that had been delivered upon her. The blindness, the failed marriage, the other child she lost, the lifetime of poverty. All that she'd been through—and yet there she was, smiling and happy, asking for no more than a good book and a comfortable place to read it. She'd been beaten down that far; she accepted everything now. She'd played the game of life and lost. That made her son so angry there were days when he felt homicidal.

Alicia came into the room via the door on the other side, the one that led into Cleona's bedroom. Cleona used to sleep on the second floor, but not since she'd lost her sight. After this adjustment, her entire world consisted of just four places—bedroom, living room, kitchen, and bathroom—totaling about two hundred square feet. She might as well be in a goddamn zoo, her son thought.

"I'm putting your pills on the table," Alicia told her, "right in front of the lamp."

Cleona nodded. "Thank you, sweetheart."

"Sure. And your soup will be ready in a few minutes. We'll eat together."

"That sounds wonderful."

"Are you enjoying the book?"

"Oh, yes, very much." It was a comprehensive history of the Harlem Renaissance. Sometimes she read fiction, sometimes non-fiction, and she seemed to have no particular preference for either.

Alicia reached for her hand, and Cleona took it briefly before letting go. If there was one bright spot in Daimon's life, it was Alicia Spencer. She understood him, understood his suffering and his anger. She had been stuck in this sorry neighborhood all her life, too. Technically, she lived two blocks over, on Magellan Avenue, but she was rarely there. Her mother had died when she was three, struck by a public bus while walking to work, and her father, an alcoholic who couldn't hold a job for more than a few months, was violent even when he wasn't drinking. She met Daimon at the New Hope Baptist Church, which she still attended but he had given up on. They were both twenty-two, although she looked much younger. She had a beautiful, fresh-faced innocence about her, which would have been an advantage under ordinary circumstances. In this town it was more of a liability.

They clung to each other, waiting for the day when they could take flight. His athletic ability appeared to be key. By the time he was fifteen, he was six foot three and weighed more than 225 pounds. He had hands that could hold on to a catch even after receiving the most punishing hits. He was fearless when it came to using his body as a weapon, throwing blocks into defenders who outweighed him by fifty pounds or more. He let his anger fuel his passion, and none of his peers could match his intensity. It gave him an edge and, perhaps most important, had earned him a football scholarship to New Jersey's Rutgers University. Receiving that letter was one of the few happy moments of his youth. He framed it and hung it on his bedroom wall.

He decided to major in business administration. He figured if the football didn't work out, the degree would have multiple applications, landing him a job pretty much anywhere, certainly beyond the limits of Atlantic City. If, on the other hand, Lady Luck smiled upon him and he ended up with a pro team, the training would be valuable there as well.

He was tremendous on the field, first as a wide receiver, then as a tight end. He never gave much thought to the latter, but his coaches felt he was a natural at the position. He was starting for the Scarlet Knights by his sophomore year. When he graduated, scouts thought of him as a promising young prospect. A few agents called. There were whispers that he might be taken as high as the fourth round, maybe even the third. The dream was in reach!

Alicia threw a party at the house on draft day. There was pizza and beer, pretzels and potato chips, and an enormous football-shaped cake. Some of Daimon's teammates showed up, plus two of his coaches. No one had ever seen him so happy. It was as if he were a different person. The unsteady, deep-set lines that had been engraved into his brow by years of disappointment and rage were gone. He looked instead like a contented young man, cheerful and hopeful—and, in a way, like the little boy he probably always wanted to be. She was seeing a side of him she had glimpsed only fleetingly in the past.

He sat on the floor with his legs pulled up, arms hanging over his knees with his hands laced together, as he watched the proceedings from New York City. The first round went by without incident, which didn't surprise anyone. A first-round pick would've been heavenly, but it was so remote it wasn't even worth considering. Besides, Daimon had already studied all the teams thoroughly and concluded that none of them needed a tight end that badly. Of course, that was a crucial factor in this situation—team needs. If no one needed you, no matter how good you were, there was a chance you wouldn't be taken at all.

When the second round passed, the mood in the room began to change. Not much, but enough to be noticed. Even a second-round signing was a slim chance—but it wasn't impossible. The feeling of complete abandon, of unbridled celebration and the "anything's possible" mentality, began to fade. As all prospective draft picks know, the phone will ring right before a team chooses them. Usually it will be the head coach or the general manager, sometimes the owner. But there's always that call, and the magic words, "We've decided to take you," from the other side. This call never came.

The draft resumed the next day, and everyone was there from the previous afternoon. Daimon was starting to look a little nervous, and the wavy pathways in his forehead reappeared. The first pick of the third round came and went, then the second . . . then the third. By two thirty, the fourth round had begun. Daimon's cell phone mocked him with its silence. People began making excuses, patting him on the back and hoping their reassurances didn't sound too much like pity. Alicia could sense his anger. Even more tragically, she could also sense the slow, epic death of his hope. In a life that had been marred by frustration from day one, here was one more dark moment to contend with. What had he done to deserve this? she wondered. Was he leading a secret life as a serial killer? A child molester? A dope dealer? It had to be something, she thought. No one should have to go through this much without a reason.

As the draft rolled to a close, Daimon's friends reminded him that undrafted free agents got signed all the time, and that some of them went on to great success—Wayne Chrebet, Priest Holmes, and Drew Bennett, to name a few. Kurt Warner won a Super Bowl MVP Award with the Rams, and Adam Vinatieri earned a reputation in New England as one of the greatest clutch kickers of all time. Daimon took their encouraging words with gratitude, but after everyone left he sat alone in his room while Alicia cleaned up. He wanted so badly to cry, but he refused to give whatever invisible forces were working against him any more satisfaction than they already had. He wanted to scream, beat his fists, break something into a million pieces. Instead, he turned on his side and went to sleep. He didn't give a damn about anything anymore.

He just wanted to disappear.

By July, the sting had mellowed into something more refined, adrift in the simmering cauldron of fury at the bottom of his soul. With his degree in hand, he found a job as a supermarket manager on the south side of town. He had to work the graveyard shift, the pay sucked, and the owner was a first-class prick. As he sat in his tiny office, which he shared with the two other managers—one of whom kept leaving stupid jokes on the marquee screen saver of the store's ancient computer in a flaccid attempt to bond with his fellows—he thought often about the opportunity that never was. He'd stood at a crossroads, with one way leading to unimaginable riches, the other to . . . this. How close had he really been? He wished there was a way to find out. Were there many discussions about him? Were there *any*? How many teams had really been interested? He knew the Bills had sent a scout, as had the Giants and the Packers. Surely their information traveled around to other teams. Scouts talked to each other. His statistics were available, both from college and from what he thought was a solid outing at the combines in Indianapolis. So was he ever a serious contender, or was he just kidding himself all along? Maybe he *was* supposed to be someone's pick, but then they changed their mind moments before their reps had to hand in that little card from their table down in the orchestra pit. Maybe it really was that close.

Then again, maybe it wasn't.

Alicia walked past him and into the kitchen, where she stirred the tomato soup on the stove one more time before pouring it into two small bowls. She set them on a silver tray along with a sleeve of saltines.

"You'd better get to work, sweetheart," she told him, already sounding like the concerned and loving wife. They had talked about marriage, and she knew he'd pop the question sooner or later. Now just wasn't the time, though, and neither of them had any idea of when that time would be. "You're going to be late."

Keeping his eyes trained on his beloved mother, he nodded absently. He hated the job so much that he forced himself not to think about it when he wasn't there. He hated everything about it—the tedium of the work, the jerkoff boss, the other idiots who worked there, and, in particular, the shitty little kids who came in there during the night to do nothing but cause trouble. He'd already broken up one knifepoint robbery and two gang fights. Risking his life for thirteen bucks an hour and substandard healthcare benefits. What a joke.

"You look nice today," Alicia said, and he suddenly realized she was standing right in front of him. She tightened the knot on his tie and reached up to kiss him. He returned it with a weak smile.

"Thanks," he said. "I guess I'll see you later."

"Be careful."

"I will."

He walked over and kissed his mother on the cheek, then went to the side door and out. The little black Honda he'd had since his freshman year, with more than two hundred thousand miles on it and barely clinging to life, started up with a rhythmic hitch. He backed out of the driveway and down the littered street.

I will find a way, that iron-willed voice in his mind spoke, as it always did when the feeling of helplessness was particularly overwhelming. *I will find a way to get all of us out of here, and I will never look back.*

The Giants called ten minutes later.

ESPN's hair and makeup artist put the finishing touches on NFL analyst Greg Bolton's face, then released him. He took his position ten feet in front of the camera. Behind him, a beautiful summer day was awakening in upstate New York, the shimmering blue sky complementing the wild green of the trees and the controlled green of the playing field where, by tomorrow morning, more than seventy hopeful young men would assemble to chase the dream of landing a roster spot for the forthcoming season.

Bolton smoothed his jacket, straightened his posture, and waited. A heavyset man wearing headphones peered out from behind the camera that sat atop a giant tripod. "In three, Greg. Two . . . one. . . ."

Inside those headphones, as well as the earpiece that Bolton wore but that could not be seen by viewers, came the voice of Tommy

Spencer, another ESPN veteran broadcaster, who was seen almost every day via *SportsCenter, NFL Countdown,* and *NFL Live.*

". . . but one big story in the league right now is still the contract holdout of Giants marquee tight end T. J. Brookman," Spencer was saying. "Our own Greg Bolton, senior NFL analyst, is on the scene at the State University of New York in Albany, where the Giants are about to open up this year's training camp, to give us the latest. Greg, what can you tell us?"

Bolton smiled as the small green light atop the camera went on. "Tommy, the Giants are so far remaining mum about the situation. I tried to speak to both head coach Alan Gray and general manager Chet Palmer as they drove in this morning, but neither was willing to comment. However, a team official who spoke under the condition of anonymity said they had, in fact, invited three free agents to try out for a tight end spot on the roster during training camp—Jermaine Hamilton, Corey Reese, and Daimon Foster. Hamilton, you may remember, was a standout tight end during his years with the Panthers, and won an Offensive Player of the Year Award after Carolina sent him to the Cowboys. But he wasn't signed to any team this year because of concerns about his age. Reese was a phenomenon from the start of his rookie season with the Ravens, then suffered multiple injuries to his right knee. A lot of experts thought he was done, but I'm told that he has successfully rehabbed himself and believes he's back in top form. And Foster is another big question mark—four good years in college, with solid numbers and a strong showing at the combines, but no one drafted him."

"Sounds like the issue is far from over," Spencer commented.

"Very far," Bolton replied. "And the New York fans aren't too happy about the way the team is treating Brookman. He's been a favorite since he arrived here, and most feel he deserves better than the league-minimum pay he's received so far. There are also those inside the league, I'm told, who agree. With training camp right around the corner, this all becomes much more interesting."

"Okay, thanks, Greg. Keep us posted."

"You got it," Bolton said. The green light went off again.

The cameraman came out from behind the camera, pulling his headphones down around his neck.

"Perfect," he said to Bolton.

"Good."

"So who's the anonymous inside source this time?"

Bolton laughed. "You won't believe this, but for the first time I have no idea. But I'm thankful I have him—everything he's given me so far on this story has been dead on."

Chet Palmer went to the bathroom around the same two times every day—ten thirty and two. He was as regular as Big Ben. He liked this because he liked things that were stable and predictable. He had long ago designed a generic daily schedule for himself, covering nearly every aspect of his life, to eliminate as many variables as possible. He accepted and tolerated a few, but when events arose that reduced his precious planning to a confused mess, he became edgy and worrisome. He clung to this habit like a drowning man clinging to a life preserver, and for the same reason—if he didn't, he would sink and die. It never occurred to him that the world simply didn't work the same way all the time, and that he was merely soothing numerous deep-seated insecurities.

At precisely ten forty-four, he emerged from the stall in the men's locker room. Players rarely came in here; it was mostly for management. There were two showers, several benches, and a tiled floor with recessed drains. Employees were encouraged to work out in the mornings, to keep their bodies healthy and their minds sharp. Palmer spent a half hour in the gym every day (from six to six thirty, without fail), then came here to shower and dress, at which time gossip and dirty jokes were exchanged.

He went to the sink and washed his hands. As he did, the door from the hallway opened and Alan Gray came in.

Spotting him in the mirror, Palmer said, "Hello, Alan."

"How are ya?"

"Okay."

Palmer shook the excess water from his hands and reached for a towel from the little pile that had been stacked on the stainless steel shelf over the basin. Gray, meanwhile, stood at the urinal.

Palmer took a quick look around even though he was already sure no one else was with them. "Uh, Alan?"

"Yeah?"

"I received a call from Barry Sturtz about a half hour ago."

"Oh? Did he apologize and relent?"

"No," Palmer said. "In fact, he wanted to know if *we* were ready to relent."

Gray laughed and shook his head. "What did you say?"

"I said we were holding our ground."

"Good."

"Yeah, good. Then he asked if that was our final decision, and I said it was."

"Excellent."

"Uh-huh. But look . . . I've been thinking a bit more about this situation, and maybe we should offer them *something*. Handling it the way we are is asking for trouble."

Gray zipped up and stepped back, triggering the automatic flush. "Without bringing in these three camp bodies, we have no leverage."

"And you have no trouble with the notion that these bodies are under the impression they've got a real shot at making the team?"

Gray shrugged. "They'll never know. That's business."

Palmer, certainly guilty of a few transgressions of his own, was nevertheless forever fascinated by Alan Gray's limitless lack of sympathy. "It's still too great a risk, no matter how well you hide your true intentions."

"Yeah? How so?"

"Well, it's pretty clear that Sturtz knows what T. J.'s worth, and he's not the type of guy who's going to just let us roll over him. We can get away with that with a few other guys, but not him. They're in a decent position."

"We're in a better position," Gray said, then walked around Palmer to get to the sink.

"I understand that. But they have a few options, like arbitration."

Gray shook his head. "They won't do that. Sturtz has a big mouth, but he won't go that far. It'd make him radioactive. Besides, if they file a grievance, who says it'll be green-lighted?"

"There have been more and more arbitrations lately. The league doesn't want a lot of these negative issues floating around. It's bad PR, so it's better just to deal with them. It also sets precedents."

"It's still not likely."

"I know, but do you really want to take that chance? Sturtz is not going to sit around and do nothing. He's not going to fold up and go home the way we want him to. He's pretty pissed off."

Gray took a paper towel from the pile, dried his hands, then examined himself in the mirror.

"I don't suppose you'd want to franchise T. J. at some—"

"No, absolutely not. I won't waste the franchise tag on . . . on him."

On an offensive player was what he really wanted to say, Palmer knew.

"At the very least, he'll probably want—"

"Look," Gray cut in, "we've got limited funds, right?"

"Well . . . yes."

"So we have to make choices. I'm choosing to concentrate on the defensive side of the ball."

That's because you don't want Dale Greenwood looking too good out there, do you? Chet Palmer thought meanly. Mean or not, most people in the organization were aware of the silent rivalry between this uninspiring head coach and the offensive coordinator who was the real reason the team had been even remotely competitive the last four seasons.

"That said," Gray went on, "I'm not eager to pour a fortune into T. J. Brookman. Everything needs to stay as is. That's the key right there—*everything has to remain status quo.* I want to invest in some of those new defensive guys we drafted, not to mention some guys during the season and next year. That money is mine."

"Even if it means we lose T. J. now?"

"We won't lose him," Gray said, and Palmer detected the faintest hint of concern. *You don't want to pay him what he's worth, but if you lose him, your ass could be on the line. That's quite a situation you've put yourself in—not to mention me.*

"He's not going anywhere," Gray assured him. He wrapped an arm around Palmer's shoulders. "We won't let that happen, right?" Alan Gray thought Chet Palmer was the biggest wuss on the planet—and thus had served him very well. Some GMs were alpha, and some were beta. The moment Gray realized Palmer was in the latter group, he made sure the team kept him around.

"No," Palmer said with a sigh. "We won't let that happen."

"And these three boys we're bringing in?" He smiled and held his hands out. "Well . . . life can be full of disappointments, right?"

"Sure."

"Good. Then do whatever it takes on your end of things, and I'll do whatever it takes on mine, okay?"

"Okay."

"Attaboy."

6

During the four-and-a-half-hour journey from Atlantic City to Albany, Daimon Foster kept telling himself that he had been invited to this training camp for a reason, and that reason was because he was *good*. The fact that he hadn't been formally drafted didn't mean a thing, other than the possibility that a lot of scouts and coaches had made the mistake of overlooking him. He was on his way up here because he had what it took to be a pro. If the Giants didn't truly believe that, they wouldn't be wasting their time.

It was this last thought that really got him pumped, inspiring him to savor the kind of grand visions he had previously kept in a dusty mental storeroom. Visions of a beautiful home for his mom and girlfriend, in some exclusive neighborhood. Nice cars and fine clothes and expensive jewelry. He would take Alicia to the best shops in the city and tell her to get whatever she wanted. He'd also stand on the sidewalk outside the house where they lived now and enjoy the sight of the hired hands loading the last of the boxes into a huge moving van, then watch it groan and belch black smoke as it bumped down that miserable street for the last time. He'd follow in his shiny BMW and not even glance in the mirror. With Alicia in the passenger seat and his mom in the back, he'd turn the corner, hit the Atlantic City Expressway going west, and begin to forget. Yes, it was true that the team was only going to pay him a pittance of just over eight hundred per week to be in camp (the vets would get just over twelve hundred), but he looked at it as merely a starting point. Hell, it was already more than he was making at the supermarket. But it would grow to much more if he could just show off his stuff.

Then there was the flip side to his euphoria—the stubborn certainty that things wouldn't work out. If there was one ugly truth he had come to believe with all his heart, it was that some people caught the breaks, and some did not. There was no profound reasoning for this; it was just the Way It Was. He'd recently read something about a woman who had won more than a million bucks in the lottery *twice*. The lottery board looked into the second win to make sure there hadn't been any foul play. There hadn't—she simply had what he liked to call "It," that certain something, the X-factor that just made life *work* for some people. Whatever It was, he often thought he didn't have It. Even a casual inspection of his life provided some evidence to support this.

Then an idea occurred to him—maybe he could beat the odds anyway. If he tried hard enough, maybe he could overcome the lack of It and succeed regardless.

Just maybe.

With his heart pounding and his mouth dry, he made a right off Washington Avenue and entered the State University of New York at Albany. Following the printed directions supplied by the team, he found himself cruising along University Drive West. A little farther up and he came to a sign for the player parking lot. He checked the printed instructions again to be sure it was correct. Then he followed the arrows with another right, and the lot entrance appeared up ahead. He was actually a little disappointed—it was no different from any other parking lot he had ever seen. There were open fields adjacent to it, and the beginnings of a hardwood forest in the distance. Nothing spectacular or dramatic. This was the NFL?

Reality stepped in when he reached the entrance and found it blocked by two candy-striped sawhorses.

He parked his tired little Honda and got out. A cursory inspection of the area told him this was the right one. It looked like a dealership for the überwealthy, with a generous selection of Lexuses, BMWs, and Escalades.

Daimon went over to one of the sawhorses and began dragging it out of the way.

"Hey! Get away from there!"

A man materialized between two long rows of cars. He was small and stout, fairly muscular. As he drew closer and broke into a slow jog, Daimon noticed that his head was shaven almost to the scalp, the silver hairs more like whiskers.

"What are you doing? Get the hell away from there!" He was dressed in khaki shorts and a Giants polo. He also had on white socks and sneakers, as if he were as athletic as anyone else.

"I'm supposed to be here," Daimon said, "for training camp."

The guard set his hands on his hips and looked him over. "Oh yeah? You don't look familiar to me." He glanced past Daimon and appraised his current mode of transportation. "And I'm pretty sure the players drive around in something better than that. Now go on, get the hell—"

Daimon handed over the driving directions. "The team sent this to me two days ago."

The antagonist stared hard into his victim's eyes, clearly unhappy that he was being argued with. Then he took the sheet and studied it carefully. He noted the Giants logo at the top, the formality of the language. It certainly seemed genuine. But then there was also the fax number printed at the very top, along with the words "ShopRite Store 557." And he didn't know anything about this kid. No, he wasn't ready to stop busting his balls yet.

"What's your name?" he said without looking up.

"Daimon Foster."

"Yeah? Never heard of you. Wait here." He took his cell phone from the holster on his belt and walked a short distance away. The conversation took less than a minute. At one point, Daimon saw the guy's shoulders droop, as if he were disappointed that he couldn't go back and give the little punk a good thumping. He refolded the phone with a snap and replaced it in its holster. He was clearly in no hurry to return.

"Uh, look," he said. "I'm sorry, but I didn't know we were expecting you. No one told me."

The change in personality was so abrupt it was startling. One minute a tough-as-nails guardian of the inner circle, the next a servile, bootlicking subordinate. It was almost a disgusting thing to see, and Daimon surprised himself by feeling a little sorry for the guy.

"I'm Ted Brodie," the guard continued, putting a hand out.

"Daimon Foster," Daimon said again, guessing Brodie didn't catch the name the first time.

"Nice to meet you. I'm one of the Giants' operations people. Tonight I'm on parking lot duty, as you can see."

Daimon nodded, wondering what kind of damage is done to the soul of a man in his fifties who spends his days bowing and scraping to people half his age with roughly five to fifty times his income.

"This is where I should be, isn't it?"

"Huh? Oh, yes. Yes." Brodie hurried over and finished the job of pulling the sawhorse aside. "Sorry. Come on in, please."

"And after I park I report to Donald Blumenthal in Chadwick Hall, is that right?"

"Yes, that's correct."

"Okay, thanks." Just before he got back into the car, he asked, "Do I park anywhere in particular?"

"No, wherever you like."

"Right."

He got back in and drove through. A strange and unexpected sensation followed—he had pierced the first layer of the league. A moment ago he was on Route 118, a thoroughfare accessible by anyone. It was still part of the public domain, so to speak. Now he was in a Privileged Area; limited access, highly restricted. He already had one person treating him like royalty, and in this small way he felt like he was no longer on the outside looking in. He *was* in. He saw Brodie replace the sawhorse in the rearview mirror. This somehow expanded his excitement—*closing and locking the door behind me.*

But the ecstasy didn't last long. He might have crossed that first border, but he realized there were plenty more to go when he puttered past vehicles whose sticker prices dwarfed his current annual salary at the supermarket. The tingle down his spine vanished as swiftly as it had come.

He saw several open spots, but he couldn't bring himself to pull into any of them. One was between a gleaming black Mercedes-Benz and a Range Rover. Another was next to a Hummer H3. *I can't park here,* he thought. *I just can't.*

He finally found what he considered to be the right place. At the northeast corner of the lot, there was a lone space next to a pile of gravel that looked like a miniature mountain. Probably dumped there for use in a future landscaping project. There were several openings on either side of it. Daimon chose to park on the side that provided the best cover. *Maybe they'll think I'm the landscaper,* he mused.

He parked, popped the trunk latch, and got out. The air was warm and heavy, and hundreds of summer insects were trilling and chirping in the empty fields beyond.

He caught sight of Chadwick Hall in the distance. The lights were on in the ground floor. People were in there waiting for him, he realized. They were waiting for many people, but he was one of them. He retrieved his black duffel bag, which contained the personal items the team had advised him to bring. Anything else he needed, they said, could be purchased at any one of a number of stores nearby. There was a Target, a Wal-Mart, and, ironically, a ShopRite.

He slung the bag over his shoulder and closed the trunk. Then he turned to see where Brodie was. He had apparently disappeared, returning to the shadows to wait for legitimate prey.

Surging with anticipation and more grand visions of the future, Daimon Foster started forward.

7

After parking in one of the spots that Daimon Foster passed up, Corey Reese took his bag from the back of his Ford Expedition and cut across the lawn to Chadwick Hall. Through two pairs of glass doors, he entered a poorly lit lobby that looked as though it hadn't received a cosmetic upgrade since the seventies. On the right was a long folding table, and behind it sat two men dressed in the same outfit that Brodie wore—Giants shirt, khaki shorts, white socks and sneakers. Several neat rows of manila folders lay on the table, each with a plain white label bearing a player's name.

"Hi, I'm Corey Reese," he said to the two men.

They did not reply immediately, but instead looked him up and down.

"Okay," one of them said finally. Then nothing again.

"I'm here for camp, and I was told to report to Donald Blumenthal."

The first one glanced at the second, and the second one got up slowly, as if he would rather be anywhere else right now. He was awkward and gangly, and he had an irritable, unkindly air to him that Reese sensed and didn't like. His face was unshaven and reddened by scores of burst blood vessels.

"What's the name again?"

"Reese, Corey Reese."

Blumenthal found the folder and came around to the other side of the table.

"I'm Blumenthal. Follow me," he said and headed down the hallway. As Reese passed by the first guy, he saw that he had a magazine in his lap.

They went past a long bulletin board decorated with a variety of leaflets and flyers—everything from school announcements to offers for tutoring, carpools, and guitar lessons—and turned left at the end. This brought them to a set of elevator doors. Corey's congenial host pushed the little button for the eighteenth floor and waited, devoting the time to cleaning out one nostril with his thumb.

"How'd the minicamps go?" Reese asked in an attempt to be friendly. It was always a good idea in this business to build alliances wherever you could.

"Oh, they were great," Blumenthal replied dryly, watching the numbers over the doors light up one at a time as the elevator progressed downward.

"Have you been with the team a long time?"

"Yeah."

He decided not to socialize further with this gifted diplomat, political potential notwithstanding. He stepped into the car when it arrived and followed Blumenthal out when it stopped again. Two more hallways, then they arrived at an unvarnished wooden door with the number 33 drawn at eye level in bold Magic Marker. Blumenthal twisted the knob, pushed the door back, and reached inside to flick the switch. He didn't actually enter the room, as if he might catch some kind of infection if he did.

"Here it is," he said, "home sweet home."

Corey stepped in and immediately caught the odor of mold. Not overpowering, but unmistakable. It reminded him of the basement in his parents' house, a place he tried to avoid as much as possible in his youth. It represented only one thing to him now—poverty.

With his stomach moving in waves, he said, "Thanks."

Blumenthal held out the folder. "Here's the information you'll need. The cafeteria is on the first floor, by the southwest corner of the building. If you leave the campus, you have to let me or Gordon know."

"Gordon's the guy you were with downstairs?"

"Yeah, Gordon's the guy. There's a schedule for the coming week in there. Breakfast is tomorrow at six sharp. If you don't show, you don't eat."

"Okay."

"Curfew is eleven o'clock every night unless Coach Gray says otherwise."

"Got it."

"And if you have any emergencies, you come to me. Emergencies only. If your girlfriend is in a bad mood and you want to go see her, that's not an emergency."

"I'm married," Corey replied. He was going to hold up his left hand and show the wedding ring, then decided against it when he noticed the guy didn't have one of his own.

"Welcome to the team."

"Thanks."

He listened to the fading echo of Blumenthal's footsteps until they disappeared, then he closed the door and opened all the windows.

He had been in plenty of dorm rooms in his life, first as a student, then as a player, and he had never seen one so small or depressing. The walls were plain beige, the overhead light a cold, clinical fluorescent. The floor was hardwood, but filthy and rotting in one corner. Someone—the previous occupant, he assumed—had covered it with an area rug, but one so ratty it wasn't suitable for fleas. There were two single beds on opposite sides, and they were dressed with plain, starchy-looking sheets that could've been stolen from a hospital. Reese wondered what kind of activities these mattresses had been subjected to through the years, then stopped himself. Completing the tableau was an aging yard-sale dresser and a tiny desk with a mismatched chair.

He threw his bag onto the desk and went into the adjoining bathroom. It wasn't much bigger than the elevator car, but the builders still managed to squeeze in a toilet, sink, and shower. At least it had been recently cleaned, as evidenced by the dizzying scent of bleach. The mirror had a small diagonal crack in the lower corner, and the tin shelves behind it were pitted with rust.

He ran the water until it was frigid and splashed his face repeatedly. Each time he brought his hands down, he looked at his reflection and realized with some trepidation that, yes, he was still here.

Back in the bedroom, he began unpacking. He crammed his clothes into the two lower drawers, leaving the top two for his forthcoming roommate—he prayed it was someone he knew. He'd also brought along a few items from home, a useful trick he had learned long ago. There were framed pictures of Jeanine and the kids, the alarm clock that usually sat on his nightstand, a small lamp, and two sets of bedsheets. He immediately went about changing the sheets, stuffing the coarse white ones underneath the bed. He would leave them there until he "checked out"—whenever that was.

Once everything was in place, he stood in the center of the room, hands on hips, and surveyed his kingdom. *It still looks and smells like a fucking dump,* he thought, making a mental note to buy a can of air freshener as soon as possible.

Then something else occurred to him, and it caused him to shudder violently. *If I don't make this team, my family could end up in a place just like this.* The image of his children being stuck—no, *imprisoned*—in such a place was so awful that it temporarily robbed him of his composure, and for just a moment he felt the insatiable hands of grief reaching for him. His kids' beautiful and confused little faces, tracked by tears, trying to figure out what had happened to the home they had before and asking when they could go back to it. Instead of being lulled by the measured twitching of the lawn sprinklers, instead they might have their sleep shattered by the pulse of gunfire in the streets. Instead of leaving their windows open at night to enjoy the cool autumn breezes, they'd have to lock them tight, keep the shades drawn, and pray to God no one ever decided to find out if they had anything valuable inside.

It all comes down to what happens in the next four weeks, he told himself, and again he redirected his attention to the knee. He could feel the reconstructed ligaments again, the reset and repaired musculature. It didn't matter that it wasn't the same as it had been before, or that it never would be. All that mattered was that it *worked.*

He took one more look at his home for the next month, then turned and went out. There was time for a quick jog.

8

It was the smallest dorm room Jermaine Hamilton had ever seen, too, but he wasn't about to complain. *I'm back,* he thought giddily. *Back where I belong.*

An old and beloved warmth flooded into him as he set his bag on the bed. Unlike Corey Reese, he had always found something poignant about the utilitarian quarters players were given during training camp. It reminded him of his early years, when all he had was his wits and his enthusiasm. He had nothing to lose and everything to prove back then. Those were good times, full of promise and excitement. He felt like he was ready to conquer the world— and succeed. All he had to do was work his magic when the right people were watching.

And now I have to show them all over again, he realized. It wouldn't be as easy this time. A guy could learn new plays, lose excess weight, and train away most mental errors, but he couldn't make himself younger. Age was truly the serial killer of NFL careers. If they thought you were too old, you were finished. The Giants obviously weren't sure in his case, so here he was.

As he unzipped his bag, the door opened. The kid who stood there was dressed in a tank top, baggy shorts, and sneakers. All of it was jet black. The only splash of color came from the wraparound sunglasses with the oil-spill reflection.

"Hey, man, you Jermaine?" the kid asked. Big smile, big teeth.

"That's right. You must be Freddie Turner."

"You got it."

He came in with the confident, cocky strut that is the sole property of the young. Although Jermaine had never met him in person, he knew Turner from watching him all last season. He was one of the Giants' wide receivers, second on the depth chart even though he was in his rookie year. He had been drafted high in the third round after breaking numerous records during his four years at Georgia Tech. Many expected him to move into the team's top spot after the legendary Malcolm Lowery retired and, after a few more years, fill Lowery's cleats quite well.

They exchanged a handshake, then a rudimentary hug that expressed just enough mutual respect without crossing into the forbidden land of genuine affection.

"It's great to see you here, man," Turner told him. "I heard about the situation with T. J. Damn. . . ."

"Caught you off guard?"

"It sure did. Caught everyone off guard."

Turner dropped his duffel on the other bed and moved his sunglasses up to the crown of his bald head.

"Would you rather have this bed?" Jermaine asked.

"No, this is fine. Thanks."

They talked aimlessly as they unpacked, plucking topics out of the air. Jermaine avoided questions about Melanie, skillfully redirecting family talk back to Turner. He learned that Turner had had the same girlfriend for the last eight months, someone he met at a charity auction. She was a model and had some money of her own. "So it's not like she'll be after mine, you know what I mean?" Jermaine nodded. He knew.

When they were finished, Turner said, "Damn, I forgot a few things. Like a fan. I had one of those big fans in here last year that go back and forth. That's a necessity."

"Yeah, I forgot some things, too," Jermaine told him. The difference was that he forgot them on purpose. During the first few years of his career, he'd always accidentally forgotten to bring something at the start of training camp. By his fifth season, however, he had the list down pat. Then something unexpected happened—he discovered he missed the frenetic midnight run on that first night to find stores that were still open. A trivial point, perhaps, but it had still become part of the ritual, and he and his roommates always went together. It was also essential to the spontaneous comradeship that needed to be cultivated.

"Let's hit that Wal-Mart that's near here."

"Yeah, I know where it is," Turner said.

"Cool."

An hour later they were back in Turner's Lexus RX350 with five big bags in the back. What had begun as a quest for a handful of items quickly evolved into a childish spending spree. Turner found the fan he wanted, and Jermaine realized he had to have one, too. They also bought a new CD player and more than thirty albums, a color TV, an Xbox system with a dozen games, a cube fridge, three boxes of cupcakes, two enormous bags of prepopped popcorn, and six gallons of cherry Kool-Aid.

Halfway back to the campus, Turner said, "Hey, I got an idea. Let's go out for a bit before we head back. I know this place about two miles away called Phatty's. It's a strip joint. Whaddaya think?"

Staying out late the night before camp started was always a dicey affair. About the worst thing you could do on the first day was show up half asleep. Guys had been cut on the spot for that. Regardless, Jermaine had thrown the dice and done it enough times— every year of his first four seasons, in fact. Again, here was a chance to recapture the magic of his early days.

Then came an alarming realization—he was damned *tired*. Not just fatigued, but worn to the bone. The kind of tired that robs you of everything. True, it had been a long day; packing, the long flight, and then the ride out to Albany. But still. . . .

I could've done it before.

"Sounds good," Jermaine said, "but, you know, I should study the playbook instead. I mean, I haven't had the time to look through it like you guys have. I haven't been to any of the minicamps."

He was thankful that Turner only nodded. "Yeah, I understand. I'll drop you off and go back out. I'm sure I'll see some of the guys there."

The younger guys, Jermaine thought.

"Cool. Have a good time."

He waved as Turner motored out of the lot. Then he lumbered across the lawn, reached the sidewalk, and went to the doors, through the lobby again (which was empty now, although the folding table still had a handful of manila folders on it) and down the hallway. He turned toward the elevators.

Just as he rounded the corner, one set of doors opened to reveal Corey Reese. He was dressed in navy shorts and a long-sleeved white T-shirt, apparently on his way out for a run. Then the door to the fire stairs opened at the far end of the hallway and Daimon Foster appeared.

The silence between them seemed to stretch to eternity; in reality it lasted about five seconds. They gave each other a cursory appraisal, their faces blank. On other teams, under different circumstances, they would all be friends. Even in the National Football League, where millions were on the line and futures were decided by the slimmest margins, young men competing for the same job usually allied with each other and got along well. But there was just too much at stake for each of them this time around. These guys were rivals, plain and simple.

Reese broke the stalemate by saying, " 'Excuse me," and breezing past Hamilton. "Sure," the latter replied flatly. He then stepped into the elevator without another word. Daimon Foster waited until the doors closed again, and Reese was well on his way, before continuing on his own journey to the vending machine.

9

Day One

The last precious moment of true peace the players would know for weeks occurred at exactly five forty-four the next morning. One minute later, alarms buzzed throughout the building, followed by the erratic rhythm of footsteps that marked a weary exodus to the elevators and down the stairways.

Reese, wearing the Giants lanyard and photo ID he'd been issued, was among the first to enter the long, sunlit dining hall, although it was filling up fast. A woman in a white catering uniform was arranging the last of the chafing dishes while another filled the coffee urns. Paper plates and cups were stacked next to tubs of cutlery—all plastic. As soon as the team was done eating, each of the thirty tables would be cleaned simply by pulling the four corners of the tablecloth together to create a "bag" and then dumping it into a rolling garbage can.

The sheer volume of food was staggering—hundreds of pounds of scrambled eggs, pancakes, waffles, bacon, sausage, corned beef hash, toast, and bagels, plus healthier items like bran cereals, smoked salmon, fruits, and vegetables. Two cooks in paper hats were on hand to make omelets. For drinks, there was a choice of low-fat milk, various juices, nutritional shakes, and bottled water.

Corey always found it odd that there were no limits to what you could eat. No stern dictums from the team, no dietary specialists designing individual plans. In some other sports, an athlete's diet was closely monitored. Personal trainers hounded your every step, slapping forbidden items out of your hand. In professional gymnastics, for example, you were lucky if you were allowed more daily calories than a parakeet. Not in the NFL—as long as you maintained your weight as prescribed by your coaches, no one cared how you did it. And if you had a heart attack in your early forties from years of high cholesterol, that was your problem.

Corey loaded his plate with high-protein items, to which he had grown accustomed since the injury. Then he looked for a suitable place to sit—and realized this might be something of a challenge. He didn't know too many of the other guys, so he couldn't just squeeze his way into a crowd. There were a few he'd played with here and there, but no one he considered a real friend. It also occurred to him that most of these players had been together at least since minicamps, and in that time some bonds had formed.

This point was never clearer than when he realized half the guys in the room were staring at him. He was the unknown quantity. He tried to appear casual while praying that someone, anyone, would wave a hand. *Yo, Corey, over here, man.* No such luck.

With as much dignity as possible, he strode to a corner table where two huge windows met like panes of glass in a fish tank. He almost felt sorry for Jermaine Hamilton and Daimon Foster when they came in less than five minutes later and ended up following the same pattern.

Three tables for three outcasts.

Breakfast lasted exactly thirty minutes. Not *around* thirty; not twenty-eight or thirty-six—exactly thirty. Like everything else, meals were precisely scheduled and regimented. Then the players were herded out of the room, up a set of stairs, and into another room—a small lecture hall. The stadium-type seating angled sharply downward and followed a gentle curve from left to right. There was a small island in the pit area and three blackboards on the wall. You were allowed to sit wherever you wished.

A side door opened, and Alan Gray appeared as if stepping onto a stage. He walked to the island and set down his notebook, then turned to face his audience.

"Welcome to this year's training camp for the New York Giants. As most of you know, I'm Alan Gray, the head coach. Before we get going, there are a few things I'd like to go over. Now that we're all past the minicamps and other off-season programs, I trust you are in good shape and at the proper reporting weight that you were assigned in May." He smiled. "If not, be on notice that you will be fined the sum of one hundred dollars a day for each pound that you are over. That means someone who is ten pounds overweight owes the team a thousand dollars today. If you're still ten pounds over tomorrow, you'll owe another thousand. If this sounds like you, then I strongly suggest you find a way to lose the excess baggage very quickly. If you don't, you will end up either bankrupt, out of a job, or both."

Players looked around uncomfortably. Those who would be writing checks to the team stood out by the bug-eyed astonishment on their faces. Others snickered and pointed at them. Reese and Foster were already at their ideal weights; thank God they'd kept up their daily workouts. Jermaine Hamilton, on the other hand, had discovered he had thirteen pounds of excess when he first spoke with Jim O'Leary. He had eleven days to lose it. He went back to fruits and vegetables and jogged five miles in the morning until he reached the required number. Stepping on the scale just before he left for the airport, he was relieved to find himself with four pounds to spare.

"And since we're on the subject of fines," Gray said, "let me discuss a few others."

The lights went out, and Gray flicked on an overhead projector. When he set a transparency on the glass, a bulleted list appeared on the wall. It was like a menu, with each line item followed by a price—and some of them were staggering.

"You'll all find a printed copy of this waiting in your rooms when you take your first break, after lunch. But have a quick look here, because anything can happen between now and then.

"As you can see, we're very serious about these infractions. Put simply, we don't want them. That's why they're so costly—when you make these kinds of mistakes, it costs *us*. It slows down the team, and we don't have time for that. The numbers on this list

TRAINING CAMP FINES

INFRACTION	FINE
Cell phone or beeper goes off during meeting	$1000 per incident
Conduct detrimental to club and league	To be determined on case-by-case basis, fine not to exceed one week's salary for contracted players
Curfew violations	$2000 per incident
Ejection from preseason game	Maximum fine of $10,000 per incident
Failure to follow rehabilitation program	$8000 per incident
Failure to join team on transportation to road games	$8000 per incident
Failure to report an injury in a timely manner	$1500 per incident
Failure to report to a scheduled visit to team physician	$8000 per incident
Failure to report to a scheduled visit to trainer	$8000 per incident
Excessive arguing with coaches	$2500 per incident
Excessive fighting with teammates	$2500 per incident
Loss of playbook	$2500 per incident
Loss of, or unnecessary destruction of, team equipment	$1500 per incident, plus cost of replacement equipment
Reporting to camp over your prescribed weight	$100 per pound, per day
Unexcused absence from team meal	$3500 per incident
Unexcused absence from team meeting	$8000 per incident
Unexcused absence from team practice	$8000 per incident
Unexcused absence from full day of camp	Maximum fine of $14,000 per day
Unexcused late reporting to team meal	$1500 per incident
Unexcused late reporting to team meeting	$1500 per incident
Unexcused late reporting to team practice	$1500 per incident
Use of telephone or Internet after curfew hours	$2500 per incident

might look high, but focus for a minute on the crimes themselves. Losing your playbook, being late to meetings, bringing your cell phone to practice—this is the stuff that hurts everyone, not just you. This is amateur crap, and I expect you to act like professionals.

"Another thing we don't have time for is bullshit personal stuff," Gray continued, clearing his throat. "Stuff like calls from mothers who miss you or friends who want to come and hang out here. We won't tolerate it. This isn't summer camp, it's *training* camp. If someone strikes us as being more interested in his life at home than his life here, we will be glad to accommodate him—by showing him the door. Don Blumenthal, by the way, will take care of that. Most of you already know him, either from your arrival yesterday or from being with the team in the past. We call Don 'the Turk.' Most teams have a Turk, and Don is ours. The Turk is assigned several unpleasant jobs, one of which is to find the guys who've been cut and bring them to my office."

Reese spotted Blumenthal standing in a far corner among the rest of the coaching staff, plus a few other front-office types. He looked as dour and uninspiring as ever. *No wonder he gets the job of cutting people. Grim work for a grim guy.*

"If this happens to you, don't even think about getting nasty with him. First off, you don't want to piss off anyone that ugly." No one laughed at this tasteless attempt at humor, but Blumenthal seemed unmoved by it. A few guys in the room even felt a little sorry for him.

"And second," Gray went on, "he isn't the one who made the decision to cut you—I did. My staff provides me with the information I need concerning who will make up the best team, but I make the final call. So if you are unlucky enough to fall into this category, the Turk will come and find you, and then I'll talk to you. But, to get back to my main point, your mind has to be right here for the next four weeks, and nowhere else. The outside world does not exist right now. If you have a genuine emergency, we'll deal with it in an appropriate fashion. If not, your entire universe begins and ends on this campus. Is that understood?"

A selection of affirmative replies rose from the crowd in an atonal jumble.

"Now, I'm sure you are all aware that this team has not performed up to its potential over the last few seasons. And I'm sure you know how disappointed I've been."

These two sentiments were followed by a deathly silence. The thought that came to Jermaine Hamilton's mind was *Five and eleven last year, six and ten the year before that. Yeah, I'd say you have some issues.*

Gray held up his right hand and splayed out all the fingers. "Five wins—that's pathetic. It is my belief that there's a losing attitude in this club, and when a losing attitude starts to spread, it's like a poison, making the body sicker and sicker until it just up and croaks. This is the first thing that needs to change. I have already cut five guys, and camp really hasn't even started yet—guys who, in spite of their skills, were losers at heart. Guys who were here only for the big paycheck, or the notoriety, or the glory, or a little bit of all three. I'm not saying I have anything against those things. But first and foremost, if you are not interested in winning football games, I will expose you and throw you the hell out of here. Mark my words—we will not have a losing attitude in this organization this season. Do we understand *that?*"

"Yes, sir," came the chorus, but another group sentiment was drifting around the room among those who had been with the team awhile—*You're pretty good at blaming everyone but yourself there, Coach.*

"Okay. I'm going to make one final point before we get going. Most of you have been in an NFL training camp before, and those who haven't probably know something about them from what you've heard, seen on TV, and been through at college. I won't paint a rosy picture—training camp is hard. It may be the hardest thing you ever do in your life. You may look back on this next month years from now and think it was the shittiest, lousiest, most painful, most agonizing, most infuriating time you ever had." Gray smiled. "I certainly hope so, because training camp has just one purpose as far as the coaches are concerned—to find out which of you has what it takes to be on this team, and which of you do not. It's survival of the fittest, period. We've got ninety-two guys here now, and we'll have just fifty-three when the day of the final cut arrives. It's going to be a race, and the last fifty-three guys standing will be the winners. Winners are who we want. They have focus, they have intensity, they have drive, and they have dedication. They are also consistent. That means they operate at the highest levels every day. If you think you're going to shine like a star for a few days, then relax the rest of the time and still make the roster, you're wrong. If we think you can function at the top, then we expect you to do it *all the time.* Not some of the time, not once in a while. Who is in the Hall of Fame? Guys who had one or two great games? No— guys who put up big numbers *consistently.* That means training camp is also about endurance. Use up all your energy during the first half, and you will fall behind in the second. Keep that in mind. And remember that injuries hurt you more than just physically.

You don't make the team from the training room. Or, as some have said, 'You won't make the club from the tub.' You better be damn near death if you're thinking of walking off the field. Remember— time not spent in camp is time when we cannot evaluate you. And we cannot put guys on the team that we haven't evaluated."

Gray trailed off here, cleared his throat again, and checked his notebook. "Boys, pay attention, try your best, keep your focus, and you'll be fine. If you follow the rules, then all it comes down to is your talent. Everything else is a constant, so the talent is the variable. Those who are the most talented will make the team. Those who have a little less talent but are still worthy might end up somewhere else. And those who have very little will go home. It really is that simple.

"So the first thing we need to do this year is find out who's ready," he told them. "Get suited up and get out there."

The Giants' practice field was located in the northwestern corner of the SUNY campus. It was set in a man-made depression about ten feet deep, and it was surrounded by a chain-link fence and many trees, which helped keep out the curious and minimize distractions. On the eastern side, however, were the university's tennis courts, where beautiful young girls in tiny skirts occasionally jarred the attention of Giants prospects, much to the irritation of the coaching staff. The field also featured a set of heavy aluminum bleachers and, outlining the perimeter, a rubber, brick-red running track.

Moving like a herd, the team gathered loosely around the fifty-yard line. Each player wore shorts and a jersey and carried his pads and helmet. They spent the first twenty minutes stretching, many of them lying on the grass like cows in a meadow. Fans happy to see the team for the first time since last season cheered from the fences.

They would be allowed to observe some practices from closer proximity later on, but not now.

Gray blew his whistle and ordered the squad into three groups—offense, defense, and special teams. Defensive coordinator Leo Miller took his boys to the western end of the field. Miller was a longtime friend and assistant to Alan Gray. Since Gray had a defensive pedigree, he and Miller shared similar minds, and their philosophies had evolved as a result of an ongoing joint effort. But while Gray was more reserved on the surface, Miller was basically a lunatic. It was he, not Gray, who was seen on television from time to time screaming from the sidelines, spitting and red-faced. It was also he who would be jumping up and down, pumping his fists and slapping helmets at every sack and backfield tackle. He hated offenses and lived for any opportunity to cause an injury. Most people around the league thought he would've ended up in prison if he hadn't found football, and his nicknames ranged from "Miller the Killer" to "Milla' the Hun." He particularly liked the second one and had someone superimpose his face over an image of the actual Hun king, then framed it and hung it in his office.

Special teams coach Frank Draybeck, who wasn't much more stable than Miller, put his men in the center of the field, leaving the eastern third for Dale Greenwood and the offensive unit. Greenwood led them to the sideline and, with clipboard in hand and a silver whistle hanging around his neck, said, "All right, boys, we're going to have some fun. Like Coach Gray said, the first thing we need to do is find out who's ready to be here and who's not." A faint collective groan came from the defensive unit at the opposite end of the field, and the other players took notice. Most of them had a pretty good idea of what was coming.

"You remember your old friend the gasser, right?" Greenwood asked, then smiled at the reaction. "Yeah," he said to his assistant coaches. "They remember."

In simplest terms, a "gasser" is a sprint used as a part of a conditioning regimen. Gassers are usually executed in a series, with minimal breaks between runs. They are arduous, often bordering on torture, and are loathed by sensible athletes. But they are also useful in gauging overall health and physical ability. Only players in the best shape can withstand a high-level gasser.

"I thought you'd be pleased," Greenwood continued. "We're going to do them in groups, by position. Last year we did a series of forty-yard dashes, but I've got enough data on your forties to smoke my hard drive." He flipped through the pages attached to his clipboard, then glanced up at Hamilton, Reese, and Foster. "Except for you guys, that is," he said, "but we'll manage. So here's what we're going to do this time." He took his pencil from behind his ear and pointed. "We're going up and back the width of the field. That's one hundred and sixty feet, or fifty-three and a third yards. Or, for you metric dorks, forty-eight point eight meters."

A few more moans drifted from the group—guys who had done this type of gasser before and remembered the experience well.

"You are going to go up and back twice." Greenwood said. "That means up and back, up and back. It'll be a total of slightly more than two hundred yards."

"Why don't we just use the full length of the field?" someone asked. It was Derrick Wilcox, wide receiver and rookie fourth-round pick from LSU. Daimon Foster glanced over at him and thought, *Was he the guy they chose over me?*

"The field isn't wide enough for all three units at the same time," Greenwood said. "We'd be here all damn day. So, first, the running backs. Let's go, get into position."

Five young men came forward, all black. In spite of this basic similarity, one stood out among them—Jason Thomas. Thomas had been the first-round, third-overall draft pick of the team three years ago. He made the starting squad without too much trouble and began performing from day one—137 yards in his opening game against the Cowboys. He would rush for more than eleven hundred that year, and over thirteen hundred the next. He was as slick as a fish, and he could squirt through the smallest of holes. Some said he had the tools to become the next Walter Payton. Whether that happened or not, he was in no immediate threat of losing his job. The second man on the depth chart, Charlie Tate, was a solid backup who had value in other roles. It was the other three guys who would be competing in this camp.

They lined up along the sideline a few feet apart. Greenwood took five digital stopwatches from a canvas bag and handed them out—one to the running backs coach, the rest among a small cluster of team gofers who were standing nearby. Most were bright young college students whose parents had landed them internship positions through their connections with team hierarchy. Everyone was assigned the task of timing a different player.

"Your goal is as follows," Greenwood said to the backs. "You will run a total of ten gassers, completing each one within thirty-three seconds. You will have another thirty seconds to rest in between, and a two-minute break after completing the fifth. Okay?"

Thomas didn't bat an eyelid, and Tate appeared only mildly disgruntled. The other three, however, looked petrified.

"Ready? On three. One . . . two . . . *three!*"

Bits of grass flew from their cleats as they sprang forward. Some of their teammates yelled in support, but none of the runners seemed to notice. When they reached the far end and turned, their faces were tightened with intensity. Thomas had the lead by a step or two, with Tate and one of the rookies nearly tied for second. The other two were doing their best to keep up. One of them—the one that appeared a bit heavier than the other four—was clearly not in good shape. Jermaine Hamilton had seen guys like this before, those who hadn't fully devoted themselves to an off-season program and figured they'd lose the weight and regain their edge *during* camp. They were almost always the first ones to go. *That's one less person on the roster*, he thought.

Thomas crossed the line first, and Greenwood clicked off his stopwatch. Four more clicks quickly followed as the others finished. Then Greenwood started his watch again and said, "Thirty-second rest, guys. Catch your breath."

The running backs kept moving, walking around slowly and in no particular direction. Perspiration had already begun to shimmer on their foreheads. A gofer without a stopwatch held out a bottle of water and a towel. No one took the water, but Jason Thomas grabbed the towel and quickly patted his face.

"Five seconds," Greenwood announced, and the backs lined up again.

The next two gassers were similar to the first, with Thomas in the lead and Tate and the one good rookie at his heels. But by gasser number four, the differences between the five young men really began to show. The rookie who had been keeping pace with Tate began to fall back a little bit, and the one who had arrived in camp out of shape was starting to wheeze audibly. During the two-minute break after gasser number five, the wheezer fell to one knee, then turned and crashed on his back. He accepted a water bottle and poured the contents over his face rather than drink it. The other two rookies were winded, but at least they were still standing. Tate appeared a bit worn as well, but he was smart enough not to show it. Thomas stood with his hands on his hips and stared into the distance, seemingly detached from it all. He had removed his shirt during the thirty-second break following the fourth run; his diamond-cut physique glistened in the morning sun.

Greenwood counted down the break in fifteen-second increments. As the five men dragged themselves to the starting line, the catcalls became louder, the taunts crueler. By the end of gasser number seven, the out-of-shape rookie looked like an exhausted puppy, his tongue actually dangling. Thomas continued his steady performance, making his time in each run. The strain was beginning to show around his eyes and in his careful, measured breathing, but that was to be expected. Otherwise, he was superhuman. Like the great Jerry Rice, Thomas subjected himself to a torturous off-season training program, and it paid the biggest dividends at times like this. Tate, amazingly, was beginning to catch a second wind. The rookies, in contrast, were not. They had expended too much of their energy trying to keep up in the first half. Now they had very little wind left. Everyone watching received a refresher course in the value of pacing yourself.

Only moments after Jason Thomas crossed the finish line for the tenth and final time, the unconditioned rookie collapsed on the other side of the field. He had not completed even half of the last run. Tate followed Thomas by about six steps, and the two surviving rookies came in side by side shortly thereafter. Tate bent forward, hands on his knees, eyes closed, and struggled to catch his breath. Some of the other players went over to the kid lying by the hash marks near the big 20 and tried to pull him up. They might as well have been moving a corpse. He turned out to be an unsigned free agent from Brigham Young and was thirteen pounds over his prescribed weight. He was carted off the field, and no one ever saw him again.

After the running backs came the offensive linemen. Since they were much heavier and inherently slower, they were given more time to complete each run—but not much. Whereas the RBs had thirty-three seconds per run, the linemen got thirty-nine. It didn't sound like much, but it made all the difference in the world—of the eighteen men who were vying for positions, only twelve completed all ten. Then came the five quarterback prospects, then the fullbacks. In each case the position coaches copied down all the times with notable indifference.

"Okay, tight ends, let's go," Greenwood said, waving them on. Glenn Maxwell jogged to the line first. He was a lanky white kid with gold hair that he kept shaved on the sides and not much longer on top. He had dark slits for eyes, a nose so long and narrow that it looked almost feminine, and a tiny mouth—which was no inconvenience since he rarely used it. His teammates thought of him more as invisible than aloof; he didn't carry an aura of superiority, but seemed comfortable waiting in the shadows until he was needed. His appearance on the field just now was a perfect example—he didn't seem to be anywhere until Greenwood summoned him. No one noticed that he'd been stretching by himself for the last fifteen minutes near the goalpost.

Hamilton, Reese, and Foster came up next, spread out about ten feet from each other, and crouched into their stances.

Jim O'Leary came alongside them. "Ready, guys? On three. One . . . two . . . *three!*"

They took off in perfect synch, four thoroughbreds competing for the same prize. Daimon Foster trained his eyes on the white line at the far end of the field, nothing else. He had learned this from one of his strength and conditioning coaches at college. *Focus on one thing and become blind to everything else. But don't focus on the pain. Focusing on something else will help you think* above *the pain.* He controlled his breathing, too, keeping it mild and steady so he wouldn't burn out too soon. He was sure he could beat the prescribed time Greenwood had given them—thirty-five seconds per gasser—in the first three attempts. He could probably even go under thirty if he really pushed himself. But after that he'd be out of steam, and by the two-minute break he'd be immobilized. So he decided not to concentrate on the time at all—just the run itself. *Steady, calm, consistent.*

Corey Reese realized Foster was ahead of him by about a half step. So far the order was Foster first, him second, and Hamilton and Maxwell another half step back in a tie for third. He decided that was okay for now. *Let Foster burn himself out. I can beat the other two regardless.* In the end, the coaches would realize he'd been the smart one, the one who used both his body *and* his brains to overcome his opponents. That would matter, because NFL coaches liked smart players. Every guy had a good body; they wouldn't have reached this point if they didn't. The mind was the make-or-break factor on this level.

Reese had also learned to focus on one thing in order to filter out all other distractions, but in this case he couldn't help thinking about the knee. It was the only thing that would keep him from landing this job. He was in better shape than Hamilton, had more experience than Foster, so the knee was the key. If it held up, he'd have no problems. So far it still felt funny. Not the best word, but adequate. Whereas he was barely aware of the movements of his other joints, he could actually *feel* things moving around down there—as if all the parts still hadn't quite settled yet, hadn't quite learned to live together harmoniously. And he considered this run the new knee's first real test. He wasn't in the comfort of his expansive backyard now, with the distant view of the other big houses. Everyone was watching, every move scrutinized. In spite of the weird sensations, the knee appeared to be holding together. As Reese pushed himself harder, his confidence increased. And as his confidence increased, so did his optimism. By the time he launched into the third gasser, he was neck-and-neck with Foster.

Similarly, Jermaine Hamilton was surprised by how good he felt. Crossing onto the sidelines for the two-minute break after the fifth run, he expected to be gasping for air. He ended up in second place, with Reese and Foster tied for first. True, he was winded— even Jason Thomas had been a little worn a half hour earlier, and he was probably in the best shape of anyone on the team. But Hamilton had feared he'd be like walking death, a machine whose parts were barely holding together. He, too, had designed and stuck with a personal conditioning program, his disciplinary fuel coming from the blind hope that someone would sign him. It had only been in the last few months that he began to slack off, when the depression struck and he started believing his career was really over. But after his agent called and said the Giants wanted him, he got back out there—literally, that same evening. He jogged five miles, feeling more alive than he had in years. He felt a lot like that now.

During the break, Maxwell vanished again. The other three tried to gauge the general condition of their rivals—without making it seem like they were doing so. They went out of their way to appear as though they were just fine. They turned down offers of water and Gatorade simply because they didn't want it to look like they needed any. In truth, they would've downed a bucketful given half the chance. Young men and their egos.

Daimon Foster noticed O'Leary talking to Greenwood, showing him something on his clipboard. The other position coaches hadn't done that. *Too slow?* he wondered. Since he wasn't focusing on time, he had no way of knowing. *I was faster than the others at the beginning,* he thought. *If I was too slow, that means we all were.*

He thought about moving closer to see if he could hear anything, but then Greenwood broke away and blew the whistle again. The break was over—five more gassers to go.

They lined up again and took off. Foster focused on a blue ice chest someone had left on the far side. In spite of this and the two-minute break, he could feel some weariness settling in. His legs no longer had the poetic fluidity they did before. They were a bit sluggish now, more recalcitrant. Making the turn at the end of the field was a drain. Nothing was automatic now; more willpower was required.

Corey Reese felt the fatigue as well, particularly in the damned knee. It was becoming painful, demanding. It was almost as if it were a separate living thing, and it was saying, *Don't push me, I can't do this much longer.* He'd be better off in practices and game situations, where you ran your heart out for a short period, took breaks between plays, then got a more extended rest on the bench after the defense took over. All this training camp crap was, without a doubt, the most physically demanding experience for a pro football player.

By the eighth run, Jermaine Hamilton was still behind Foster and Reese, and struggling to hang on. They were finally beginning to slow down, as he'd predicted—but so was he. He felt like his lungs were on fire. He figured his careful pacing and measured breathing would carry him through, and this was where he'd claim the lead, but the early symptoms of age were unavoidable. He simply did not possess the stamina he had ten years ago; it was *gone*. There was nothing in the world he wanted less than to do two more runs. He turned away from the crowd during the thirty-second break, closed his eyes, and dropped his head. He wasn't even certain if he would make it. Then he thought about life outside of here—his dying marriage, and that little prison in the basement. Now that he'd been able to put some time and distance between himself and that world, he began to see how poisonous it really was. Amazing how many people became trapped without even knowing it. Through the agony, he hazily remembered something about that from psych class in college—*environmental factors*. Something about influence. He thought it was all double-talk back then, but it made sense now. He felt happier right now, in spite of the pain, than he had in ages—simply because he'd changed his surroundings. How much longer would he have lasted in that misery? he wondered. Did he really want to go back?

Greenwood blew the whistle to start the ninth run, and Hamilton found himself jogging up to the line. When he burst forward, it was with an enthusiasm that surprised everyone. He forgot about the visual focusing tricks and thought about Melanie, about watching the games from his couch and having no desire to answer the door or the phone. That was part of the past, he decided, and he was running away from it—and toward the future. He still felt the pull of the years, the greedy fingers of age wrapping themselves around every joint and muscle. But he was moving forward anyway.

Corey Reese had no intention of coming in second to a veteran like Hamilton, or a kid like Foster. His mind was trained on keeping that gorgeous home and those beautiful cars, fending off the embarrassment of bankruptcy and the pity of fans, friends, and family. If he performed as he knew he was capable of performing, it would all be nothing but an unpleasant memory. A nightmare he woke up from and could then forget about. All he had to do was run. . . .

Daimon Foster remembered the two women who had sole claim on all the affection he was capable of. He knew he could outshine the others, knew he could carve out a niche for himself in this league. The Giants were offering more than an opportunity to make their team—they were offering an opportunity to *escape*. He thought about that dream-moment that would come in four weeks when he could deliver those four magic words to Alicia: *I made the team.* Everything would be different then *everything.* Even if he didn't land a zillion-dollar contract, he'd have enough to lower a bucket into the well of their despair and raise them up to the light of day. This was actually—*finally*—within reach now. He had no intention of blowing it.

They crossed the line for the tenth time, their bodies unwilling to go any farther. Amazingly, they finished at the same time, with Maxwell not far behind. It took the greatest effort of their collective lives to remain standing. They spread out from each other in a way that seemed choreographed. No one refused fluid this time. Reese finished a bottle of lime Gatorade in seconds and reached for another. Hamilton poured most of the water from his container over his head. Foster kept moving in small circles because he was afraid he would collapse if he didn't.

Twenty feet away, Jim O'Leary conferred quietly with the other three timekeeper-gofers. Greenwood watched from a distance, puzzled. After a few moments, O'Leary left the group and approached him with a frown on his face.

"You're not going to believe this."

"What?"

O'Leary handed him the clipboard and tapped a figure at the bottom with his pen.

"What's that?"

"Their times."

"You're kidding."

"No, I checked and double-checked."

Greenwood kept staring. "You're sure this is right?"

"Positive."

The three new prospects had mostly recovered now and were lingering, waiting for their next challenge.

"Damn," Greenwood said.

That first practice session ended just after eleven thirty. The final offensive group to run gassers was the quarterbacks. There were five prospects, two of whom had been on the roster for several years—Mark Lockenmeyer, the starter for the last three seasons, and Blair Thompson, thirteen-year journeyman and veteran backup. The rest were rookies, one acquired in the seventh round of the most recent draft, the other two free-agent signings. Lockenmeyer, a long-time Greenwood favorite who many said had much greater talent than his record and his statistics suggested, logged the best time, with Thompson logging the worst; it didn't matter, he knew they'd keep him. He was experienced, competent, affable, and—of paramount importance—relatively cheap. One other highlight of the gasser session was that two more players had to be removed from the field, both massive defensive linemen. Gray screamed at one of them as the kid lay in the grass.

The team walked wearily to the dining hall, where another lavish layout awaited them. They ate greedily and silently, eager to replenish their carbs and electrolytes for the afternoon session. Jermaine Hamilton found himself sitting alone again, hunched over a heap of roast chicken and new potatoes. His legs ached already. *On the first damn day*, he thought worriedly. He prayed it was merely a symptom of the torture he had just endured and that it wouldn't get any worse. Corey Reese wanted desperately to sit with somebody—*anybody*. He knew how important it was to socialize, to make it appear that you were accepted by your teammates, that you fit in. It was the kind of political thing coaches would notice. It might not be a make-or-break factor, but it helped. Daimon Foster didn't have as much of an issue with the idea of sitting by himself. He had a feeling he'd done pretty well with the gassers. He still felt like an alien, totally out of place in his surroundings. He didn't know anybody, didn't know where anything was, and didn't feel particularly welcome. He was already learning that the world of pro football could be fairly cold and impersonal. So he focused on his performance. *That's what really counts,* he told himself.

After lunch came a one-hour break, followed by drills with no pads. Nothing unusual, just one-on-ones and other basics. Then dinner, and finally a series of meetings—first the whole team with the head coach, who recapped the day by saying he wasn't pleased with anything, then smaller group sessions. The tight ends met with Dale Greenwood and the rest of the offensive coaches and players, getting the itinerary for the rest of the week, and finally with Jim O'Leary, who was friendly and upbeat and did most of the talking. While Maxwell was his usual stoic self, O'Leary could sense that the other three were uncomfortable around each other, and he tried to ease that. When it became clear he couldn't, he focused on the playbook, giving everyone a heads-up on what would be expected of them in the coming weeks and what the Giants were looking for, overall, in a tight end. He was impressed by how thoroughly his three new students had studied the book so far. They were asking questions of greater depth than others in the building were probably asking at the moment. He sensed they also wanted to know about T. J. Was he really cut from the team? If not, why were they here? And what happened that caused all this controversy in the first place? They wanted to ask these things, but they didn't.

By ten o'clock, every person in the dorm who was hoping to be in a Giants uniform come September was asleep except one. Sitting on the toilet with the lid down, the bathroom door shut, and the lights off, an exhausted Jermaine Hamilton opened his cell phone and, with his oversized fingers, phoned home. His heart pounded harder with each ring, and a part of him wanted to kill the call before anyone picked up. Melanie would be furious—she'd know he was checking up on her. She hadn't been around much. He'd seen her only three times since he was contacted by the team, in fact, and only in passing. She breezed in, then out. The conversations were terse, chilly. Anger seemed to be her default position now. He didn't want to argue with her, didn't want to fight, but he wondered if that was the only way to get her attention. He couldn't believe this was the same woman he had fallen in love with seven years earlier, the one who seemed so loving, attentive, and cheerful. She used to hang on him like a Christmas ornament, her arm wrapped around his and locked so tight he thought it might become gangrenous and fall off. Could it really all have been a scam? Could a person be that shallow, that conniving? He'd been warned by a handful of people to be careful of her through the years, that she matched the profile of the classic gold digger, ready to latch on to anyone who could provide the luxuriant life she craved. But he didn't believe it—he thought that kind of stuff only happened on soap operas. Sometimes in real life, but not as often as some people seemed to believe. No, Melanie Nemus wasn't that way.

Was she?

Four rings later, he heard a familiar voice. "Hi, you've reached the Hamiltons. Leave a message after the beep." The voice was familiar because it was his. Was she there, listening? If so, was she alone? Had she returned to the house only after he left? Was she stretched out on the couch with some guy she picked up at one of the clubs? Were they doing all the things that *they* used to do, in a time so distant now that it seemed like it belonged to someone else? The thought of it made him sick to his stomach. Other images, hopefully fictional, came rolling off the assembly line of his imagination. Amazing how efficient the human mind can be at tormenting its owner.

He terminated the call without leaving a message and, after some hesitation, tried her cell phone. Voice mail again. He left no message, for he knew it would never be returned.

He sat there in the dark for what seemed like a long time and debated what to do. The disciplined part of him issued the order to go to bed so he'd be fully rested for the long day tomorrow. *You're not going to make this team if you don't.* His body simply did not function without proper rest anymore, and this was *training camp*, for God's sake. If you didn't do the things you were supposed to do, the coaches would know it and you'd be gone. There were ten guys waiting in line to take your place, and ten more behind them. Finding someone to play on an NFL team wasn't too tough. It was the ultimate buyer's market.

Another part of him wanted to keep dialing, call and call until Melanie got so fed up that she answered just to scream at him, tell him to leave her the hell alone. That wouldn't be pretty—but it would be *something*. Was that where his feelings had settled? he asked himself. Was that all that was left? *Even if she yells, at least it's attention in some form.* He knew guys like that, whose wives treated them like shit, and their rationale was *Hey, it's better than being ignored.* This made him feel even sicker, and it was an inward-facing disgust. He couldn't help it, though. Part of him still loved her, still wanted her (the *old* her, his mind emphasized), and that part was

writhing in pain over visions of her infidelities. If he could inter-
rupt them just by pushing a few buttons on this tiny, toylike device
in his hand, why not?

He tried the home number again.

Text of letter sent by Barry M. Sturtz via registered mail on
August 3:

> *Alan Gray, Head Coach and Director*
> *of Football Operations*
> *Chet Palmer, Vice President and General Manager*
> *c/o The New York Football Giants*
> *Giants Stadium*
> *East Rutherford, New Jersey 07073*

> *Gentlemen:*
> *   This letter concerns the matter we discussed as a group on*
> *July 14, which was then briefly revisited by Chet Palmer and*

myself one week later over the phone—that of the desired contract renegotiation between my client, Thomas James Brookman, and your organization. To restate the matter, it is the belief of my client and myself that the former is fully within his rights and within reason to request the aforementioned renegotiation, as he has, statistically and provably, performed at a level above and beyond that of his peers since his entry into the league. Over the course of the last season, in fact, he has carried out his duties in a fashion that could readily be termed "best" at his position. And yet, he is earning a salary commensurate with players at the lowest-performing levels. When I requested that his salary be increased to that of his contemporaries playing on the same level—not that his salary be higher, but only representative of an average of the other three top players at his position—I was firmly rebuffed, and in fact threatened to have my client "benched" for the course of the upcoming season. When I suggested several other options, all were met with a similar response.

Therefore, after careful consideration, I regretfully submit this as notice to the following: 1) that my client will continue to remain at home rather than in training camp until this matter can be resolved fairly and amicably, and 2) that this be considered a formal grievance filed by myself on behalf of my client.

I would like to state again that I hope we can settle this matter in a fashion that is fair to both parties, and move forward. It is requested that the parties to whom this letter is directed kindly furnish a response, in accordance with the Collective

Bargaining Agreement (Article IX, Section 3) within seven days of receipt.

Thank you.
Sincerely,
Barry M. Sturtz, Owner and President Performers LLC
CC: NFLPA, NFL Management Council

Greg Bolton knew he needed to improve his diet. He'd been making that promise to himself for . . . *what, two years now?* His physician—the same guy he'd been seeing for the last six years after finding him randomly in the United HealthCare search engine just one week after he and his family moved to Michigan—told him repeatedly that he needed to mend his high-cholesterol ways or earn honorary membership in what he called "Club Cardiac." "You're thirty-nine now, Greg, not seventeen," the bastard said sternly, sounding like a grandmother. "Your body doesn't bounce back the way it used to."

Sitting in the darkened corner of a Chili's restaurant in North Carolina's Raleigh-Durham International Airport with an almost-finished cheeseburger on the plate next to his laptop, Bolton thought about this and shook his head. *What the doc doesn't realize is that I'm going to kill myself from overwork anyway, so I'm going to eat whatever I want in the meantime.*

The pace had indeed been murderous these last few weeks. ESPN had him back in the hot seat of the third-straight "Greg Bolton's Training Camp-Palooza." The first one had been a monster hit two years ago, featuring a not-so-subtle mix of humor, behind-the-scenes investigation, and solid reportage. Bolton discovered, to his astonishment, that he actually had some on-screen charisma. He didn't see what the big deal was, but if the fans enjoyed it, that was good enough for him—and certainly good enough for the network. The gods rewarded his newfound fame with a salary bump and a new title, which was great. Of course, it also meant longer hours, more work, and more stress and strain. In turn, that meant less time at home with his wife and five-year-old son, Chase, whom he adored and couldn't wait to see in a few hours. Still, this was what he'd always dreamed about since he came out of Kent State with his journalism degree. John Clayton (whom he secretly thought of as one of the most encyclopedic minds the sportswriting world had ever seen) had his own thing, and draft guru Mel Kiper Jr. had his. Now he had one, too.

He finished off the burger, and when the waitress came to clear the table, he ordered some ice cream (disregarding the tiny barbs of guilt over not making it frozen yogurt or sherbet instead; *screw that*). An easy evening glow had settled along the horizon, somehow making the concrete of the tarmac and the steel of the airplanes postcard-pretty. He appreciated the view for a moment, but it was more to take his eyes away from the screen than anything else. When he wasn't in front of the camera, it seemed, he was staring into the damn thing. He didn't wear glasses yet, but he knew they, too, were in his future. Most of the ESPN folks pulled double duty as writers, and he had a syndicated column in more than a hundred papers around the country, plus a handful overseas.

The piece he was working on right now was an update on the Panthers' camp. Coach Martello had been helpful but reserved. Once again, Martello and his staff had pulled off a very quiet but very excellent draft, and once again they managed to get all their new guys signed and on the field in plenty of time. Jerry Richardson ran a tight ship over there, and Bolton was, like countless others around the league, very impressed with the organization. Martello was a formidable coach, and the Panthers always produced a competitive team. *Solid*—that was the word he always thought of, although he had already applied it to them so many times in his writing that he had to find other ways to get this point across. This afternoon he'd shot about two hours' worth of film from their camp in Spartanburg. Maybe three minutes would end up on television. And nothing of great note occurred, so there wasn't much to write about. During one-on-one drills, a rookie receiver got into a shoving match with a veteran safety, and it descended into an all-out brawl. Bolton was standing no more than twenty feet away. It wasn't the first such altercation he'd ever seen, and it certainly wouldn't be the last. But he didn't mention it in the article. Neither player ended up getting injured or tossed off the team, so there really wasn't anything to say. What he found personally interesting about these incidents, however, was the way the coaches seemed to like them. It showed fire in the souls of the participants, a certain competitive spirit that was essential to success in the NFL. He even knew of several fights that had been purposely precipitated *by* the coaches, who instructed a veteran player to push a younger guy around to see what kind of guts he really had. Bolton didn't think that was the case here, though. Just two idiots losing their temper in the heat.

He turned back to the glowing screen and discovered the waitress had left the ice cream without a sound. He picked it up and dug in. Just as he put the first spoonful in his mouth, the Instant Messenger box popped up in front of the Microsoft Word document. The text was brief and to the point, and Bolton was awake again.

CMC88: Are you there, Greg?

He dropped the bowl back onto the glossy table, where it slid a few inches and almost went over the edge, and set his hands on the keyboard.

GEB@ESPN: Yes, I'm here. Thanks for the note. What's going on?

He hoped that sounded casual enough. There was very little equality in this relationship, but he didn't mind as long as the information kept flowing.

CMC88: A new development today. Barry Sturtz has filed a formal grievance against the team. He's going to keep T. J. Brookman out of camp until they get a new deal.

GEB@ESPN: That's incredible. Gray and Palmer didn't think Sturtz would take this step, did they?

CMC88: No, they thought he'd give in.

GEB@ESPN: What are Gray and Palmer going to do?

CMC88: I don't know yet, but they're shocked that it's come to this.

GEB@ESPN: Do you know what Sturtz is asking for? How much?

CMC88: He wants the average of the three highest-paid tight ends in the league.

GEB@ESPN: Do you feel he's worth that?

From a reporting standpoint, this was a pointless question. Bolton had no idea who the source was, so the response would have no value. He slipped it in there anyway, hoping the answer would shed some light on the identity of the person on the other end of this dialogue, which had been going on sporadically for two weeks now.

CMC88: I'm not close enough to the situation to be able to answer that with any authority, but I know Brookman's statistics have been good since he arrived in New York.

Smart, safe answer, Bolton thought. *Whoever this guy is, he's no fool.* Someone in the front office, most likely. An assistant, or maybe an executive trying to undercut Gray or Palmer so he can take a step up.

GEB@ESPN: How is the rest of the team responding to the conflict?

A dual-purpose question—again, to gain insight into the mystery person, but also to dig up more information for the next piece.

CMC88: I don't think the mood around the club is very good, but it's probably due more to other things than to this. But this isn't helping.

Bingo! What a terrific sentiment, definitely usable. *The natives are restless.*

GEB@ESPN: What other things? I'm guessing you can't tell me everything, but can you tell me >> some << things? Anything?

CMC88: There's a losing attitude around here, a sense of hope-lessness. The team hasn't had a winning record in a while. I'm not saying a mutiny is about to occur, but the players, I think, are beginning to lose faith.

GEB@ESPN: That's interesting. How about the other three tight ends? The new ones? How are they doing?

CMC88: Too early to say.

GEB@ESPN: Any chance one of them could replace Brookman, and Brookman could be released?

CMC88: Again, too early to say.

GEB@ESPN: What about the—

CMC88: I have to go now, Greg. Sorry. I'll be in touch.

GEB@ESPN: Wait, please. One more question.

Bolton waited, but after a few minutes it was obvious his source had abandoned him. That's how it always ended, abruptly, without warning. He was a little disappointed, but not much—once again, he got the scoop. His competitors were going crazy trying to figure out how he knew so much about the story; everybody wanted to know who was feeding him. A little professional jealousy, but that was life. He frankly wasn't even sure he *cared* who the source was. He had begun to think of the guy as his personal Deep Throat—the NFL equivalent of Mark Felt, the former assistant director of the FBI who gave *Washington Post* reporters Woodward and Bernstein the information that eventually led to the exposure of the Watergate scandal and the downfall of President Richard M. Nixon. What was more of a mystery to Bolton was why this person had chosen *him.* There were other sportswriters and broadcasters with more experience, more respect, more prestige. Why Greg Bolton? He was certainly thankful for it, but he couldn't help wondering about the rationale.

Now he had to call around the Giants' offices and talk to a few people, follow up on the information to confirm it. He knew it would be solid; so far it had been dead-on. Still, this was the procedure. He got the feeling the front-office folks over there were beginning to hate hearing from him. The last person he spoke with was so nasty that he knew he was on the right track. *A bitter employee?* he wondered, then replaced the word "bitter" in his mind with "disgruntled." It was an adjective that had become popular in recent years, the buzzword for people who were angry with their employers and decided to strike back in whatever way they could. If they were postal workers, it usually involved weaponry and bloodshed. In this case, however, the method of vengeance was a bit more subtle.

Pure gold.

With renewed energy and less than an hour to go before his plane departed, Bolton closed out the yawner of a Panthers story and opened a new document. Forty minutes later it was traveling to his editor via the miracle of cyberspace.

From there it became one of the lead stories on *SportsCenter.*

Training camp, Daimon Foster realized after a few days, was all about one thing—*execution.*

You didn't make the team because you were the biggest or the fastest. You didn't make it because you went to the best school or had the most impressive stats at the combines. You made it because you could execute. A lot of guys who appeared to have everything going for them, at least on paper, couldn't do it. They had the strength of bulls and the speed of gazelles, but, for one tragic reason or another, they just couldn't make the plays happen. *It's all about getting it done.*

When he pitched this notion to Jim O'Leary on the sixth day, as they walked to the fields in the morning, the O'Leary smiled and nodded. "You got it." Foster thought he was impressed, perhaps because he had figured it out so quickly whereas some who had been to camps three or four times never made this crucial realization. "No team in the league can afford to keep a guy who can't make plays," O'Leary added. It was as simple as that—nothing else mattered. You could be a walk-on who was working as a car mechanic the week before, and if you could make amazing throws as a quarterback or amazing catches as a receiver, they'd sign your ass to a contract.

Foster stood on the sidelines, along with Reese, Hamilton, and most of his other teammates, and watched Greenwood take small groups through one drill after another. Everyone who had played organized football—from Pop Warner to the pros—knew about drills. There were literally thousands of them, each with a different purpose. Some focused on the running game, some on passing. Some were for the benefit of the defense, some for the offense. Some exposed weaknesses in single positions—and, to that end, a few matched up only two guys in what amounted to little more than tests of raw strength and willpower. There were drills being used that had been dreamed up by coaches half a century ago, and others that had been designed within the last few weeks. They produced nothing but data.

Greenwood started the session with a drill for the offensive line. He wanted to see who could stop the blitz. He borrowed some of Gray's defensive hopefuls, and he purposely made the situation disproportionate—five O-liners against seven D's in a 4–3 formation. They were in full pads, but the quarterback was redshirted and therefore untouchable. The belief was that if the O-line could hold off all seven of them for a respectable amount of time, they could more than handle similar pressure in a real game, where they would have the added support of the rest of the offense. The quarterback made the count, and the D-backs bounced and jittered, juiced by the challenge and hungry to prove their worth to their own coaches. Greenwood clicked his stopwatch the moment the ball was snapped. The defense would, of course, eventually penetrate and collapse the pocket; the issue was how long this would take. At one point, a second-year linebacker knocked starting quarterback Mark Lockenmeyer to the ground, which earned him Dale Greenwood's considerable, albeit rarely displayed, wrath. There were some shoving matches as well.

At just after eleven, Greenwood turned to his three new tight end prospects and said, "Okay, you guys are next. Daimon, you first, pal."

With butterflies in his belly, Foster jogged out to the field and waited for the others to line up. This would be another lopsided drill in favor of the defense. The goal of the offense was to open a lane for the running back. The defense also had the ridiculous advantage of knowing exactly what play was coming, so the challenge for the O-guys was even greater. Again, it was believed that their success in this one-sided situation would prove their ability to execute in a normal game, where the opponent would be much less likely to know what to expect.

Foster positioned himself in the traditional three-point stance on the right side, and his butterflies turned into bats when he saw Jared Kirch, the 255-pound, six-five outside linebacker, move directly in front of him. Kirch was a walking oak tree. In his fourth year with the team after being drafted in the third round out of Fresno State, he looked more like a creature from a sci-fi novel than a human being. The dark face framed inside the helmet was carved from granite and featured the wild eyes of a serial killer. There was little doubt that Kirch would make the team, but he wasn't taking any chances. He was the perfect Alan Gray–type guy, bordering on madness and eager to inflict pain. *This guy could snap my head off and eat it*, Foster thought, mustering all his strength to appear casual. In that moment, for whatever reason, he also remembered something he read way back when he was preparing for the combines. *Everything is faster in the NFL. Forget what you saw in college.*

As Lockenmeyer called the count, Foster realized Kirch was staring him down, looking not just at him but *into* him. At this level, the psychology was as important as the physics. *If they successfully intimidate you, they've already beaten you.*

When the ball was snapped, Kirch came off the line as if he'd been fired from a bazooka. Foster had watched other guys do this for the last five days, yet it was an entirely different experience when you were part of it. He compared it to watching a baseball game. On TV, you could actually see the ball move from the pitcher to the catcher. In person, it appeared as little more than a blur.

Kirch's monster-hands came up and pushed Foster off his feet in a span of perhaps half a second. The next thing Daimon Foster knew, he was staring at the blue sky and being serenaded by the humiliating sound of his teammates' laughter.

"Sonofa*bitch*!" he growled, jumping back up.

"We may want to try that one again," Greenwood said flatly. Foster was too embarrassed to make eye contact with him, but with his peripheral vision he could see Jim O'Leary smiling. He seemed to have been granted a pass on this first error. A little comedy to ease the tension.

As Kirch jogged past Foster to return to his side of the line, he quipped, "Get used to it, princess."

Few things shifted Foster's motivation into high gear faster than being kicked when he was down. Sci-fi freak or not, Jared Kirch was not going to get the better of him twice. And Foster realized something else, something that would prove invaluable in the future. *I've established an image of myself in his mind, so now he has an expectation of me. I can use this to my advantage.*

They lined up again, and when the ball was snapped, Foster didn't make the mistake of moving upward, where his body would be an easier target. Instead, he attacked low and in, applying his hands to Kirch's considerable torso while planting one foot a bit behind the other. He pushed with all available power, and the world spun around crazily. For a fearful moment he thought Kirch had somehow gotten the better of him again. When he opened his eyes, however, he found he was still standing, his running back zipping past him on the left, and Jared Kirch lying on the grass at his feet. There was more laughter, accompanied this time by sporadic applause.

"Holy shit," Daimon said so quietly that no one heard it. A smile began forming on his lips, too, but he squelched it.

"Lucky motherfucker," Kirch said as he scrambled up. Foster wanted to say, *Not bad for a princess, huh?* but thought better of it. He had made his first enemy, one who no doubt would have him in his gunsights for the next few weeks. There was no point in throwing more fuel on the fire.

Corey Reese was next. He faced off against one of Gray's rookies. The kid wasn't as big as Kirch, but he had the unmistakable fire and intensity of a greenhorn.

"I'm gonna getcha," the kid kept saying, bouncing on the balls of his feet. He said it so fast that it sounded like one word. *Umgonna-gitcha. Umgonnagitcha.* Reese ignored him, watched Lockenmeyer, and waited for the count. When the ball moved, the kid lunged forward—but his target was almost gone before he got there. Reese dropped low and inside, and the rookie missed him completely, stumbling over Reese's well-conceived chop block and sailing to the ground. The laughter was almost deafening, and the kid walked sheepishly away, quickly dispatched and a little wiser. Everyone remembered why Corey Reese had once been one of the best in his position—he was a notch or two smarter than most.

Turning randomly to one of his teammates, Reese said with a grin, "I love doing that." The teammate, who had had no earlier exchanges with Reese, smiled back and said, "Sweet."

Jermaine Hamilton lined up opposite another kid, one who had remained quiet throughout most of camp. His name was Dorwin Leer. Like Kirch, Leer was a giant and in immaculate physical shape. Hamilton had seen him around, knew that he wore little round glasses and read classic literature when he wasn't on the field. He kept himself well groomed and moved in a careful, measured way. An intellect—a guy who reflected upon football in an *intellectual* way. If he hadn't been gifted with his physique, he'd probably be a professor somewhere. Hamilton had seen his type before.

Leer lined up on the opposite side. His stance was picture-perfect, as if he were posing for a photograph in a how-to guide. When the snap came, he launched flawlessly off the line, leaning forward just enough to produce leverage without risk of losing his balance. He'd probably practiced this in front of a mirror a few hundred times.

Hamilton couldn't help laughing as he ducked low, reached out, and actually grabbed a hunk of Leer's stomach with both hands.

The stunned defensive end wanted to push Hamilton away, but he instinctively realized this would likely cost him a skin graft about a foot long. Hamilton then drove his hopelessly perplexed victim back far enough to create a lane wide enough for an ocean liner. The running back participating in the drill didn't even bother going through it.

"You won't find that one in a book," Hamilton said, putting his arm around Leer as they walked away, "but you better watch out for it." Hamilton then made the good-natured gesture of showing Leer how to defend against it—by slapping the tight end's hands down first, then continuing the motion with an upward push against the chest.

At the end of the morning session, some of the players took the time to sign autographs for fans who'd lined up along the fences. Neither Hamilton, Reese, nor Foster joined them—at first. All three were eventually recruited by the pleas of a small but growing contingency of fans who had been watching them and following the saga of T. J. Brookman in the media.

Greenwood and O'Leary took note of this.

"What did you think?" O'Leary asked.

Dale Greenwood said, "I think we may be onto something here."

Barry Sturtz had been a fan of the James Bond movies all his life. Ever since he saw *Dr. No* as a child, he'd been hooked. The action and adventure were irresistible enough, but the fact that the guy was impossibly handsome and never failed to get laid was even more so. He could shoot the balls off a gnat at a hundred paces, wore the best clothes, had the coolest gadgets, and ate in the finest restaurants while tramping through the most magnificent cities in the world. Put simply, he was living the life every red-blooded heterosexual male dreamed of living but never would.

Yet now, on this warm and sunny August day, Sturtz couldn't help feeling just a little bit like his old hero.

The restaurant in this case wasn't quite up to Bond standards—it wasn't a candlelit bistro or a society tearoom, but rather a pancake house called Ellie's. And it wasn't Paris or Melbourne, but a suburb he'd never heard of and wouldn't have found without the aid of MapQuest. Nevertheless, there was an undeniable Bond-esque feel to this visit. He'd heard about stuff like this going on in the league before but never imagined he'd one day be a part of it.

The little silver bell above the door rang out, as it had done every minute or so. Sturtz looked over but didn't see his man come in. Couple of guys in jeans and plaid shirts, most likely a pair of truckers stopping in for a meal. Sitting at the counter sipping his black coffee—as opposed to a vodka martini, shaken not stirred—Sturtz realized this was a busy place. And, the businessman part of him noticed, it appeared to be fairly well run, too. The person in charge, as far as he could gather, was the crusty old bastard doing the cooking. Like something out of a '70s TV show, he had the paper hat, the crewneck T-shirt, the filthy apron, and the big beefy arms (no military-service tattoo or dangling cigarette, though). When he spoke, the waitresses jumped. They looked panicked, frantic. Sturtz had a feeling they were the last—and therefore the best—in what was probably a long line of employee "tryouts." The part of him that understood people and had tremendous intuition for what made them tick grasped the dynamics of the situation almost immediately. In here, customers got what they wanted, period. If they didn't, someone paid dearly. And yet, as busy as they were, everything was spotlessly clean and in its place, the food was delivered in a timely fashion (and smelled pretty damn good), and every customer-employee interaction came with a smile. The only other steady sound Sturtz noticed apart from the bell over the door was the glorious melody of the electronic cash register.

Fifteen more minutes passed, a dozen or so people came and went, and he was still alone. He checked his watch again and wondered, with a touch of fear, if he was in the wrong place. He took the little slip of paper from the outside pocket of his blazer—it was a wrinkled dry-cleaning receipt, actually—and reviewed the notes he had jotted feverishly while trapping his cell phone between his ear and shoulder two days earlier. Twelve thirty, Ellie's, and then the address. Yes, this was right.

A kid of perhaps eighteen or nineteen came up and sat next to him. Jeans, T-shirt, black lambskin jacket. Brown hair combed in a single, dramatic sweep to one side. He looked like he'd graduated college within the last week and was now thinking about going to the West Coast to try his hand at acting.

"I'm sorry, but can you sit somewhere else?" Sturtz said as politely but firmly as possible. "I'm supposed to meet someone here."

"I know you are," the kid said, rubbing his hands together and staring straight ahead. His smile was faint, almost smart-alecky, but there was something in his voice and in his face that suggested intelligence. This wasn't just some arrogant teenager.

"You're . . . the guy?"

"No, I represent the guy. My name's Mike." He put his hand out and smiled, still looking away. "Nice to meet you, Barry."

Sturtz was stunned.

"You, too," he said, giving the hand a quick shake.

One of the waitresses came over and removed the pencil from behind her ear. "Hiya, cutie," she said to Mike.

"Hey. Can I have a Diet Coke, please?"

"That's it?"

"Yeah, for now."

"Okay."

The waitress walked off, and Mike watched her go. Although she was an attractive woman, Sturtz's new friend didn't seem to be appraising her in the way that most men his age would. It was almost a passive, clinical study, as if he were taking mental notes for an anthropology class currently covering the blue-collar segment of society.

"So, we understand your client is interested in perhaps moving on," he said quietly.

Sturtz already knew the team that was interested in T. J. He hadn't contacted them, as that was explicitly against league rules. Technically, they weren't permitted to contact *him*, either. But. . . .

One didn't need to have a professional cardplayer's instincts to sense how uncomfortable—and potentially explosive—this situation really was. Sturtz realized this kid wasn't making eye contact specifically because he didn't want anyone to know they were interacting. So, in keeping with the spirit of the moment, he also turned away, setting his elbows on the counter and focusing on the big menu board that hung just under the ceiling in a forward tilt.

"Yes, that's true. And I understand you might be interested in providing a place that he can move to."

"Correct."

"So you've heard about the grievance, then?"

"We have a copy of it," Mike said simply. Sturtz had no idea how in hell he obtained such a copy, but something told him the guy wasn't lying. By this point he was in serious doubt as to whether his name was really Mike. What was even more intriguing, however, was that he didn't look the least bit familiar. Sturtz had been involved in professional sports for almost fifteen years, most of it with the NFL. He knew everyone on every team—players, coaches, executives, lower echelon. He even knew the guys who worked at every stadium, most of them on a first-name basis. He'd never seen this individual in his life. He trusted his memory for faces, even more than his memory for names, and he had no mental file on this Mike or anyone who faintly resembled him.

Regardless, he plowed ahead. "Okay, then you should also know that, should we get his team to agree to a trade, it won't be cheap."

"We've anticipated that."

"No, I mean he won't be cheap to obtain *in the first place.* My client and I have already been assured that, should the team decide to trade him, they're going to want a bundle."

"Because they don't really want to trade him."

"Right."

"Of course. We know."

"And you're still willing to explore it?"

"Definitely."

Going over it in his mind, Sturtz realized this freewheeling attitude wasn't really all that hard to believe. The team Mike was representing had acquired, just last year, a quarterback with the third pick of the draft. He was a stellar choice, with amazing stats and, most agreed, a limitless future. Thinking about it reminded Sturtz, with some lingering bitterness, that he'd been about one nanometer away from signing the kid as a client, but one of his biggest competitors snatched him up at the last minute. Sturtz still had no idea what the rival agent offered that sealed the deal, but he was certain, knowing the agent as he did, it wasn't something that would've held up in an ethics review.

"And even if we get to that point, my client does not come cheap. That's why we're in this situation to begin with."

"Fully understood," Mike said without flinching. In fact, he seemed the tiniest bit irritated by what was apparently information he already knew and had thoroughly discussed with his superiors. The quarterback in question had been surrounded by great receivers in college, including a superb tight end, who went to Denver early in the second round of the same draft. It came as no surprise to Sturtz that they wanted to make sure the kid continued to have that safety net. So they were building an entirely new offense around him, and they wanted T. J. Brookman to be a part of it.

Perfect.

"So what happens next?" Sturtz asked. "What do we do now?"

"We wait and see what happens with your grievance."

"Ultimately, does it matter?" Sturtz said.

"It might, it might not," Mike replied. "If the league grants your wish, you'll be in a very good position indeed."

"Well, it's easier to get a date when you have more than one interested party."

Mike took a long sip of his Diet Coke before saying, "To be sure." Then he turned and faced Sturtz directly for the first time, put on a devastating smile, and added, "Which is why we wanted to get in touch first. We'll pay your guy what he wants. We know how much you're thinking, and we know he's worth it. And we've got the money to spend, too."

This much Sturtz knew. After four abysmal years, the team in question was going through a vigorous rebuilding phase, and one bright spot in the gloom was that all of their high-priced players had gone out to pasture and their back-loaded contracts had been covered. Put simply, the financial wounds had finally healed.

"Sounds great," Sturtz said. "Then I assume you'll follow proceedings and be in touch?"

One more long sip and the soda was gone. Mike pulled two ragged bills from the pocket of his black leather jacket and tossed them on the counter.

"I will indeed," he said casually, as if this were nothing more than the end of a lame date. "Gotta run, but thanks for your time. We appreciate it."

"Sure," Sturtz replied, and he watched one of the most unusual characters he'd ever met walk out the door and disappear into the sunny afternoon.

They would never see each other again.

13

The door to Deluxe Suite Number Six in London's Royal Garden Hotel flew open, and Dorland Kenner, forty-two-year-old owner of the New York Giants, zoomed through like an overwound toy. He pulled off his jacket and tie and tossed them on the loveseat, then nimbly undid the buttons of his white dress shirt and tossed that, too. He was a handsome individual, with neatly groomed dark hair and a sharp-featured, Ivy League face. He glanced at his wristwatch, a Cartier his wife had given him this past Christmas, and shook his head.

He passed through the sitting room and went into the bedroom— then came to an abrupt halt. The fresh shirt and tie should've been hanging on the closet doorknob, adorned in lightweight dry-cleaner's plastic. But they weren't. Standing there in the dying afternoon sunlight in his dress pants and crewneck undershirt, he looked around briefly to see if perhaps they'd been hung some-where else.

"Hell," he said softly. He skirted the queen-sized bed and got to the phone, tapping the speed-dial button for the laundry service.

"Hi, yes, this is Dorland Kenner in Suite Six. There was sup-posed to be a shirt and tie waiting for me, but I don't see them any-where. What's that? Oh, okay. No, that's fine. Just please bring them up right away. I have a dinner appointment, and I have to leave shortly. Sure, thank you."

He set the phone back into its cradle and, as a reflex, checked his watch again. It was roughly one minute later.

The dinner was with the heads of an investment firm, one of several that the Kenner family dealt with in Europe. This one han-dled mostly real estate. It was a pretty boring group, all things con-sidered, but they got results. Dorland's father had done business with them since the late '70s, and once William Kenner liked you, he kept you around forever.

The family's landholdings were just one facet of the Kenner em-pire that had been placed on Dorland's shoulders after his father's death from colon cancer five years earlier. Each of the Kenner siblings—Jared, Michael, and Denise were the other three—got a piece of the pie to manage as he or she saw fit. Jared, a Stanford law school graduate, had his own practice and therefore handled all le-gal matters. Michael ran the textile industry that made his father wealthy in the first place. Denise took care of the three philan-thropic organizations. Dorland, the youngest, inherited all invest-ments, several smaller profitable companies, and a football team known as the New York Giants. Dorland suspected his father handed him this responsibility because he'd been the most athletic of the children, a star in college in both football and baseball. But he wasn't good enough to go pro, and he knew it. Besides, his heart was in business, and he breezed through Duke with sterling grades on his way to an MBA that he planned to put to good use.

He had no clue how to run a football club, however, and the first few years were unsteady. His heart was in the right place, though, and he tried to learn the ropes. It was a slow process, as the other sectors of his late father's universe absorbed most of his time. Plus, he was determined to be a dedicated husband and father. So he made the decision to leave the team under the command of Alan Gray (football side) and Chet Palmer (business side) early on. It was only in the past year that he had begun making quantifiable progress as the club's president and CEO, with the goal of having a firm grip on its daily operations by the end of the fifth year and thus being able to independently make sound decisions concerning its future.

While speaking with his wife, Annie, he heard a voice in the other room.

"Hello?"

He went out there and found a smallish woman of Asian decent in a maid's uniform, his shirt and tie hanging from her finger.

She smiled. "Here are your things," she said sheepishly, as if it were her fault they hadn't been ready. The mixture of Eastern and Western accents created a peculiar hybrid.

Kenner smiled back, reaching into his pocket. "Great, thank you for getting it up here in such a hurry. I'm sorry, but I have to go right back out or else I wouldn't have called." He handed her twenty pounds.

The woman looked at it as if he'd just placed a snake in her hand.

"No, no, only seven," she said.

"You keep the rest," he told her. "I appreciate you getting it to me so quickly."

"Oh, okay. Thank you." She performed a spare, awkward bow and retreated to the hallway, closing the door.

Kenner returned to the bedroom, tearing off the plastic and slipping into the shirt as he moved along. He finished the call with his wife while doing the tie, then grabbed the remote and clicked on the TV. He went through the stock prices, seeing nothing of note, and switched to ESPN. His timing couldn't have been better—or, depending on your perspective, worse.

". . . and now that this grievance has been officially filed with the league, the situation could spiral downward into a nasty spitting match, much in the spirit of a contentious divorce," Greg Bolton was saying. He was standing in a studio somewhere, in a suit and tie, with a black backdrop covered by ESPN logos in red. "So the relationship between T. J. Brookman and the New York Giants appears to be getting worse instead of better."

The broadcaster back at network headquarters thanked Bolton for his fine reporting and told him to keep on the story, then moved along to a baseball update.

Kenner was on the phone again in seconds. He switched to speaker and sat down on the bed, leaning forward with his elbows on his knees and his hands folded. The first person he spoke with was Amanda Bellwich, Alan Gray's assistant. Then, a moment later, Gray himself.

"Dorland! How are things going over there on the other side of the pond?"

"Busy," Kenner replied. "Very busy."

"Nothing wrong with that," Gray told him.

"No, nothing at all. Hey, listen, I'm in my hotel room, on my way back out, but I just turned on ESPN and saw this story about a grievance that T. J. Brookman filed against us. Is this true?"

There was a pause, and then Gray said, in a grave tone, "Yeah, I'm afraid it is. It looks like he's turned on us."

"Why?"

"He wants more money. He and that asshole agent of his."

If there was one feature of Alan Gray's personality that Kenner never cared for, it was his generous use of profanity. Kenner was sometimes guilty of it himself, but he believed a little went a long way. Gray used it as if he were being paid by the word. Some conversations with him were like watching lost scenes from *Scarface*.

"If I'm not mistaken," Kenner went on regardless, "T. J.'s one of the best tight ends in the league. He's done some great things for us, hasn't he?"

"There's no doubt the kid's talented," Gray replied, "but he signed a contract, and Chet and I expect him to honor it."

"But what about—"

"He only has one year left—this coming season—on the damn deal anyway. After that, we'll be happy to come up with a new one, something that's better suited to his current skills and contribution. But if we give him a new contract now, they'll all be coming in with their asshole agents. It'll be a stampede."

Another pause, this time from Kenner's side.

"Don't worry, he'll be properly compensated," Gray assured him. "But for right now, what with the vast complexities of the salary cap and everything, we really can't screw around too much with our current setup." Gray had inserted the words "salary cap" on purpose, because he and Chet Palmer had determined, via previous conversations, that they had a magical effect on Dorland Kenner. He had some idea of how the cap worked, but the finer points of it were still out of reach. This was why the team had hired a cap expert full-time. In truth, Alan Gray didn't know much more about the cap than Kenner did, but he did recognize its manipulative value. When in doubt, bring "salary cap" out, and amazing things would happen.

"Next year will be different," Gray went on, "but this year, we just can't."

Kenner was nodding. "Okay, and what happens with this grievance? It's not making us look too good, is it? As I'm watching this report, looking at it from a fan's perspective, I'm thinking the Giants are the bad guys here."

"Only for the moment," Gray said. "Only for the moment. I'm very confident this will fizzle into nothing."

"Why do you say that?"

"Well, mainly because T. J.'s claims are unfounded. Yes, he wants more money. Don't we all? Doesn't everyone? And he and that little prick of an agent waited until right before training camp to pull this. Why not back in April or May, when we would've had time to deal with it? Why right now? Because he thinks it gives him leverage, that's why. Frankly, I think it makes them look bad, not us."

Kenner nodded. This made some sense, he thought. "And in the meantime, he's not in training camp, right?"

"That's right. We're trying out three other guys, all of whom have some real talent. If worse comes to worse, we'll have to play one of them instead."

"But they won't be as effective on the field as T. J.," Kenner noted.

"You never know," Gray said quickly. "We didn't think T. J. would turn into the player he's become, either. But I had a feeling about him."

Kenner sighed. "Okay. I guess the situation's about as good as it can be, all things considered."

"Don't worry," Gray said. "This'll work out in the end. T. J. will be here, playing and contributing."

Kenner nodded again. Then he remembered why he was back in his hotel room in the first place. When he checked his watch for the third time, his heart skipped a beat. "All right, Alan, thanks as always for your time."

"My pleasure."

"Please keep me updated on what's happening with this."

"I sure will."

Kenner terminated the call with a hard tap on the speaker button and zoomed out, grabbing his jacket and sliding his arms into it before he reached the door. A moment later he hit the London sidewalk and jumped into the first available cab. It melted into the traffic flow and was gone.

Back in northern New Jersey, at the team's offices in Giants Stadium, Chet Palmer was sitting at his computer, typing out an e-mail that would be sent to everyone in the organization, when his phone rang. Without taking his eyes from the screen, he grabbed the receiver.

"Chet Palmer."

"It's Gray," the coach said gruffly from 135 miles away, in Albany.

Palmer instantly knew something was wrong; he'd been dealing with the guy long enough to spot that certain tone in his voice.

"What's the matter?"

"The boy knows about the situation with Brookman and Sturtz."

Anytime Gray spoke to Palmer about Dorland Kenner, he referred to him as "the boy." Put simply, Gray was the type who believed that the young should have no function in society other than to serve at the pleasure of those who were older—and they most certainly should not be the *employers* of those who were older. Although Gray never came out and said as much, Palmer could sense that he loathed, with every fiber of his being, the fact that the man who provided his paycheck was more than twenty-five years younger. Palmer was also of the belief that Alan Gray enjoyed being a coach, at least in part, because it gave him limitless opportunity to push kids around—many of whom were already wealthier and more highly regarded than he would ever be. And if they disobeyed or displeased him, he could exact whatever punishment suited his whimsy. It was yet another nasty thought about Alan Gray, but he couldn't deny what he'd seen over the years.

"How'd he find out?" Palmer asked.

"It was on fucking ESPN, Chet!"

"Oh, good God."

"Yeah, good God."

"Well, don't get all riled. It won't go anywhere."

"That's what I told the sonofabitch," Gray said, and Palmer was thankful the phones around here weren't bugged—whereas in some clubs, or at least he'd been told by some reliable sources, they usually were. "He's concerned anyway. Wants to know what's going on. Wants to be updated."

"Okay, so we'll keep him updated. We'll manage the situation, and we'll keep him updated."

"Yeah," Gray said, then let out a quick, irritated sound. "You know, I liked it a lot better when that fucker wasn't so interested in how things worked around here."

"I know," Palmer said.

"One thing's for sure," Gray went on.

"What's that?"

"We have to find our mole."

"Our who?"

"The mole. The scumbag who's feeding all this inside information to the media."

"Alan, that could be anyone," Palmer said. "Teams always have moles. Sometimes more than one. How are we going to accomplish that?"

"I'll find out who it is, trust me," Gray told him, and Palmer detected the slightest touch of excitement in his voice—like a hunter in the hour before the fox is released, almost twitchy with psychotic eagerness. Suddenly Palmer wanted this conversation to end.

"Trust me," Gray said again, "I'll find him . . . or her."

Then Palmer got his wish—the call was terminated, followed by the dull single note of the dial tone.

"See how the outside linebacker cuts in right here?" Jim O'Leary asked, using his laser pointer to place a small, glowing dot on the player in question. The slightly blurred frame was frozen to the markerboard in the tiny classroom assigned to the tight ends. O'Leary sat behind a black IBM laptop, an overhead projector humming alongside it. "When he does that, you need to break from the outside lineman you're covering and let the left tackle step in."

Jermaine Hamilton, looking as serious as ever, nodded. "My initial assignment is the outside lineman, unless the back moves in," he said.

"That's right. Since we place a second tight end on the opposite side, along with a receiver," O'Leary continued, moving the dot over, "the defense may be lured away from the sweep, so this scenario shouldn't be that common."

"The left guard pulls at the snap," Daimon Foster said, "leading a blocking line in the direction of the run."

"Correct."

"Along with the center," Corey Reese added, "to create a curtain so the back can turn the corner."

"You got it."

It was a toss-sweep play that the team had used sparingly over the last season. Greenwood had swiped it from the Cowboys' playbook and made some modifications to fit his own personnel. When properly executed, it all but guaranteed minor upfield progress, ideal in short-yardage situations. Occasionally it provided a bit more than that. Once, when running back Jason Thomas found himself hemmed in, Lockenmeyer yelled for the ball to be tossed back to him in an impromptu flea-flicker. He then mailed it twenty-eight yards downfield to T. J. Brookman, who had found a lane on the weak side and was wide open. Brookman went twelve more yards for an easy score against the 49ers. It was almost a sandlot play, unplanned and undisciplined, but Greenwood liked it so much that he put it in the book. He even had the unit practice it from time to time, although he hadn't used it in a game yet—it was such a big deal in the highlight films that defensive coordinators watched for it.

"By putting one of you on the far side of the action," O'Leary continued, "we create a dual threat. The linebackers aren't sure where to commit." He told them the pseudo-flea-flicker story. "We just got lucky with that one, but it made us realize we could turn this into a passing play if we wanted to. And, psychologically, our opponents now worry about us doing this any time we run it."

"The advantage of a two tight end set," Reese said, almost to himself.

"No weak side" was Foster's comment.

"You could do almost anything," Hamilton added. "This could become a pass play, starting off in an I-formation as if you were planning on running up the middle or to the outside."

"With two tight ends," Foster said quickly, not wanting to be out-done, "the defense couldn't cover them both, *plus* a receiver."

"The tight end who throws the initial block on the left side could even break away and move into the interior for a short pass," Reese said. "Shit, even the back could throw it. It wouldn't be more than five or six yards."

O'Leary smiled in the dark. These three were like excited children, such was their enthusiasm and focus. It was almost ten o'clock at night, when most players were barely able to walk and only wanted to fall into their cots, and these three were still hard at it. Furthermore, they were going over a play that was late in the book—they were studying ahead while most of the other hopefuls were running just to keep up. What started out as merely another training camp was quickly materializing into one of the most enjoyable experiences of Jim O'Leary's thirteen-year coaching career. This really was what his profession was all about—guiding eager young talent so they could fulfill their potential and succeed. Even Hamilton, who supposedly was past his prime and ready for the broadcasting booth, seemed like a rookie again. O'Leary couldn't recall a time when he'd had such attentive pupils. The only sad part was that he and Greenwood could only have one of them. The other two would have to be thrown back into the water, two fish who were allowed to get away. Glenn Maxwell, who was also in the room but had said nothing all evening, was the mainstay, the grunt worker. So their other tight end had to be someone special. At first O'Leary wondered if such a person was to be found in these three prospects. Now he would have trouble deciding which of the three it would be.

"The opposite-side tight end could even run a post pattern," Reese went on, "going up about ten yards, then cutting out. . . ."

Through the dorm window two hours later, Daimon Foster watched the full moon in the night sky. He lay on the cot, hands folded across his chest, with his cell phone between his fingers. His roommate, Howard Jenner, another undrafted player who was hoping to nab a spot on special teams, was snoring softly on the other side of the room. Foster barely knew him.

Everyone else was asleep now, as it was almost midnight. He knew damn well he should be asleep, too. Adequate rest was essential during training camp, and the last thing he wanted to do was take unnecessary risks with his future. But he couldn't help it—he couldn't turn his mind off now. Not after the call from Alicia.

O'Leary ended their meeting just before eleven. He told all four of them that they were doing great, that he was pleased with their progress. Foster believed him—he seemed like a very decent man, very honest and straightforward. Daimon thought he was slightly ahead of the other two, Hamilton and Reese. Maxwell apparently was going to make the team regardless. He had two years left on his contract and knew what he was doing. The Giants wanted to replace T. J. Brookman, and Daimon had begun to believe he just might be the one they'd choose. He was by far the fastest of the three. Since he was the youngest and in the best physical shape, he had greater speed and quickness. He didn't have the distraction of Reese's rebuilt knee, nor the weight of Hamilton's years. He was just as smart as they were, too. Smarter, maybe. True, they had more experience. But what was experience except knowledge? He would learn in time. He had good studying habits, he was observant, and he had plenty of native intelligence. *Anything they can do, I can do better.* This had become his new motto.

When he first arrived, he was scared of his competition. Hamilton and Reese had already been there, knew their way around. He figured he was the long shot. Then he got on the field and began studying them, looking for places where he could outdo them— and he found many. Hamilton sometimes seemed winded. He didn't have the endurance of a young man. He compensated for it with excellent hands and remarkable knowledge of the playbook. He also knew every defender's trick imaginable, and he overcame them with a few of his own. But Daimon watched and learned. *Let the guy show off,* he thought several times in the relentless August heat. *The more he shows them, the more he shows me.* And Reese had lost a step or two since his glory days. Foster sensed the knee still worried him. Maybe it really was fully healed and fully functional, but Reese didn't seem to think so. Physical scars and mental scars were two different things. When the former healed, the latter often lingered. Maybe all Reese needed was for someone to walk up to him and say, "You're doing fine. Don't worry about the knee. It's working just the way it's supposed to." If so, Daimon sure as hell wasn't going to give it to him. Perhaps that was a cold way of looking at it, but that was how he believed he had to be now. There was too much at stake here. Far, far too much. . . .

That damn phone call.

He tried to talk to Alicia every night before he went to sleep. A few times he was just too tired and couldn't even bring himself to unfold the phone. Once he even dozed off in midconversation. On this night, though, he was feeling pretty good. Two great practice sessions in which he'd made several solid plays, some words of encouragement from Coach Greenwood plus a few teammates who'd barely noticed him during his first few days of camp, and then the meeting with O'Leary. He was walking two inches off the ground as he headed back to his room. He couldn't wait to give Alicia the news.

But something was wrong; he could hear it in her voice. She was excited for him, but it was forced. She was distracted, upset. He knew her too well now. They weren't married, weren't even engaged, yet she was an open book to him.

"What's up?"

"Nothing."

"Come on, I know you better than that." He was trying to keep his voice low, trying not to wake the snoring Jenner. "What's happened?"

She told him—two break-ins on their street in the last week. One woman was viciously beaten; an elderly woman, no less. Her house had been ransacked, all her silver and jewelry stolen. She'd been taken to the hospital, and Alicia hadn't heard any more. There was yellow tape around the house. The police were looking into it. They had no leads yet. Bunch of kids, someone said. A gang, most likely, but there were many in the area. There had been a spree of murders, too. All prostitutes. Some were comparing it to the famed Jack the Ripper killings of 1888 in London. Again, the police had no clues. The same kids? Maybe. Then again, there were a lot of loonies who came to the casinos for a few days, did their thing, and left. Could've been anyone. Atlantic City was a transient's mecca, as all casino towns must be. Solving crimes in such an environment was a near impossibility. Could it actually be getting worse? What happened to the civic improvements that were advertised by the politicians when the casino owners began building their glittering towers? What happened to the feel-good promises of a greater, happier, healthier Atlantic City? A place to have children, build a home, and receive your slice of the American dream? What happened to all of that?

Daimon's blood boiled as she spoke, his temperature rising with every grisly detail. The urge to run to his car and zoom down the New York Thruway itched like maggots under his skin. Alicia was a strong individual, but even she lost her composure a few times. She hitched and sobbed, struggling to keep her voice low so as not to disturb Daimon's mother. They were helpless down there. Helpless to defend themselves. A gang? Hell, even one punk would have no trouble taking the two of them. If they were willing to attack some old lady, what chance did Alicia have? She was a natural beauty, rarely wore makeup and didn't need to. Daimon was sure they'd seen her around the neighborhood, sure someone had tabbed her as a future target. Sometimes he wondered if he was the only reason they hadn't made a move yet. He was a big guy, and he had a few friends who were also big—and straight, and didn't like those little bastards any more than he did. They feared some form of retribution. But what if word got out that he wasn't around now? What if they noticed his car hadn't been in the driveway? *What if they already noticed and made their plans?* It could happen any day now—any minute.

His mind swirled with the grim possibilities, the images so stark and clear that he was more awake than ever. The break-in, the screaming, the beating and possible rape. His heart pounded, his tongue was dry. He couldn't sleep, even though he was exhausted in every way. He wanted to be down there, protecting both of them. It was the police's job, of course, but they couldn't be relied upon to do shit. They didn't waste their time on that side of town. Not while the zillionaires on the other side were paying their salaries in one way or another. The only two people in the world he truly loved were goddamn sitting ducks.

It was the discipline that kept him here—the discipline, and the beyond-his-years wisdom that made him realize the true answer to all these problems lay in this place at this time. If he earned a spot on the roster, he'd never have to worry about this kind of thing *ever again*. If he didn't, he be back down there in hell right alongside them. Going down there now would only provide a temporary solution to the problem. Making the team, however, would pay dividends forever. But the strength required to stay the course was like none he'd ever known. Meanwhile, he—*they*, really—would have to continue playing the odds and hope the numbers fell in their favor. Because that's all it really was—mathematics. Every time the sun sank into the west, the wheels began to spin and the cards began to fly in Atlantic City, and a very different form of gambling began, where the winners claimed their prizes in the shadows and the losers lost more than their money. So far they had been lucky. But Foster knew as well as anyone that luck ran out eventually.

He found his playbook and dragged his weary body into the bathroom.

"How has Krueger been doing at fullback?" Gray asked, unscrewing the cap from his bottled water and taking a sip. He then set it down in the only bare spot left on the table, which was covered with a variety of spiral notebooks, looseleaf sheets, and open copies of both the offensive and defensive playbooks.

"Coming along pretty well," said Tony D'Angelo, who was in his seventh year as the Giants' running backs coach. D'Angelo, with his baggy eyes and carefully trimmed silver mustache, was a quiet type, competent and utterly reliable. No pretensions, no delusions of grandeur. Most important to Alan Gray, he had never expressed any interest in being a head coach in the NFL, so Gray decided to keep him around when he took over the team.

"He looked pretty sluggish to me," Gray said. "I saw him drop two handoffs last week."

D'Angelo wasn't the least bit fazed. "He has some possession is-sues, no doubt. I'm not going to deny that. But he is also very quick, very tough, and very competitive. If I can get him past his fum-bling problem, he can be first-rate."

Gray ran a hand over his hair, then twiddled his pencil. "All right, keep me updated. What else on offense? How about receivers?"

Camp had been in session for just over one week, and this was the first day that Alan Gray had assembled the coaching staff to re-view the team's progress. Because of this, it was also the first day that he gave the players off. Most of them slept late to let their bod-ies heal, then fled into the town of Albany to hit the bars and restaurants. Hamilton and Reese chose to stay in their dorm rooms and study their playbooks. Daimon Foster wanted to do likewise, but instead hopped into his ancient Honda and zipped down to At-lantic City to make sure everything was all right. He brought the playbook with him anyway, which technically was a violation of team rules.

"Bowen is not the same guy we saw in the combines," Green-wood said. "He seems slower than he was, and he sure as hell can't take a hit."

"Another guy who pulled it all together in Indy," added Kevin Jefferson, the team's receivers coach, "so he could get into a training camp. Another weight-room warrior. Knows how to look good just long enough to take the next step."

"But on game day," Greenwood went on, "he won't contribute much. I guarantee it."

Gray, with his elbows on the table and his hands bunched to-gether, adopted an air of profound introspection. He was playing God with this young man's future, so it was his dire responsibility to carefully consider all options before making a call. But it was all a façade—complete and utter bullshit. And everyone in the room knew it. They were so used to it by now, however, that no one displayed the slightest hint of dissension. Alan Gray knew as much about evaluating an offense as he did about bioengineering, and his capacity for compassion wouldn't register on a jeweler's scale.

"Okay, let's cut him," he said gravely, as if the responsibility of making the decision hurt him deep down. "Have the Turk take care of it."

Don Blumenthal had been a busy man already, which was fairly unusual within the first week or so of an NFL training camp. The heads typically started rolling around the third week, after the first preseason game. But Alan Gray considered himself a quick study, and he was, in truth, uniquely gifted at estimating what went on in the hearts and minds of others. Throughout his life, more than a few people had accused him of a certain degree of paranoia, but he knew better—that "paranoia" was in fact a finely honed instinct, almost a sixth sense. He knew within days which guys in camp were on the weak side of the spectrum, which eight or nine definitely had no shot at making the team. Sometimes it was due to a lack of physical talent, but that was rare; the combines, plus four years of college performance and piles of statistics, gave a pretty clear picture of a young man's physical abilities. Most of the time it was mental shortcomings—too easily distracted, unable to maintain consistency, bad attitude, not motivated enough, only here for the glory and the fame, only looking for a big payoff, etc. He had been in the league long enough to know a loser when he saw one, and he didn't want to waste time on losers. So it became a characteristic of Alan Gray's training camps that a handful of guys were out the door when other teams were just getting started with the paring process.

He twiddled his pencil some more and said, "Okay, I think that about covers everything, right? We've got to prep for the first preseason game this Saturday." He gathered his books and papers into a neat stack and began to rise. "See you all back here after lunch, when we—"

"Hang on, Coach," Dale Greenwood said. Jim O'Leary sat on his left. "We didn't go over the tight ends."

Gray froze halfway up. He looked like he was waiting for a doctor to do a prostate exam.

"It'll only take a minute."

The coach settled back into his seat. "Okay, tell me about the tight ends."

"Well, strange as it might sound, we're having trouble figuring out which of the three new guys is the best."

Gray had taken his defensive playbook back out and was absently flipping through the pages, but this made him stop and look up. "What's that?"

"Hamilton, Reese, and Foster," Greenwood said, "they're pretty damn good."

"All three?"

"Yeah. They ran the gassers faster than T. J.," Greenwood told him.

"They *all* did?"

"Yeah. Not by much, but they did. Even Hamilton."

O'Leary: "Reese hasn't dropped a ball yet."

Greenwood: "Hamilton knows the whole playbook already. I think they all do."

O'Leary: "Foster is the quickest tight end I've ever seen. And he's got competitive fire to burn."

Greenwood: "He got into a fight with Kirch yesterday. *Kirch.*"

O'Leary turned to Greenwood and said, "They've all got fire. I've never seen three guys so motivated."

Greenwood nodded. "Yeah, it's like they've got the devil at their heels."

Gray was looking back and forth between them, absorbing every word. "And you're telling me they're all *better* than T. J.?"

Greenwood said, "Well, I don't know about that. If we used one of them, we'd have to make a few minor modifications to the system. They're all close."

"Yeah, they're all very close," O'Leary put in. "Each has his own weaknesses. Hamilton's aging body means he'll run out of steam sooner rather than later. He's showing no signs of it yet, but it's only a matter of time. You can't escape that. He's got so much experience in the league, though, that he almost makes up for it."

"And Reese," Greenwood said, "has clearly lost a little speed due to that injury. He's still fast as hell, but he's come down one level. Plus he has great hands, and he knows how to get open and block. He's still very reliable."

"Foster," O'Leary finished, "is a special kid. I don't know how everyone missed him. He's so fast, so smart, and so intense. He's about as focused as anyone I've ever seen. He's made a few typical rookie mistakes, but he learns from them and self-corrects. There's no doubt he's going places."

Now Gray was smiling, something he hadn't done all day. "Interesting, very interesting. If you had to make a decision right now, who'd get the job?"

"Impossible to tell," Greenwood said. "Too close to call."

"Yeah, too close," O'Leary said. "But I know this much—all three are a pleasure to work with. Three good guys with real talent. We were incredibly lucky to get them." He shook his head and added, "Too bad we can't sign them all. We could use two for trading fodder."

Gray was staring off into space, his moronic grin still pasted to his pudgy face. This *was* a good idea, but unrealistic. Spots on the roster were precious, and he wasn't about to start playing Monopoly with these guys; they were serving an entirely different purpose for him at the moment. Furthermore, agents rarely went along with tactics like this unless it meant a sweet deal for their clients. More trouble than it was worth.

"Okay," Gray said finally, "I appreciate the information. Please keep me informed."

"Sure."

With that, everyone rose and left the room.

Instead of leading the pack this time, Gray took up the rear. As he went out, Jim O'Leary's words replayed themselves in his mind. *We were incredibly lucky to get them.*

He was still smiling when he broke from the rest of the group and headed to his office.

Text of letter sent by Chet Palmer via registered mail on August 12:

Barry M. Sturtz, President and CEO
c/o Performers LLC
1152 Skyline Drive
Huntersville, North Carolina
28070

Mr. Sturtz:

This letter is in response to yours of August 3 concerning the ongoing "stalemate" between you and your client, T. J. Brookman, and the New York Giants. First off, let me apologize for not responding in a more timely fashion, i.e., within seven days of its receipt as per the terms outlined in the CBA. As you know, the team has been involved in the opening of its annual training camp activities and, as such, Coach Gray and myself have not had a chance to respond sooner.

That said, we would now like to address the matter at hand. After careful consideration of all facts, we have decided not to revisit the possibility of renegotiating your client's current contract. Instead, we reaffirm our belief that he should honor the terms as they stand, and again offer to put together a "new-and-improved" contract at the end of this season, when the present contract naturally terminates. At that time, we will be willing to forge a deal that is beneficial to both parties; one that will take your client's improved skills and contribution to the team into full consideration. In turn, he will be paid adequately in respect to other premium performers at his position around the league, as you have requested. But, in the interim, we do not feel that it would be appropriate to alter, in any way, the agreement he has with us now.

In consideration of the above, Coach Gray and myself would therefore like to request, for the second time, that your client report to training camp as soon as is reasonably possible, where he can join his teammates in preparation for the coming season. Failure to do so, as we have stated before, may result in disallowing him to participate in all team activities going *forward. We would, naturally, prefer not to take this course of action. But we will do so if we feel no other reasonable choice is afforded us.*

At your convenience, kindly let us know how you wish to proceed.

With Best Regards,
Chester T. Palmer, General Manager
The New York Football Giants
CC: NFLPA, NFL Management Council

one of his old jerseys yelled, "Corey! Corey, up here!" The kid gave him a thumbs-up. When Reese returned the gesture along with a smile, the boy turned around to report the exchange to his father.

Preseason games have their detractors, most of whom usually define them as pointless, a waste of everyone's time, and so on. Players understandably don't want to get hurt during a battle that has no bearing on the regular season. And many fans, even hard-cores, find it challenging to keep their attention on games that are ultimately meaningless. But coaches place great value on them—every one affords yet another angle from which to evaluate their talent pool. They can put young prospects through every drill in the book, show them countless hours of film, and force them to memorize playbooks as thick as phonebooks—but nothing compares to being out there.

Furthermore, anyone who thinks the preseason lacks competitiveness simply because the outcome has no impact on a team's chances to reach the eventual postseason doesn't understand that, individually, every man out there is fighting for a roster spot. There are, of course, a handful whose jobs are more or less safe, like players in the prime of their careers who performed solidly the previous season, but those cases are rare. A head coach's job during training camp, above all else, is to assemble the best group of first-stringers possible. If that means replacing a veteran with a rookie, so be it. Very few guys have the luxury of avoiding this pressure, and those who think they do are often the first to go. So while the actual score of a preseason game has little meaning in the big picture, one kid's performance during the course of that game can mean the difference between the rewards of an NFL contract and toiling in a nine-to-five job for the rest of your life. What it boiled down to was this:

With both a fullback and a halfback behind him, Lockenmeyer ran a long count, and second tight end Glenn Maxwell went in motion in the hopes of acting as a decoy, possibly for a blocking role in a phantom running play to the right side. When the ball was finally snapped, most of the Jets' linebackers did drift to that side. But one—Jacob Harvey—wasn't fooled. He came forward a little but stuck to his zone, obviously suspicious. The problem with misrepresentative formations, of course, was that it was so easy to *over*sell them, and Harvey got a sense of this. Hamilton jogged the first five yards of his pattern, then cut in and turned on the afterburners. Lockenmeyer, by this time, had already faked the handoff to both backs and turned to find his mark. Harvey followed his eyes and began screaming, "Here! Here!" while pointing to Hamilton. The ball came at bullet speed, which was a necessity. Unfortunately, it was also thrown a little ahead. As Hamilton reached out for it, he saw Harvey charging toward him. Everything began slowing down, as it always did before a collision. Incredibly, although he knew this phenomenon would occur, he never got used to it the way some guys apparently did. As he felt the leather slide into his fingers, he clamped down and pulled the ball inward. A nanosecond later, he absorbed Harvey's bull-charge impact. That was when the situation elevated into something like an out-of-body experience— distantly, he felt himself spin around, the ball hit his gut as he tucked it in, then the cool of the grass as it zoomed up to meet him. He was aware of the bounce as he came off the ground for an instant, then the repeated thumps of other players piling on top of him. Once all motion ceased, the sluggish dream-sequence linearity cleared away. He heard several whistles blowing, and he could feel the bodies being lifted off one at a time. He knew he had taken a monstrous shot, but he also knew he had held on to the ball. Some luck had been involved, of course, and he knew that. But still . . . in simple terms, he had made one hell of a catch.

Eight minutes further into the quarter, Corey Reese was called in. His knee felt tight this morning, when he first got up. That wasn't unusual, but the fact it hadn't loosened since then was. After some stretches and a brief jog, it was usually fine. Not so today. This made him worry about it—but not half as much as that great grab by Hamilton. Outdoing his competition was his primary objective. It had to be.

His assignment on this play was fairly simple: move first inside to block as if you were punching a hole for a running lane, then head upfield fifteen yards and drift outward, at which time the ball should be sailing toward you. Again, two backs were used as decoys, and again most of the Jets' defense bought into it. But the safeties stuck to the zone defense, and Nelson McCann, on the strong side, didn't trust the sight of Corey Reese—whom he had covered in years past—zipping toward him. Reese tried to stutter-step to the middle to break McCann's concentration, but the veteran was too experienced to fall for it. There was a time, many seasons ago, when it might have worked; Reese's mental file on him was a bit outdated. McCann simply moved back a yard, buying himself another precious moment to determine the receiver's true path. When Reese cut back outside, McCann became glued to him. Far in the back of his mind, Reese noted the improvement in McCann's coverage skills. He was so close that they were almost sharing the same damn jersey, yet he wasn't so intrusive that he risked an interference call. In other words, Nelson McCann had become a damn good safety.

As the ball launched from Lockenmeyer's hand, Reese saw that he'd have to go up and get it—not only because it was slightly overthrown, but also because McCann's leaping ability was considerable, and both men, by rule, had a right to the reception. Sluggish knee or not, Corey Reese would have to earn this one.

He leaped off the grass with a grunt, McCann hanging over him like a mugger. All four hands grazed the bottom of the ball as it moved along its downward trajectory, causing it to pop back up slightly, spinning end over end. As it came down a second time, Reese, who focused on it so rigidly that the rest of reality was effectively blocked out, managed to get his fingers around both sides as he, too, continued downward. He could feel McCann's arms slither over his shoulders, and then the pounding fist that tried to knock the ball free. Reese yanked it down and tucked it away just as he crashed in a heap at the Jets' thirty-three-yard line, McCann landing painfully on top of him. It had been a fairly tough catch, but he managed it. When he got back on his feet, the crowd was cheering wildly. He held the ball high—intentional drama—as he jogged it back to the ref. What made the triumph even sweeter was that the knee, while still a little tight, was in one piece.

Daimon Foster stepped in four plays later, when the Giants had moved the ball down to the Jets' eleven. His heart thudded as he prayed everything went smoothly on this, his very first play in the National Football League. He knew thousands of eyes were on him, knew there was a good chance some of the commentators were speaking his name, broadcasting into millions of homes in the area, and he knew Alicia and his mom were watching, as excited and as nervous as he was. This would not be the best time to make a mistake. As he broke the huddle and took position just behind the line of scrimmage, he went over the assignment in his head. He would not be the receiver, just a lure. He was on the right of the front five, opposite Glenn Maxwell on the left, so there was no strong side. Receiver Willie Knight stood next to him, on the outside, and would be getting the ball in the end zone. That was the plan, anyway—but the Jets' red zone defense had allowed just twenty-one touchdowns during the previous season.

The ball was snapped after a short count, and Foster followed an inward slant pattern, moving to the center of the field. The Jets had given up the zone for man-to-man, and Daimon quickly acquired one of their linebackers. Since the guy was pacing him on his right side, executing his assignment was now problematic. He had to cut back to the outside to draw at least one more coverage man off Knight. Now he had to improvise.

He took two quick steps forward, as if to break free from the coverage and continue across the center of the field, and the linebacker fell for it. As soon as he turned on the gas to follow, Foster pulled back and cut right. The linebacker spun to stay on him but lost his footing and went down.

Foster's momentary satisfaction evaporated when he saw that Knight had miscalculated his own pattern—instead of cutting left in the end zone, he went right. Lockenmeyer, who had to rely on the synchronicity of the play, had already released the ball, which was now drifting toward the spot where Knight was supposed to be—and where a Jet defender who also noticed the error was heading.

Foster discarded the design in his mind and charged full-bore to the site of the forthcoming disaster. As much as he would love to be able to put his first pro touchdown into the record books—and on his first play, no less—he didn't think he'd be able to get to the ball in time. Personal gain aside, what he needed to do here, he knew, was play a little defense of his own.

The ball came down, and the Jet safety had both hands out, ready for the interception. As in a dream, it seemed so far away to Foster—much too great a distance to cover in such a short time. He dove headfirst, arms outstretched, and screamed something unintelligible. The safety did manage to get both hands on the ball, but Foster knocked it loose before he had the chance to pull it in and gain full possession. It then fell harmlessly to the ground and bounced crazily away.

Up in the Giants Stadium press box, Sal Clinton, the color commentator, said into his microphone, "Not bad. I thought that would be Jets ball for sure."

Ken Vreeland, who handled the play-by-play, responded, "I agree. A very good heads-up play. That's one of Big Blue's new tight end hopefuls, Daimon Fostek... er, Foster, wearing number eighty-two."

"All three of their TE prospects have looked fairly sharp so far. First Jermaine Hamilton, the veteran, looking as youthful as any rookie out there. Then Corey Reese, with a rehabilitated knee you'd never suspect if you didn't already know about it, and now this kid. An interesting little saga so far, if you think about it, with the reported benching of T. J. Brookman, who has had such an impact over the last few years."

"Just goes to show you no one's job is safe in the league these days," Vreeland added.

"You're not kidding, Ken, you're not kidding."

The Giants made another first down on the next play, then ran a left-side sweep two plays after that for the first score of the game—one in which Maxwell had been placed on the right side while Foster carved a lane for his running back with one of the play's key blocks.

As Foster jogged off the field, Alan Gray pulled his headphones down around his neck and clapped effusively, slapping him on the back as he went by. This was a purely cosmetic gesture, as Gray figured the cameras would be on him at that moment. He imagined—correctly, as it turned out—that both Barry Sturtz and T. J. Brookman would be watching the game somewhere, and he wanted to communicate the message that he was pleased with his new tight end talent. More leverage . . . always more leverage.

"Pretty good, huh?" Dale Greenwood said from a few yards down the sidelines. Gray had told him to make sure all three were given plenty of time on the field so he could better evaluate them.

"Yeah, not bad," the head coach called back, grinning like a demon. "Not bad at all."

Hours later, Corey Reese was sitting toward the back of the team bus, watching the miles go by. The sun was setting on the New York Thruway, reducing the Appalachian Mountains to an uneven run of dark shapes against a canvas of muted reds and violets.

They had pulled out the victory, 21–20, against the predictions of the broadcasters, bookmakers, armchair quarterbacks, and, apparently, everyone else who'd bothered to form an opinion. It hadn't been easy, though. They lost one prospective starter on the offensive line to a broken foot, and a promising young safety blew out his Achilles tendon. His career in the National Football League was likely over before it had begun.

That aside, Reese'd had a fantastic game. He kept going over his performance in his mind, scanning for places where he could make improvements. This constant self-evaluation was a vital component of success, because you were expected to push yourself to get better. At the same time, however, he was aware that his rivals had also done well. Hamilton made several key blocks, including one that paved the way for the team's second touchdown, plus a pair of against-the-odds receptions. And Foster was absolutely fearless, going head-to-head with everyone during the Jets' fearsome blitzing schemes. Plus, the little bastard was *quick*. His ability to find dead zones in the secondary and get open was pretty damn good. Whereas Reese was reacquiring his mechanics, Daimon Foster had the seeds of real vision. He sensed where the holes would open up before they did. This wasn't something you could teach—it was a gift. It wasn't fully developed yet, as Foster was simply too young and inexperienced for that, but it was on its way.

Nevertheless, Reese thought with a wicked smile, he was the one who ended up with the ball in the end zone, not Foster or Hamilton. It was a fourth-quarter leap that gave the Giants the lead for good. And that was the stuff people remembered.

He waited until the guy sitting next to him—defensive tackle Bryan Pettit—was asleep before taking out his cell phone. It was otherwise quiet on the big charter, with most guys either out cold or listening to their iPods.

Jeanine answered on the second ring.

"Hey, sweetheart," Reese said, keeping his voice to a whisper.

"Hey."

"Did you see me? Did you see the game?"

"We saw most of it, but the kids were running around crazy."

"Did you see the touchdown?"

"Yes, we saw that."

"Wasn't it great? Man, I'll tell you, I didn't think I was gonna get it. Mark was throwing a little ahead of everybody today, but he'll get better."

"Uh-huh."

"And Coach Greenwood, he was all excited, telling me how great it was. Gray wasn't too happy, though. The defense made some mistakes that nearly cost us at the end. We got lucky, though, but he was screaming at them in the locker room. Man, he was *pissed*."

Silence.

"My knee feels all right. A little sore, but not as bad as I thought it would. It was tight when I got up, but it was okay by the time I jogged out onto the field."

More silence.

And then, listening close, Reese thought he heard—

"Jean?"

No response.

"Jean? Are you . . . crying?"

It'd been faint, almost like the high squeal of a door. Then the chilling, choking sound as she tried to catch her breath.

"Jean, oh my God, what's wrong? Baby . . . what?"

More squealing, then a feeble attempt at speech. One thing Corey had always found oddly endearing about her was the child-like quality of her grief. It made her seem so frail and vulnerable—and made him that much more protective of her.

"A man came to the house today," she said finally, and he could picture her wiping her face with her hands, trying to gather herself. "Two men."

"What did they want?"

"They wanted your car," she said. Enhanced by her emotion, it sounded sinister. *They came for your car today. . . .*

With his elation gone, Reese asked, "From the bank?"

"I guess so. But they didn't look like . . . bank people."

Repo guys, Reese thought, and a slithering disgust moved inside him. *Not exactly the kind of people I want near my family.*

"Did they . . . do anything?" This was the only way he could think of putting it. The more generic the better.

"They scared the *hell* out of the kids!" she screeched, and in that one reply Reese realized just how frightened she really was. This was about much more than the car—this was the Ugly Monster they had been fearing for the last year and a half. It was like death after a prolonged illness. You knew it was coming, yet you were never fully prepared for it. No matter how much you braced yourself, it was still a jolt to the system.

"Okay, okay. Take it easy, sweetheart. Did they do anything else?"

"One of them went over to the garage and looked in the window, as if I might be lying when I said you weren't around. *He looked in our goddamn window!*"

"All right. Anything else?"

"He said he'd be in touch."

"Did he leave a card?"

"No, nothing. That scared me, too—he said he'd be in touch but he didn't leave any information. My God, Corey, those two guys could've come from anywhere."

No, not anywhere, Reese thought, *just whatever part of hell repo people call home.*

She started sobbing again, and Reese pressed the phone even harder against the side of his head so no one would hear.

"Okay, look, baby. I'll give Dennis a call first thing tomorrow.

Maybe we can hold them off with a minimum payment or something, all right?"

She calmed down just enough to say, "Okay."

"In the meantime, relax. I'm doing pretty good out here. Remember that I love you, and that we'll get through this one way or another."

"Right, right."

"And tell the kids I love them and I miss them."

"I will."

"Okay."

Another moment of silence, broken by his wife saying, "Corey?"

"Yeah?"

"I'm so scared."

The figurative light frost that had settled over his skin turned into an arctic freeze. Everything that he had been fighting back all these months had now, literally, come to his front door. Today's visit, he knew, was just the beginning.

"Don't be, baby," he said in a whisper, a lump forming in his own throat. "We'll be all right."

They ended the call by wishing each other good night. As Reese folded the phone and replaced it in his pocket, he caught Daimon Foster staring at him from across the aisle. Then Foster turned away.

Look all you want, kid, Reese thought. *Take a real close look at the guy who's gonna beat your ass right off this team.*

"And now," Tommy Spencer said into the studio camera and, simultaneously, millions of homes, "we turn back to the NFL and the continuing story of the New York Football Giants and their future at the tight-end position. And to help us, as always, is our own training camp stud, Greg Bolton. Greg, what's the latest?"

A chuckling Bolton appeared on the right side when ESPN switched to the split-screen perspective. He was wearing a navy blazer with a light blue shirt and no tie. Behind him, blurrily, the Giant players were going through more drills in what appeared to be an afternoon session.

"Hey, Tommy. When I spoke with Coach Gray today, I wasn't surprised to find him elated—almost giddy—about the situation with the three new prospects that were brought into camp: Jermaine Hamilton, Corey Reese, and Daimon Foster. I've been told that all three have continued to impress everyone here with their intensity, their focus, and their physical skills. In fact, one unnamed team source said offensive coordinator Dale Greenwood and tight ends chief Jim O'Leary still have no idea which one they like best."

A surprised Spencer said, "Is that right?"

"That's what I heard. None of the three is quite on Brookman's level, but they're close. Judging by their performance in Saturday's first preseason game, a lot of fans in the area seem to agree."

"And what's the latest on Brookman and his agent, Barry Sturtz?"

"Well, the story there is that the two of them are still waiting for a judgment from the league on their grievance. As I reported earlier, Sturtz's formal complaint was rejected by the Giants in what was the first step toward independent arbitration. Put simply, both sides said they were going to stand their ground, so nothing was resolved. The next step, then, was for Sturtz to request a third-party review of the situation, which he has. As you know, his argument is that Brookman deserves a new contract due to his exceptional performance for the team over the last two seasons, and the Giants' feeling is that, with only one year left on his current contract, everything should remain status quo until that one runs out."

"At which time he'd get a new one."

"Right," Bolton said. "But, as you know, so many things can happen between now and then. I tried to call Sturtz on his cell phone earlier today, but he didn't answer. So we just have to wait and see if the league allows them the arbitration they're hoping for."

"And what's the probability of that?"

"Hard to say these days. Most formal grievances are worked out before a third party has to step in, mainly because the league doesn't feel they deserve arbitration in the first place. They prefer that both sides work out their differences on their own, quietly if possible."

Spencer nodded. "With Hamilton, Reese, and Foster performing so well, it sounds like Brookman and Sturtz are losing more leverage each day."

"It certainly seems that way. A lot will depend on the league's decision, Tommy. It doesn't look good for the superstar tight end and his agent at the moment."

"Okay, well, thanks, Greg, for that update to this ongoing saga. Please keep on it."

"You bet."

18

Barry Sturtz stared blankly through the north-facing window of his home office in Huntersville, North Carolina, watching a trio of deer graze on the edge of his property. In some distant sector of his weary mind, he wondered if he would ever get the chance to go out there, back to the little stream that was hidden within the brief tract of untamed forest that served as a border region between his land and that of his closest neighbor, and maybe try his hand at fishing.

He absently massaged the stubble on his cheeks. He didn't go for the unkempt look anymore; it was too much like the New York street punk he used to be, another lifetime ago. He had since taken up the practice of shaving every morning, trying to appear relatively well groomed and maybe even a little cultured. It was either that or let it grow nice and thick, but that made him look like a member of a country-and-western band. He'd tried the beard on two separate occasions but never kept it.

This time it wasn't so much a personal choice as a simple matter of not having found the time to deal with it. The situation with the Giants was pushing him to the brink of his sanity, a maddening puzzle of circular logic for which a clear resolution could not be found. In spite of all his experience, wisdom, extensive business training, and considerable intelligence, he couldn't determine the right approach—at least for him and his client. Incredibly, it seemed as though all roads led to a decisive victory for his opponent.

Did I miscalculate? Was it all a mistake?

No, he decided. This was the point he kept coming back to. *No, it hadn't been a mistake.* The act of going in there with both barrels blazing, demanding a better deal, had been the right move. T. J. deserved it. The two of them were far from being the only ones who thought so. If only he had a dollar for everyone who had raised the topic with him. "He's not still earning league minimum, is he?" "The Giants are making out like bandits." "They're making you and T. J. look like fools." On and on. It was all true—T. J. was an incredible performer and contributor. He had given his lifeblood for those vultures. All he wanted was fair compensation, "fair" being defined as commensurate with those who were posting similar results.

It hadn't been a mistake.

Once he was comfortable with that point and had fully established it in his mind, he moved on. That's where the problems started. He kept trying to figure out where it all went wrong. He felt he had the edge going into the meeting, felt the team needed T. J. badly enough (there was ample evidence of this) and Gray was concerned about his own future (also ample evidence). There were no other tight ends on T. J.'s skill level available (utterly inarguable); plus, the position had continued to evolve and was more important than ever (also inarguable). It seemed like all the stars had aligned to make the negotiation little more than a formality.

So what happened?

The wireless headset in Sturtz's hand twittered. He didn't need to check the little screen to know who it was. He thumbed the button and nestled the device into his ear.

"Yeah."

"We're *dying* over here, man."

"T. J., calm down."

"*Calm down?!* Are you kidding? Did you see the three of them on Saturday? Were you watching the game?"

"Of course I watched the g—"

"Christ, they looked like Pro Bowlers! Hamilton knows more about the damn position than *I* do! Reese is a friggin' acrobat! And Foster—just who in the hell is this guy, anyway? I can't believe no one drafted him!"

"You're still better than they are."

"Not by much! They could put one of them in there instead of me and they'd barely miss a beat."

"They're not going to do that. They want you there, believe me. Those three, I'd be willing to bet anything, were brought in just for show. For leverage."

"Well, that's what they got—and plenty of it."

Sturtz knew this was true. If he was right and those players were meant to tip the scales in the Giants' favor, unethical or not, it was working.

"We've still got the possibility of arbitration," he said, amazed at how calm he sounded.

"From what I hear, that's a long shot."

"I'm not going to try to second-guess the process. I'm just going to wait and see what happens."

"And what if it doesn't work out? What if they won't hear the case?"

Sturtz sighed. "Then we'll try something else."

"Like what?"

"I'm not sure yet."

"What about talking with other teams? Weren't you going to t—"

"Let me worry about that. Don't ask about that. You don't need to know anything there."

"Well, you've got to come up with something."

"I will."

"Like what?"

"I don't know, T. J., okay? I'll figure that out when the time comes!"

It came out in a roar, spit flying from his lips. Sturtz would later swear he could actually feel the rise of his blood pressure. He had no idea where all the anger came from. Just seconds earlier, he seemed to be fully in control of himself.

The silence that fell between them lasted perhaps ten seconds, but it seemed more like ten minutes.

"Dammit," Sturtz finally said, all the fatigue and stress laid bare in the hoarseness of that one word, "I'm sorry, I didn't mean to lose it like that."

After another pause, Brookman said, "Shit . . . I'm sorry, too. I know it's not your fault."

"No, it's all right. I understand. Believe me—I understand."

"I know you're doing everything you can."

"I just . . . I don't know."

"Maybe we should've given in."

"Huh?"

"Maybe we should've just played along for another season, until the contract ran out, then shot for a better deal, either with them or with someone else."

Sturtz had considered this several times over the last few days, played out all the scenarios. None of them seemed particularly appealing. Best case was that T. J. chalked up another phenomenal season, coasting them into a sweet bargaining position. Then he'd have to hammer out a new deal consisting of a fair amount of guaranteed money, much of it up front. That was the best case—but it wasn't the most likely. There were too many variables. T. J. could become injured, he could stay healthy but have an off year, he could find himself written out of schemes and spend a fair amount of time either on the bench or, perhaps even worse, on the field but not featured in enough plays. Sturtz didn't put it past a serpent like Alan Gray to purposely squelch a player's performance solely to keep him from gaining the upper hand in a postseason negotiation—especially an offensive player, knowing Gray's preference for the other side of the ball. No, there was no point in second-guessing now. He and T. J. had made the right decision last month. They were in a sweet position, and that was the time when you talked about renegotiating.

"I think what we did was right," Sturtz said, focusing on the three deer again. One of them swatted a fly away with its little tail. Another—the male, he assumed, judging by the branchlike antlers—looked up quickly, as if he knew the owner of the property was watching.

"Yeah, I guess it did at the time. So now what? We just wait?"

"Uh-huh. Look, if they agree to arbitrate, I like our chances. If they don't, and then the team signs one of these other three and makes you sit, then I can file a new grievance, and that one, I believe, will most definitely go to arbitration. And I think we'd win it, too."

"Yeah?"

"Yeah."

"Good, 'cause I don't want to spend the season watching from my couch."

"That won't happen," Sturtz said. "You're not going to be warming any furniture." He thought about legendary running back Marcus Allen, whose career suffered tremendously after the Oakland Raiders' owner and then–head coach Al Davis, in what appeared to be a purely spiteful gesture, purportedly reduced his playing time to keep him from reaching several records he'd been chasing. In the end, he retired just short of some of them.

"I hope not."

"No, you won't."

Brookman took a deep breath. "All right, I'm going."

"Hang in there. We'll get it done."

"I hope so."

The call ended, and Sturtz could not remember a time when his client sounded so defeated.

This is bullshit, he thought angrily. *Pure and total bullshit.*

He took the phone off his belt and dialed another number. Just before the call went through, however, he killed it. One more look out the north-facing window; the deer were gone now. He closed his eyes and pinched and rubbed the bridge of his nose in a useless attempt to drive away the monster migraine he had developed. Then he dialed the number again.

This time he let the call go through.

Only two thoughts were running through the young man's mind as he came off the elevator and started down the sunlit dorm hallway: 1) *You can't be seen . . . you can't be seen . . .* and 2) *This is the most underhanded thing you've ever done. You're a goddamn WEASEL.*

Underhanded or not, however, he had come to the conclusion that he no longer had a choice in the matter. Too much was at risk now, far too much. It had been different in years past, when his skills and talents had carried him through. This time he needed an edge. *A little insurance, that's all*, he had rationalized it. Even then he knew it was total bullshit. *Once you have to convince yourself, then you know you're doing something wrong.* But these kinds of thoughts had to be pushed far to the back of his mind, where they could be dealt with later. This was no time for morality. Again— there was just too much on the line. *This was war.*

Weasel hurried down the corridor and came to room 1833. He set his hand on the knob, praying it was unlocked. It should be— he'd made a dry run two days ago and was astonished to find it that way. Corey Reese, as well as his roommate, should've known better in such a hypercompetitive environment. But they didn't; they made the choice to be trusting instead. *Once again, the nice guys finish last.*

The knob turned smoothly, and he went inside. In spite of the open windows, the room still reeked of perspiration and filthy clothing. Both beds were unmade, playbooks lying on nightstands alongside candy wrappers, half-filled bottles of Gatorade, cell phones, and who knew what else. Reese had framed pictures of his wife and two children, whereas his roommate was apparently unattached and had only a photo of his parents. Each player also had a small shaded light, and under Reese's Weasel found what he was looking for—a digital alarm clock.

He studied the controls quickly, always keeping one ear trained on the hallway and one eye on the window. The rest of the organization was still in the dining hall, having lunch after the morning session. If everyone kept to the schedule, they wouldn't be heading back here for their naps for another thirty minutes. Of course, the only certainty in life was that there were no certainties—one guy might not feel well and decide to skip lunch; another might finish early just to get an extra twenty minutes of rest. You never knew.

Weasel had always been a smart individual, and he figured out how to accomplish what he'd come here for in a matter of maybe twenty seconds. He pressed the ALARM SET button, and 1:30 P.M. appeared in glowing red on the LCD screen. Then he pressed a button that bore just one character—a plus sign—and watched contentedly as the 1:30 zoomed forward until it reached the 3:00 region. The last two characters were just a blur. He had no specific time in mind. As long as it was well beyond what Reese needed, that was fine.

He set the clock down again, careful to position it precisely as it was before. Then, just to be safe, he went into the bathroom, pulled about two feet of toilet paper from the roll, and wiped away any fingerprints. It was a ridiculously anal gesture (*as if the FBI might come in here and investigate the crime*), but you never knew. Better safe than sorry.

He peeked down the hallway before stepping out, then closed

the door and gave the knob a quick wipe, too. He headed toward the elevators, but stopped when it occurred to him that he might come face-to-face with someone he didn't want to see when he emerged on the ground floor.

He turned swiftly, his sneakers squeaking with each step, and went the other way. At the end of the hall, he opened the fire door that led to the stairwell. It would bring him, he knew, to a side exit facing away from the dining hall; the odds of being seen there were slim. The door drifted to a close as he disappeared, and all was quiet again.

The elevator doors at the other end parted exactly twenty-three minutes later, and Corey Reese, along with four of his teammates, walked out. With full stomachs and aching bodies, they separated to their respective rooms. Reese kicked his cleats off, dumped his helmet and pads in the corner, and collapsed onto the cot—sliding back up on one elbow just long enough to activate the alarm. Then he crashed onto the pillow, pulling the thin woolen blanket over his head.

He was snoring within minutes.

When he awoke, his first thought was that he felt more refreshed than usual. *Deepest sleep I ever had.* Then it occurred to him that he had awakened naturally—not because of the alarm. Unable to believe that he had been asleep for less than an hour, he turned his head to look at the clock.

3:34.

"Shit!"

He jumped up and scrambled for his cleats. Then he rolled back into a sitting position, pulled them on, and tied them at light speed.

"What's wrong with this fucking thing?!" he snarled, smacking the clock with his open hand. Then he picked it up and inspected it quickly. The current time was correct, the volume was turned up to maximum (a necessity), and the alarm button had been pushed to the ON position.

What the hell?

He'd brought the unit from home. He had several alarm clocks, in fact, and purposely chose this one because it was historically the most reliable. He found it impossible to believe it had simply failed.

There wasn't time to figure it out now—he was already in enough trouble. He gathered up the helmet and cleats and turned to go out. Just as he reached the door, however, the alarm exploded—a series of urgent beeps that sounded more like an intruder alert in a military base.

Reese stopped and stared at the clock for a moment. Then he walked back slowly, set his gear down on the cot, and lifted the clock for the second time. It was so loud that he could actually feel the beeps through his skin. He shut it off and pressed the ALARM SET button.

3:36.

"What the f—"

That wasn't right. How did it change? A power outage?

You can't worry about it now. Get moving.

He set the clock down again and rushed out.

By the time he emerged from the building, the others were on their way back. Standing there waiting for them, he'd never felt like a bigger idiot.

As the crowd engulfed him, the comments began.

"Have a good sleep?"

"All rested up now?"

"We didn't disturb you, did we?"

"Must be nice."

No one seemed to find any humor in it—especially Coach Gray, who gave him a look of disgust that he would remember for the rest of his life. The fact that he added a muttered "Nice of you to join us, Reese" didn't help. Greenwood and O'Leary didn't say a word, but neither looked pleased. There was also a touch of disappointment in their faces, which, for some reason, cut deeper than anything else.

Reese wanted to shout, *Hey, it wasn't my fault! My alarm got screwed up!* But, of course, he didn't. That would be an excuse, and you didn't get far with excuses in the National Football League. *But it wasn't my fault, I swear. . . .*

This was the moment when he realized someone might have intentionally changed the alarm just for the sake of getting him into trouble.

Could that be what happened? Would someone actually do that? If so, who?

He tried to locate Daimon Foster and Jermaine Hamilton in the group. Foster was nowhere in sight, but he spotted Hamilton walking among a cluster of four others, still in his pads and carrying his helmet.

He's smiling at me, Reese realized. *The sonofabitch is looking in my direction and grinning.*

It wasn't exactly the right kind of look—it wasn't smug or satisfied. Then again, Hamilton was an old pro, knew all the tricks.

That's what they've been saying about him, right? He's a tricky guy— compensates for his age by doing things others wouldn't even think of doing. Just the type who would pull something like this.

Reese and Hamilton remained in their staring match for a few moments, during which time Hamilton's smile bent to a frown and he appeared more confused. But Reese wasn't buying it.

If it was him, he's gonna pay, Reese vowed. *He's gonna pay like he's never paid for anything.*

Text of letter sent by Michael V. Soltis, Esq., via registered mail on
August 18:

Alan Gray, Head Coach and Director of Football Operations
Chet Palmer, Vice President and General Manager
c/o The New York Football Giants
Giants Stadium
East Rutherford, New Jersey 07073

Barry M. Sturtz, President and CEO
c/o Performers LLC
1152 Skyline Drive
Burlington, North Carolina 27216

T. J. Brookman
215 Hope Street
Franklin Lakes, New Jersey 07417

Gentlemen:

Concerning the ongoing dispute between Mr. Sturtz, his client, Mr. Brookman, and the New York Football Giants organization, I am notifying all parties involved that I have decided to let the matter continue on to a formal arbitration hearing, where, it is hoped, it can be settled in a way that is acceptable, even if not preferable, to all sides, and the matter can be put to rest. That said, I am appointing William T. Serra, Esq., to act as independent arbitrator. Mr. Serra, as some of you may know, has handled similar cases in the past and has firmly established himself as a fair, objective, and impartial overseer. I am confident that his final decision will be satisfactory.

Having stated the above, I now request that all sides kindly deliver whatever records, documents, and other evidence they feel will be necessary to Mr. Serra no later than ten days after receipt of this letter, per Section 5 (Discovery), Article IX (Non-Injury Grievance) of the current Collective Bargaining Agreement.

Thank you.
Sincerely,
Michael V. Soltis, Esq.
Notice Arbitrator
CC: NFLPA, NFL Management Council

20

The last two days had been dreamlike for Greg Bolton. At last—a break. Much needed; very much needed. The ESPN gods decided to cut him loose for seventy-two hours, lest he suffer a mental meltdown of unprecedented proportions.

Just one week earlier, he had been at the Cardinals' camp, held at Northern Arizona University in Flagstaff. The heat was such that two players collapsed from exhaustion. Then it was on to Nashville to watch Jeff Fisher and the Titans. The next day Bolton had to make two stops—the Falcons in Flowery Branch, Georgia, and the Saints at Millsaps College in Jackson, Mississippi. He and his crew filmed more than four hours' worth of material, of which perhaps twenty minutes would ultimately appear on national television. After the Saints visit, a Wednesday, he begged for a breather. His producer told him to go home and see his family until the following

Sunday, when he would be due at Minnesota State in Mankato to cover the Vikings.

Bolton came through the door that evening with a bag full of presents. Chase, to his amazement, ignored them and leaped into his arms. Bolton played with his son for the next two hours. When the boy finally lost steam and fell asleep on the living room couch, he grabbed the opportunity to sneak upstairs with his wife, Alexandra, for some practice in the art of conjugal privilege (which, incidentally, would result in the birth of their second son, Kenneth, nine months later).

Over the next three days, all work-related matters were ignored while he and his family patronized a string of amusement parks, shopping malls, and restaurants. He took Chase to and from school on Thursday and Friday, taking time to speak with his teachers. On Friday evening they visited Alexandra's parents, whom he actually liked, and didn't return until well past midnight.

Saturday was spent just hanging around and generally enjoying the art of doing nothing. But he knew he'd have to get back into the swing of things, at least in a preparatory capacity, that evening. His flight to Minnesota left at eight twenty-two the following morning, so he had to get ready—pack, review notes, get onto the Internet and find out what had been going on for the last few days. He also wanted to field some e-mails, lest his in-box become overloaded and unable to receive any more.

By nine thirty, Chase had been read his favorite Pooh story, Alexandra was upstairs reading the latest book by her own favorite author (Amy Tan), and Bolton was sitting in his den, going through the formidable pile of letters and packages that had accumulated over the last four weeks. So much of it was just garbage, but she didn't like to throw anything out. Who knew what might be important? He appreciated her discretion, but certainly some of this crap could've gone. *A flyer from ShopRite? An offer for a credit card? A coupon from the local deli?*

He had already tackled the e-mails, deleting about two-thirds of them out of hand and responding to the rest, in most cases, with just one or two sentences. At precisely nine forty-seven, as he was navigating through NFL.com at his desktop computer (his ESPN-issued laptop was "resting" in its case on the other side of the room), his Instant Messenger popped up in front of everything else. His first thought was *Oh, shit, not now.* Then he saw the name of the sender.

CMC88: Greg? Are you on?

His fingers moved in a chattery blur across the keyboard.

GEB@ESPN: I sure am. How've you been?

How've you been? What a ridiculous response. As if he were talking to someone at a funeral.

CMC88: I'm okay. I see you've been busy.

GEB@ESPN: Yes, very. But I'm home now for a few days, taking a break. What's new?

CMC88: Well, there's been a development today. Something I figured you would want to know about.

Okay, so I'm getting back to work a few hours earlier than planned. He'd sworn he wouldn't, yet he didn't feel the least bit guilty considering the circumstances. It'd been almost a full week since he last heard from the guy (he was pretty certain it was a guy, anyway).

GEB@ESPN: Sure—I'm listening.

CMC88: The league has granted arbitration in the matter of the team vs. T. J. Brookman and Barry Sturtz.

Bolton read the line several times.

GEB@ESPN: You're kidding.

CMC88: No. The letter was received earlier today. They're going forward with it. The hearing will commence in less than two weeks, and then the decision will be handed down fairly quickly.

GEB@ESPN: This is incredible. How is Gray taking it?

CMC88: He was shocked at first, then angry.

GEB@ESPN: I'm not surprised. Most of us in the media figured it would be denied. We assumed the league would want the team to work it out internally.

CMC88: That's what Gray thought would happen. But more of these issues have been turning up in recent years, so the arbitrators probably feel they have to deal with them or else they'll never go away.

GEB@ESPN: I guess this doesn't bode well, right? I mean, if they're willing to review the situation, then it seems more likely that they'll rule in favor of Brookman, won't they? Why would they bother otherwise?

CMC88: I'm not going to speculate on that. I have no idea what kind of hidden meaning, if any, this decision has.

Bolton nodded. *Playing it safe. But he sounds a little disappointed, too. I wonder if my Mystery Man is Chet Palmer?*

GEB@ESPN: Is Chet Palmer upset, too? I would imagine he would be.

A pause. *Is that significant? Or did the guy just reach over to get a tissue and blow his nose? How much should I read into this?*

CMC88: No, he's not happy either. They're both a little concerned. If the ruling goes against them, they could be in a lot of trouble.

Trouble? What did that mean, exactly?

GEB@ESPN: What kind of trouble? Can you elaborate?

A second pause, longer than the first.

GEB@ESPN: Are you still there?

CMC88: I have to go now. Sorry.

GEB@ESPN: Wait—just one more thing. What did you mean by Gray and Palmer being in trouble?

Nothing else came. The person on the other side—whether it was Chet Palmer or not—was gone. As always, Bolton felt short-changed, but he was electrified. *Lead-story material.*

Ignoring the rest of his mail, the NFL.com news page, and pretty much everything else, he opened a new Word document and began typing. Within thirty minutes he had the piece ready to go; it landed in his producer's in-box seconds later. Then he had to figure out how to work it into the Vikings segment tomorrow morning.

The minivacation was over.

Bolton's report the following morning was short and sweet, delivered in a segment that would be run separate from his Vikings visit. Everyone around the United States and the world saw it—including Dorland Kenner, who had been on his way out of his London hotel room en route to Heathrow Airport.

As he settled into his first-class seat for a quick flight to Spain, he called Alan Gray on his cell phone. He got Gray's assistant again, who said she didn't know where he was but would try to locate him. Kenner was then placed on hold.

"Yes, Dorland, what's up?" Gray said gruffly after a nearly ten-minute delay.

"Did I catch you in the middle of something?" Kenner asked,

glancing at his watch. "I figured you'd've been in your office by now."

"No, it's fine. What's up?"

"I'm sitting on a plane that has yet to leave the runway. I'll be in Madrid for most of the day."

Kenner waited for the obligatory response—a grunt, an "okay," or whatever—but there was nothing.

"When I was leaving my hotel, I saw the report on *SportsCenter* about the arbitration hearing."

Another pause. Then Gray said, "What about it?"

"What's going on with it?"

"I don't know yet. I'll know more when the hearing begins."

"Okay. But I'm surprised. I thought there wouldn't be one. During our last conversation, you were fairly confident the league would deny the request."

"I guess I was wrong," Gray said.

"I guess so. How confident are you that the arbitrator will rule in the team's favor?"

"I have no idea. I can't read his mind."

Kenner didn't have to be a psychologist to realize he'd caught Alan Gray in a bad mood. "I understand that, Alan. But what's your sense of it? If you had to make a call right now, from your gut, what—"

"I don't know, Dorland, okay?!"

A frigid silence followed, during which an embarrassed Kenner scanned his immediate surroundings to see if anyone nearby had heard the outburst. "Okay, Alan, take it easy. I'm just trying to get a grip on what's going on."

"Yeah," Gray said, now sounding more tired than angry. "Sure."

"I'll call back tomorrow, all right?"

"Uh-huh."

"Okay. Talk to you later."

The line went dead without so much as a good-bye from the other end. Kenner watched absently as the airport workers loaded the baggage into the belly of the aircraft. His current itinerary required him to be in Madrid for the next three days, then on to Brussels, and then back to the States for a series of meetings in Dallas.

Now he wondered if it might be better to forgo Dallas and head straight to the Meadowlands.

Since coming to Giants training camp, Daimon Foster had discovered a peculiar quirk about himself—he was incapable of eating dinner without showering first.

After the second session each day, the players had one more short break before heading to the dining hall. Then it was on to the usual trio of evening meetings: first the whole team with the head coach, then splitting into three groups—offense, defense, and special teams—and then into further groups with the position coaches.

Foster chose to use this break to run back to his room (or walk back, depending on how he felt), take a quick shower, and put on a fresh tracksuit. He had already permitted himself one luxury—he'd hired a service to come and do his wash once a week. Almost everyone on the team used the service, so it was fairly cheap. He stuffed everything into a canvas bag, pulled the tie-string shut, and set it in the hallway. By the following afternoon it was back, everything inside washed and folded.

He came into the room just after five o'clock, set his gear down on the rickety little student desk against the far wall, stripped naked, jammed everything into the canvas bag, and went into the bathroom. He didn't wait for the water to warm up—the initial cold spray did wonders for the aches and pains. He grabbed the soap and started lathering everywhere. As he did, he reviewed the day's work in his mind. He'd had two terrific sessions, making almost no mistakes. He couldn't help but constantly arrange and rearrange the ranking, as he imagined it, of himself, Reese, and Hamilton in the eyes of the coaches. Some days he felt like he was in last place, other days in second. At the moment, however, he was definitely on top.

He turned the water off ten minutes later and stepped out. After drying himself thoroughly, he got dressed. The clock on the nightstand read 5:44—sixteen minutes before dinner began. It only took five to walk over there, but he liked to be a little early. Being late was always a risk.

Before he headed out, he pulled back one of the desk drawers to retrieve his playbook. There were some things he wanted to go over while he ate. He had finally developed a small group of friends—although he still thought of them more as colleagues or associates—that he sat with at mealtimes. They would needle him about his over-the-top focus and determination, but ultimately they would leave him alone.

When the drawer opened, however, Foster saw to his alarm that the book wasn't there. He opened the other drawers in a rush but found only an ancient No. 2 pencil with a broken point and a chewed-off eraser.

He searched the room up and down, flipping the two mattresses and digging through both laundry bags. This killed about ten more minutes, leaving him no safety buffer before dinner. His heart was racing, his throat dry. It wasn't just a matter of not being able to squeeze in some bonus study time—*the fine for losing your play-book.* Twenty-five hundred bucks! Christ, where was he going to get that money?

"Shit!"

He gritted his teeth, kicked his helmet into the corner, where it spun at great speed for a few seconds before winding crazily away, then turned and stormed out. The slamming of the door echoed dramatically through the hallway. As he strode to the elevators, he went over the problem methodically in his mind. *Where did you last have it? Did you leave it there? If not, then where?*

He wondered if his roommate took it by accident. This was unlikely. First, that guy was trying for a shot at special teams. Second, failing that, he'd been a safety in college. *Even if he lost his book, he wouldn't have any use for mine.*

It wasn't until the elevator reached the bottom floor that Foster was struck by the idea that it might have been stolen. By the time he exited the building and started across the lawn, he had calculated that this was, in fact, the most likely possibility. He was making enormous strides in ability. He was becoming a genuine threat to the other two, a force to be reckoned with. Maybe they felt they couldn't beat him any other way. Maybe this was a sign of their desperation—*time to play dirty, huh?* He'd seen his share of underhandedness in college. Plenty of it, in fact, and it always made him sick to his stomach. He hated people who dragged things down to this level. Was it Reese, or had it been Hamilton? He didn't know.

One way or another, he promised himself, he would find out.

21

The next day, a Saturday, began with noticeably fewer bodies. Four more players, it was reported around camp, had been cut the previous evening. Don "the Turk" Blumenthal was now regarded as a spectral, horror-story type of character, the gridiron equivalent of the Grim Reaper; the only time anyone saw him was when he came to fill his death-bag. Even then, only his victims and their roommates could claim a sighting. Where was he the rest of the time? they wondered. Did he stay in the same building? Was he even on campus? Whatever the case, he scared the hell out of everybody, with his cruelly ugly face and permanent scowl. A few players even claimed to have had nightmares about him.

What started as a squad of ninety-two hopefuls was now down to seventy-eight—just three over the required number of seventy-five by August 29, which was ten days away. As the number went down, the tension went up. Every little mistake mattered now. Everything you did was studied and judged. Gray wanted to get them away from tryouts and into practice mode for the real season as soon as possible. Many said this was foolish—too anal and over-efficient. Alan Gray did it anyway.

The team would be leaving on the buses tonight for tomorrow's second preseason match, in Buffalo. So today's two sessions would be a bit more like a formal practice, with fewer drills and more strategy.

Daimon Foster walked to the fields already wearing his pads and helmet, keeping to himself and still reeling from the sting of the playbook theft. He asked a few guys during dinner if he could borrow theirs for study, but the only ones who had brought them did so for the same reason. When he got to the second meeting, with Dale Greenwood and the rest of the offense, the first question was "Did you bring your playbooks?" When Daimon sheepishly admitted that he hadn't—and couldn't—the room fell silent. He made a point of watching Reese's and Hamilton's reactions. Reese just stared, mouth slightly open but with no particular emotion. Hamilton, on the other hand, shook his head and turned away. *What the hell is that all about?* Could it be translated as suspicious? Did it suggest he knew something? *Or is this sonofabitch actually judging me?* If so, where did he get the goddamn nerve? It was hard to tell. They were both hard to read.

Greenwood wasn't, though, nor was O'Leary. Their disappoint-ment was clear on their faces. Greenwood even looked a little pissed. He mumbled something to a nearby assistant—a gangly, pimple-faced kid wearing the obligatory khaki shorts and team polo—who then unlocked a rolling crate, took another playbook from inside, and walked it up to Foster. Greenwood went on to remind the guilty party about the fine for the oversight. This produced a few snickers around the room, and Foster nodded before taking his seat.

Oddly, he didn't feel any anger toward the two coaches. He had already decided they were honest men who were giving him as fair a shot as he could hope for. He felt that he had sufficiently impressed both of them, and that they believed in his chances to find a place in the league. Their disappointment in the lost playbook, regardless of the reasons, stemmed from their desire to Get Things Done. Nice guys or not, they were here to win, and you didn't do that if you couldn't hold on to your goddamned playbook.

So, as he strode onto the field that Saturday morning, he had just one objective in mind—to make up for the incident by dazzling them. As ticked off as they had been, Foster knew they'd forgive and forget when he demonstrated how he could be a difference maker. Other guys had incurred fines and were still here. It wasn't the end of the world. It sucked, but it wasn't the end of the world.

By late morning, the team was practicing in full pads, with eleven men on each side of the ball. They were focusing on the running game (because of the perception that Buffalo had a weak defensive front) and the strength of their secondary (since Buffalo's offensive coordinator liked to stretch out the passing game).

Foster's blocking had been fierce, earning praise from his teammates and, most rewarding, an eventual slap on the back from O'Leary. Then came a sweep play to the right side—his side. With a double tight end set involving him and Jermaine Hamilton, the ball was snapped after a short count, and fullback Benny Krueger cut left while running back Jason Thomas moved right. Hamilton had already gone in motion in the backfield, suggesting that he could be slicing open a running lane for Krueger in the gap between the blind-side guard and tackle. When quarterback Mark Lockenmeyer confirmed this by handing off to Krueger, the defense shifted in that direction. Then Krueger pitched the ball back to Thomas, who found an easy lane waiting for him, courtesy of Foster. They broke beyond the line of scrimmage, and Foster cut inside to continue leading the way. Unfortunately, he quickly came upon a considerable barrier—not a defensive player but Jermaine Hamilton. Surprised, he tried to slam on the brakes but slammed into Hamilton's massive bulk instead. As he hit the ground, he realized he was supposed to cut out instead of in—this was one of the new plays he'd wanted to study earlier but had been unable to. He'd gone over it late last night after the meetings, but, with so little time to absorb it, he simply forgot the assigned route. Thomas managed a few more yards on his own, but, without his lead blocker, he was taken down.

As Foster rose with a curse, he heard Hamilton say, "If you had your playbook, you would've known better." Foster turned, his eyes wild.

He made sure Greenwood and O'Leary heard him, too.

As Hamilton turned away, Foster, unable to swallow another ounce of pride, attacked. He pushed Hamilton down from behind and jumped on him, striking one blow after another. Hamilton was able to twist around and give a few swings of his own. But since both men were still in their pads and helmets and thus fully protected, the effort was largely futile.

With dozens of players and coaches rushing in, the incident was over in a matter of seconds. One of the first on the scene and pulling Foster off, notably, was Corey Reese. Foster was too enraged to hear him saying, "Hey! Get ahold of yourself!" When Hamilton rose, he stepped away to leave—then turned back and shoved Foster hard. Daimon tried to lunge, but one of the linemen held him while two other guys set themselves in front of Hamilton.

"Little piece of shit!"

"Fuck you, you bastard!" Foster spat back. "Where's my playbook, huh?"

"What?" was Hamilton's perplexed reply. Through the cloud of his fury, Foster registered that he seemed genuinely surprised by the accusation. If it was an act, it was a damn good one.

"You're crazy, man. You watch too much TV. Shit."

"Yeah, right." Foster finally yanked himself free of Reese's grip. "Let's check your room and see."

"Yeah, let's *do that*," Hamilton said firmly, gesturing with his finger for Foster to come forward. Although careful not to show it, Foster was shaken by his confidence. *Could I be wrong?*

Before either one got the chance to continue the discussion, Dale Greenwood inserted himself between them and said, "If you children are finished, I'd like to continue with the practice."

Foster and Hamilton stared hard at one another. Then someone tugged on Foster's jersey and said, "Come on, let it go."

Eventually the crowd dissolved and the session rolled on. Foster and Hamilton kept clear of each other for the rest of the day.

22

Looking down upon the field at Buffalo's Ralph Wilson Stadium from the dimly lit pressroom, their noses almost touching the smoked, one-way glass, were WWGR's Don Cummings and Howard Kayland. The pair had been calling the Bills' play-by-play (Cummings) and color (Kayland) commentary for more than a decade. Cummings, although in his midforties, could still pass for a college boy. He had a clean-shaven face and dark brown hair combed neatly to one side. Kayland, conversely, looked like a carefree academic, with his corduroy coat, tousled golden hair, and beard-mustache combo that he only trimmed when his wife nagged him about it. He was heavyset and sloppy, often wearing clothes decorated with old food stains. He had the diet of a man secretly trying to commit suicide, augmented by the occasional cigar. He also had a sterling sense of humor that dovetailed with his cohort's button-down straightforwardness.

Kayland shook his head as he watched Buffalo's third-string quarterback, a fifth-round pick named Justin Miller, get sacked for the second time in as many minutes. They had just begun the fourth quarter, and the only players anywhere near the field were unknowns—undrafted free agents, late-round picks, and also-rans. These were the guys who hoped for nothing more than to make a roster spot, names you saw once on a uniform, if you watched preseason closely enough, and never saw again.

"Our boys just couldn't seem to get anything going today," Kayland said into the microphone, a device he barely noticed anymore. "Just terrible." He glanced at the end-zone scoreboard and winced at the numbers—41 and 6.

"Yeah, this has been pretty ugly," Cummings replied with his deep, handsome voice. "But I have to say, to be fair, the Giants looked pretty good, particularly on offense."

"Their running backs zoomed around like banshees today. Did we even have a D-line down there?"

Cummings laughed. "I'm not sure."

"No second-guessing where we've got some gaps in the depth chart, hmm?"

Cummings paused the discussion to announce the next play—a Bills shotgun formation. The line did manage to fend off the Giants' six-man rush for a few seconds, but the pass that Miller eventually released was tipped at the line, then spun high into the air before sailing harmlessly out of bounds.

"And how about those three tight ends New York's got, huh?" Kayland went on. "I have to tell you, they look decent."

"They do indeed."

"According to the stats we've got in front of us, Jermaine

Hamilton posted a total of fifty-two yards in the first half alone, along with one touchdown. Corey Reese didn't reach the end zone today, but he caught six passes, including one bomb for forty-eight yards. And that kid, Foster."

"Yeah. . . ."

"Who knew he could throw the ball? Only his second NFL game, and he tosses a little blooper to Todd Kardinski for their third touchdown. Unbelievable."

"And what's going on with T. J. Brookman?" Cummings asked in an easy, conversational manner.

Kayland held his hands out as if the listeners could see this. "I have no idea. He and the Giants are still having their little spite match. As far as I know, he hasn't officially been cut or traded or anything."

Cummings laughed again. "So they've got *four* choice tight ends, then. And five if you count Glenn Maxwell, the mainstay."

"They're trying to corner the market, it seems."

"Well, something has to give. No one needs more than two."

"That's right. Somebody's going to be heading home soon."

He felt as though he'd been hit by a goddamn garbage truck.

Every bone, every joint, every muscle—barely movable. From the dull, relentless throbbing in his head to the creakiness in his feet, Jermaine Hamilton had never experienced a hurt with this kind of depth.

When it began, just after the game while he was jogging back to the locker room with his teammates, he thought, *Oh, yeah, here it comes. . . .* It was normal—of course you felt like this after a game. Considering the beating your body took, it was a miracle you could move at all. Some guys didn't even do that—they were carted off or carried off, depending on the extent of the damage. This wasn't Ping-Pong or chess, after all. Pain was a natural part of football, and he'd felt plenty of it through the years.

But this was something different. This was *wrong.*

The healing period had never been particularly long for him. He'd been in battles that made Custer's Last Stand look like a dance recital, and never once did he feel the way he did right now.

It's taking longer now, he realized. *I'm not bouncing back like I used to.*

That hadn't been the case in the first preseason game, but then he hadn't absorbed some of the sadistic blasts he did today. There was one in particular—a draw play in the middle of the second quarter. He had a standard blocking assignment, but just before the snap the two linebackers rushed up to blitz. Hamilton chose to get in front of one of them, and the guy barreled through him as if he weren't there. When the play was over, he felt like his brain was spinning. Yet he managed, somehow, to get on his feet and make it to the sidelines without attracting any attention. It was like driving mildly drunk—through the alcoholic fog you were still able to perform the basics. The failed play resulted in a fourth down, so he had a chance to rest. He slumped onto the bench and put a towel over his head, the universal signal that a player wanted to be left alone until further notice. The swirling feeling didn't stop for another five minutes, during which time Hamilton felt nauseous and thought he might vomit. But he struggled against it, for he knew what everyone would say. *Old man. Too old to play this game anymore. See? Can't take a good hit. How will he be when the regular season starts and they're* really *whacking him?*

He got lucky in another way, too—Greenwood wanted to see more of Reese and Foster when the offense got the ball back. By the end of that series, he felt all right.

But now. . . .

He waited for everyone else to clear out of the showers in the visitors' locker room. Now it was empty, the only sound being the lonely drip of the shower heads on the tile floor. His teammates were busy getting dressed or whatever. Some were already on the bus, talking to their wives or girlfriends on their cell phones.

After he washed off, he sat in the last stall, wrapped only in a towel. He kept his eyes closed, breathed deep, and waited. . . .

For what? For everything to feel better?

That's how it worked before. But not tonight. Maybe not ever again. He'd never felt like this; *never.*

Maybe the time really has come for—

He looked up, alerted by the echoey footsteps. He realized he would've heard the guy sooner if he hadn't been so deep inside his own thoughts.

The visitor stared hard at him for what seemed like a long time, and there weren't many people Jermaine Hamilton would've wanted to see less than this one.

"I'm sorry," Daimon Foster said with surprising civility. "I just came looking for my toothpaste."

An opportunity was presenting itself, they both knew—to finish what they started the day before, and without the impediment of their colleagues. They could beat each other into comas before anyone realized what was going on.

Yet nothing of the sort happened. More unspoken information was transferred between them. Hamilton somehow knew that Foster was aware of what he was doing back here, and why. Foster knew that Hamilton was worn down, more so than he should be. And he knew it was because he was past his prime, with each day carrying him closer to his inevitable exit from the game.

"I'll just get another one," Foster said finally, as if Hamilton gave a damn, and turned to leave.

Then, to Hamilton's astonishment, he turned back.

"Did you take it?" he asked plainly. He didn't appear to be making an accusation—he really just wanted to know.

"And Corey Reese's alarm clock. Did you reset it so he'd be late?"

Again, this inquiry came across without the slightest trace of nastiness. He could've been in a department store asking a saleswoman if she had the same sweater in green rather than blue.

Now the silence stretched on forever. The dripping became louder, the space between them smaller, and the air heavier.

"Of course I didn't do any of that. I don't do that shit."

"Well, someone did. And it seems reasonable to believe—"

Hamilton said wearily, "Look, I didn't do any of it. You'll have to believe that." He set his head back into his hands. "Now leave me alone."

Foster lingered for a few more seconds, studying the man's body language for more clues.

Finally he left.

23

Dale Greenwood could barely hold his head up. His eyes burned, his joints ached, and there was a dull throbbing in the core of his brain. In spite of all this, he maintained an upright and professional demeanor. It was killing him, but he did it. Midnight was less than twenty minutes away.

"I think we're going to have to let go of Cleveland, too," he said with great reluctance. Darryl Cleveland was a guard from the University of Texas, an undrafted free agent in whom Greenwood saw some potential. He was surprised no one grabbed him back in April—both Tennessee and Arizona were in the market for some depth at the position. He was also a good kid who got solid grades in school and kept out of trouble. Greenwood always placed a high value on character, and Cleveland had it. His fatal flaw was his inability to read defenses; he simply could not absorb data and quickly convert it into an appropriate action. Linebackers zipped past him left and right, diving onto his hapless quarterbacks. His blocking skills were adequate, but complex defensive schemes left him befuddled. He'd managed to get by in college, but in the accelerated world of the NFL, he had no chance.

Alan Gray, who by no means burdened himself with Dale Greenwood's concern for etiquette, yawned like a lion. All the players were asleep, most of the front-office people had gone home, and a million stars speckled the night sky. It was too late for deep thought.

Although coaches often met during these hours—for them, training camp really was a 24/7 affair—Greenwood knew that Gray purposely saved the offensive discussions for last. Still, it was his job to give these reports.

"I think I'm also going to have to cut Maloney."

"The running back?"

"Fullback."

"Right."

"He drops the ball too much."

"I agree," Gray said, turning to his computer. There was a spreadsheet open, a defense-only roster that was heavy with statistics. At the bottom was a short list of players he wanted to sign if and when they became available.

"What about those three tight ends? Who's the top guy there?"

Greenwood managed a laugh. "We still can't figure that out. Jim and I have been discussing it, trying to get a grip on it. They're all performing well."

He couldn't understand why this made Alan Gray smile.

"Yeah? Well, that's good for you guys. I'm glad it's working out.

You've got to make a decision at some point. Don't rush and get it wrong, but don't take forever. Every spot on the team is precious."

"We'll puzzle it out."

"Good. All right, that's it for today. Thanks for the update."

Gray closed the door after Greenwood was gone and went back to his desk. He studied the spreadsheet for another moment, relishing the fantasy of signing *all* of the guys on his wish list and moving another millimeter closer to his dream of being a revered defensive mind. Then he saved the file and shut the computer down.

On the other side of the room, hanging on the wall like a modern masterpiece, was a flat-screen plasma TV. As a matter of routine, Gray turned it on at the end of each day to catch up on the latest ESPN stories. Part of the reason for this was to see if there was anything happening around the league that he could benefit from—players being cut or released, players on rival teams sustaining injuries, etc.—but he also had to admit he enjoyed seeing stories about himself. Some, of course, were less complimentary than others, and he didn't care for those any more than anyone else would. Even then. . . . He had long ago accepted the fact that he had a sizable ego.

He grabbed the remote from the chrome-and-glass coffee table and settled into the couch. *SportsCenter* was going over some baseball scores, then on to a quick mention of some multiplayer deal that had been made in the NBA. When they shifted to the NFL, a Giants logo appeared in the right corner, floating by the broadcaster's head. A little smile broke out on Gray's pudgy face. He might be mentioned.

He wasn't—at least not directly.

"The latest incident at Giants camp involved an on-field fight

between their three tight end prospects—the ones who are supposedly competing for T. J. Brookman's position. An anonymous team
source told ESPN that all three, while performing well in preseason, have still not reached Brookman's level of play, and that their
bad behavior is putting a strain on their chances of making the
team. . . ."

In spite of a fatigue that he could feel in the core of his brain,
Gray scrambled from the couch and grabbed the phone on his
desk.

Chet Palmer answered right away. "Yes?"

"Have you seen ESPN?"

"No, not since this afternoon. Why?"

Gray repeated the report.

"Jesus," was Palmer's distant reply.

"Who told them this? Where did they get this information?"

"Now how do I know that?"

"Who the *fuck* is this goddamn 'anonymous source'?"

"I'd tell you if I knew."

"God *dammit*!"

"Calm down, Alan."

"This guy—or girl, or whatever—is *killing* us! I'm trying to get
Brookman and that asshole agent of his into a certain *position*!"

"I know that."

Chest heaving, heart pounding, Gray looked back to the screen.
The Giants logo was now replaced by the official team headshot of
T. J. Brookman. Gray couldn't hear what was being said, but it
didn't matter. It was time to issue a decision he'd been planning for
a while now.

"I want you to bring our guy in here to find out who's doing this."

Another pause, and then Palmer said, "A witchhunt?"

"That's right. That's exactly right."

"You sure?"

"*YES, I'M SURE!!!* I want him here, first thing tomorrow, working his way through everyone and everything until he finds our mole. Not in a few days, not next week—first thing tomorrow. Got it?"

"Sure. But. . . ."

"What?"

"Well, what are you going to do to the person responsible if and when you catch them?"

"I'll take care of that."

Garrick Hart had a problem. Actually, he had four—and they were all in the form of speeding tickets.

"You've got to get me out of this," Hart pleaded. "They're going to take my license away!"

Maybe they should, Freddie Friedman thought. *You drive like a damned lunatic.*

"All right, take it easy" was what Friedman actually said into his headset. The wire down ran into his shirt, snaked around his back, and connected to a cordless phone attached to his belt.

Friedman was a small, spare man of forty-six, with dark hair that he kept well oiled and combed straight back. He was the president and CEO of Good Sports Ltd., an agency that represented over two dozen pro athletes, most of whom were in the NFL. He had built the company from nothing, starting with a gifted basketball player who had gone to high school with him back in Brooklyn and eventually landed a contract with the Dallas Mavericks. Friedman had a gift for numbers and powers of retention that bordered on freakish, but his most endearing quality from his clients' perspective was his integrity. He could be so brutally honest at times that it stung, but he always played it straight. In a business infested with maggotry, this was by far his greatest asset. He kept his client list relatively small, but they were all big-ticket people. He didn't steal their money, didn't sleep with their wives, and didn't ignore their phone calls. In return, all he asked was the standard 15 percent of their earnings—which they happily gave. As a result, he had become a very wealthy man.

One of the only disadvantages, he had come to discover, was having to deal with the antics of mental toddlers like Garrick Hart.

"I just bought that Alfa, man!" the four-time Pro Bowler whined on. "Over two hundred grand! If I can't drive it around—"

"I said take it easy," Friedman repeated, firmly but kindly. "I'll make some phone calls and see what I can do."

"Shit, they'll want me to go to one of those driving schools with all those losers."

If there's anyone on this earth who needs to be schooled in the art of driving. . . .

"You won't have to go to school. But look, if I manage to get this cleared up, you've got to start driving a little more responsibly."

"Re*spons*ibly?!"

"That's right. Doing ninety through a mall parking lot might be a bit much."

"They were *closed*, Freddie. I just wanted to see what she could do."

"You could've killed yourself, or your girlfriend. Or both."

He knew the mention of the girlfriend would get him to back

down. Friedman didn't even know the woman's name. It might be Alexandra; or maybe that was the last one. He'd lost track at some point and didn't really care enough to follow up. What he did know for sure was that Hart's wife wouldn't be too happy if she found out.

"Shit . . . all right. I'll try and slow down."

"I hope so, because next time they'll stick you in the cooler for a month. That'll mean the end of your endorsements, too. And I won't be able to do anything to help you if that happens. You've got to behave yourself."

"I know, I know."

There was a beep, and Friedman snatched the handset from his belt. The tiny screen displayed a phone number with an 816 area code, and the words above it read KANSAS CITY CHIEFS. Since Friedman didn't have any clients with them, he was a little puzzled.

"Garrick, I've got to go. I've got another call. I'll let you know what happens."

"Okay, thanks."

He thumbed the FLASH button, and Hart disappeared.

"Hello?"

"Is this Freddie Friedman?"

The voice was familiar, but he couldn't quite put a name to it.

"Yes, that's right."

"Oh, good. I was afraid I might've had an old number. Freddie, this is Derek Knudsen, general manager of the Kansas City Chiefs."

"Hey, how are you?"

What's he calling for?

"I'm fine, very well. How are things on your end? I'll bet it's beautiful in upstate New York."

Friedman, who was already standing (he rarely sat when he was on the phone; moving around helped him think), turned and admired the view of the Adirondack Mountains through two panoramic windows.

"It certainly is. What can I do for you today? Is there a problem?"

"No, not at all. I'm calling about one of your clients."

"One of *my* clients?" Odd—they were all under contract.

"Yes. Now, you understand, Freddie, this call is strictly off the record. . . ."

Friedman had a digital recording device on his desk that could be activated simply by pushing a button. What stopped him from doing just this was Knudsen's reputation. He was a brilliant man with a razor-sharp understanding of how the National Football League worked. He had degrees in law, business, and sports psychology. He was too smart to say anything over the phone that he shouldn't, so there would be little point in capturing the conversation.

"Sure, that's fine."

"Good. We're just having a discussion here about one of your boys."

"May I ask which one?"

Knudsen laughed. "I suppose I should mention him at some point, right? It's Corey Reese."

Another surprise.

"Corey? What about him? He's in camp with the Giants right now."

"We know. And we've been watching him. Pretty impressive."

"Yeah, he's done well so far." Never disagree with a compliment from a prospective customer.

"A lot of us thought that knee injury two seasons ago signaled the end of his career, but he seems to have bounced back."

"Amazing, isn't it?"

This was no lie—Freddie Friedman *was* amazed at how Corey Reese had brought himself back from the brink of ruin. He'd seen other athletes suffer the same injury, and most of them never saw action again. They all vowed they'd return, but it rarely happened. It was like battling lung cancer—a fraction won the battle, but the majority did not. Reese, through discipline, education, and raw determination, had defied the odds.

"It is indeed. That's why we decided this call was necessary."

"I'm not sure I understand."

Knudsen's voice dropped. "Freddie, I realize the comment I'm about to make isn't in keeping with league policy and is a violation of unwritten ethics, but we wanted you to know that, should Corey fail to make the final cut in New York, we'd be very interested in having him here in Kansas City."

There it was, as plain as day. Yes, making an offer for a player who was already under contract was a great whopping breach of rules and regulations. But Knudsen, Friedman noted, was careful not to make a specific offer. All he did was make it clear that they were *willing* to make an offer. Dancing along the edges, that's what Knudsen was doing.

"How interested?"

"I can't get into the details, of course."

"Of course."

"But I assure you it would be worth investigating further."

Friedman was doing quick numbers in his head, getting a general idea of where he would want to go with the negotiations. One factor, unfortunately, was Corey's dire financial situation. He had urged and pleaded with Corey to keep it as quiet as possible. Amazingly, the media had never caught wind of it, but that didn't mean people within the league weren't whispering about it. Did Knudsen know? He had a reputation for thoroughness, and he rarely went into a negotiation without digging up as much information as possible.

Most important, however, was that this new twist meant Freddie now had some leverage. There was a time when it appeared as though Corey Reese would be doing TV commercials and magazine ads for the rest of his life. Now he was on the radar screen of two different teams. After a few more showcase performances, maybe there'd be four or five.

"Freddie? Are you still there?"

"Huh? Oh, sure. I'm sorry."

"Well, what do you say? If things don't work out, can I count on a phone call from you?"

"I believe I can promise you that, yes."

"And to us first?"

Friedman almost laughed. *He's trying to find out if anyone else has called, too.*

"Sure."

"Great, great. Okay, I'll let you go now. I appreciate your time very much."

"My pleasure. Have a good day."

"You, too."

Still staring at the beautiful view that he didn't take the time

24

Hunched over his laptop and sitting in the bathroom with the toilet lid down and the lights off, Giants defensive lineman Howie Abraham reviewed what he'd just written.

Gray is the biggest jerk I've ever played for. He won't let me get in there, doesn't pay attention to me when I'm doing drills. I've played just fourteen downs in two preseason games. He only wants *his* guys on the team, guys he's known for years. Antonio Burgess has been with him since he was an assistant coach with Minnesota. But Burgess is an old man who has the grace of an elephant. I was playing better than him in my freshman year at Cal. I honestly don't even know why I was invited to this camp. I got a bad vibe from Gray on day one. He clearly doesn't like me and isn't interested in what I can do. What a waste of time.

He looked like a mad scientist, the way his face was lit by the diffused glow of the monitor in the otherwise darkened room. He made a few grammatical adjustments to the text, then clicked the SEND button at the bottom of the IM box; thank God for the free Wi-Fi in the building. There was so much more he wanted to say, but he was exhausted. These occasional late-night writing sessions always took a toll, and he'd pay for them tomorrow, but he had to get this stuff off his chest, had to do something to strike back at Alan Gray. He certainly couldn't vent to any of his teammates. They were good guys, but trust only went so far when there was so much on the line. The competition was tight now.

After a few minutes, a reply arrived.

I know it's tough, but it'll be worth it in the end. If the Giants don't take you, someone else will, I'm sure. I'm glad that you're confiding in me this way. What else is happening?

Abraham smiled; he had a feeling the man at the other end would ask this—he always did. He set his fingers on the keyboard and started pouring out more thoughts.

The loud *BOOM!* that shattered the night silence and caused Abraham's heart to lodge in his throat was caused by someone smashing the door open in the main room. Seconds later, the bathroom door was yanked back and a hand reached in and flicked on the light. Abraham, momentarily blinded, never had the chance to shut the laptop and kill the connection.

"Hey, what the *fuck*?" he heard his roommate say.

"Shut up and stay still," came an authoritative, deep-voiced response from someone Abraham couldn't see. The reason he couldn't see the guy was that there were two other people in the bathroom doorway—Don "the Turk" Blumenthal and, just behind him and smiling broadly, the subject of Abraham's last message. In spite of the fact that it was at least two o'clock in the morning, both Gray and Blumenthal were fully dressed and as clear-eyed as if it were high noon.

"What's going o—"

The Turk snatched the laptop from Abraham's knees with a speed that few would've believed he possessed.

"Hey! No!"

The Turk passed it back to Gray, then put a hand on Abraham's massive chest when the latter stood up. In spite of the ridiculous difference in their sizes, the Turk wasn't the least bit intimidated.

"A little late-night correspondence, Mr. Abraham?" Gray said with a chuckle. He set the computer down on the student desk—an exact copy of the one in Daimon Foster's room, although in slightly better condition—and pulled out the chair.

"That's a private message," Abraham said.

"Oh, nothing's too private around here, son. You should know that."

Abraham pushed himself far enough forward to observe the rest of the room. He noted with faint horror that the third man—the one with the deep voice—was now leading his roommate, safety Brandon Wade, into the hallway and closing the door. "Come on out here with me," he told Wade. "This doesn't concern you."

Abraham was petrified but refused to show it. He remained

motionless until Gray was finished going through the dialogue he and his correspondent had exchanged for the last half hour.

"Hmm . . . I'm quite a guy in here, Howie. You've got me one notch below Hitler."

No response.

Gray read a little more, then stood and faced the defendant. "Tell me, how much are they giving you?"

Abraham's face made a slow transformation from defiantly blank to genuinely puzzled. "What?"

"Over at ESPN. How much? Are you getting cash, or is it something else? Promise of better coverage for yourself?"

Abraham looked briefly to Blumenthal—who, he realized for the first time, was studying him *very* carefully—then back to Gray. He felt like he was being interrogated by the CIA. *Was this even legal?*

"I have no idea what you're talking about. Those messages—"

"Who else sends e-mails—"

"It's an Instant Messenger."

"Whatever. Who sends messages in the middle of the night?"

"I do—to my *father*."

For the briefest moment, Blumenthal and Gray appeared uncertain. Abraham realized then that this was, both literally and figuratively, a shot in the dark for them. They were trying to smoke someone out, but they had no idea who it was. *Someone leaking information to ESPN?* That's what it sounded like. A mole in the organization. *But why me?* he wondered. *Why did they pick me? How did they even know I was doing this?*

Did Wade squeal? Abraham always kind of figured he knew. He never tried to hide it—he only went into the bathroom so he wouldn't keep Wade awake with the typing. *No, he wouldn't tell anyone.* They had become good friends, and there was no benefit to selling him out. He wasn't a spy. Abraham knew about spies, knew every team had them—guys who weren't as talented as they should be, so they needed some kind of an edge. This sometimes came in the form of spying, being a coach's eyes and ears during the private moments when the players talked freely, in the weight room, the dorms, the huddle, and so on. The information was priceless, and they were always rewarded for their services.

But not Brandon, Abraham thought again. *No way.* He was sure of this, absolutely certain.

Gray scrolled down the column of messages again, trying to confirm or deny Abraham's claim.

"I'm going to check a little further into this person you've been contacting," he said finally. "I'm going to make certain it is who you say it is."

"You do that," Abraham replied. The disgust was plain in his voice and on his face. The damage was done, so he might as well be honest.

Gray stood. "In the meantime, I'm going to keep watching— you and a few others. I'm going to keep my eyes and ears open, and so is our friend the Turk here, understand?"

"Yeah."

He turned and went out of the room with the Turk on his heels. No sign of remorse, no apologies. Just a cut-rate dictator and his disappointed minion fleeing into the night.

After they were gone, a terrified Wade crept back into the room. "What the hell was *that* all about, man?"

Abraham, his eyes glazed with rage, said, "Nothing. Don't worry about it."

———————

Six floors up, while Howie Abraham was receiving the third degree, another member of Big Blue was sequestered secretly in his bathroom. Again, the toilet lid was down, the lights had been turned off, and there was an electronic device involved.

Jermaine Hamilton sat hunched forward with his arms folded across his knees, as if suffering from a tremendous stomachache. His cell phone was wrapped inside his enormous hand, a wispy-thin cord running out of the fist and connecting to a plug in the outlet next to the mirror. He'd had no choice but to charge it about an hour ago; that's what happened when you made so many calls.

He'd tried her at home at least a dozen times, then her cell phone another dozen, maybe more. He hadn't heard from her in over a week, and their last conversation, which he'd initiated, lasted less than a minute. The jealousy, the agony, the rage—all of it had congealed into a slippery, squirming thing in the pit of his stomach. It kept him up at night, sapped his concentration during meetings and practices. It would affect his play in the third preseason game tomorrow, and that would be costly. He had to get some answers one way or another. As the saying goes, it's the *not* knowing that kills you.

He called his brother, Lonnie, just after midnight. Four years younger, Lonnie lived about two hours from Jermaine's home and had his own key. Jermaine asked him to make the trip to see if he could learn anything. Lonnie said it was no problem. He knew about the troubles they were having. When Melanie first came into Jermaine's life, Lonnie did his best to get along with her. There were even isolated moments when he thought he might actually like her. But when she turned nasty—around the time that Jermaine's career

seemed over, he noticed—he felt like an ancient suspicion had finally been confirmed. He didn't get on Jermaine's back about it; he
figured his brother didn't need any more hassles. But he wasn't surprised.

When the cell phone vibrated, Jermaine unfolded it quickly.
"Yeah."

"I got here and got in," Lonnie said.

"And?"

At first there was only a fine, hissing static, and Hamilton thought
maybe the call had been lost.

"Lon?"

"She's gone, J."

"How do you know?"

"All her stuff has been taken out," Lonnie said. He was speaking
softly, gently. "The closets are empty, the drawers . . . everything.
I'm sorry, bro. I'm just . . . I'm sorry."

His voice barely above a whisper, Hamilton said, "It's okay."

"There's a note here, too. In an envelope."

"A note? Where?"

"On the kitchen table."

Hamilton took a deep breath. "Would you read it?"

"What? Now?"

"Yeah."

"J., I don't think I should. It's for you. It even says so on—"

"No, I can't wait. It'll be the only thing I think about. Read it,
please."

He knew Lonnie wanted to protest further, but he heard the dis-
tinctive sound of an envelope being torn open, then a sheet of paper being unfolded.

The sentiments, though not unexpected, were still chilling, and the words harrowing—divorce . . . settlement . . . attorney. . . .

When Lonnie finished, there was more silence. And then—"J.?"

"Yeah."

"Is there anything I can do?"

"Umm . . . no, not right now."

"You sure?"

"Yeah. You can go back home. Tell Ma what's happening, and I'll call you tomorrow after the game."

"All right. . . . Look, man, I'm sorry, I really am."

"Thanks. Thanks for doing this."

"No problem."

Hamilton closed the phone and set it on the marble basin. There would be no more calls tonight—for now he *knew*. No more wondering, no more being distracted. The matter was settled.

He returned to his leaning-forward position and waited for the tears to come—but to his amazement, there were none. There had been plenty in the past, but not now. He felt only numbness and detachment. In a strange way, it seemed as if the divorce had been settled years ago and he was merely thinking back on it. Then he realized why—it was because the relationship really *had* been over for years. This declaration by Melanie, followed by the eventual legal proceedings, was just a formality. Once the affection was gone, the rest was insignificant. Her love for him had probably drained away—if it ever really existed—ages ago. It was only his unwillingness to admit it that kept the marriage going as long as it had. He'd been looking for something that simply wasn't there.

Staring into the blackness, he made a wise decision then—to get on with his life. To starve whatever pain remained until it was as dead as the relationship itself. It had done enough damage, and now it had to be purged. He had some potentially great days ahead, but he'd never get to them if he kept dwelling on this. He would hire lawyers, they would handle the situation, and then it would be over; done and gone. Someday, hopefully, the memories would fade as well. For now, he had to think of the future, because it was all he really had.

And maybe that's not such a bad thing.

25

After almost two years, Corey Reese finally rediscovered something he called the Zone.

He tried explaining it to others, but he couldn't. You had to experience the Zone for yourself. You had to be the type of person who *could* experience the Zone. It was like another dimension of reality. You couldn't see it, couldn't touch it or smell it. When you were in it, you just knew.

And he knew on the evening of the following Saturday. Third game of the preseason, at Giants Stadium in the New Jersey Meadowlands, against the Cleveland Browns. After countless dismal seasons since their rebirth in 1999, the Browns had finally begun a steady upward climb, finishing the previous year with a 9–7 record and barely missing a wild card berth via the wacky playoff mathematics that about eight people on earth understood. Still, they were getting better in all respects. A team on a mission.

On the second play from scrimmage, Lockenmeyer hit Reese for a short screen pass on third down that the tight end parlayed into a twenty-nine-yard gain. Later in the same quarter, he took a lateral from two yards behind the line of scrimmage, slipped out of three tackles, and waltzed into the end zone for the first of two touchdowns. He would catch all eight passes thrown to him, run one kickoff back to midfield, deliver more than a dozen key blocks, and even act as fullback on two plays. And through all of it, he never felt like he was breaking a sweat. It came easily, effortlessly. It was like there was some otherwordly force working with him, guiding him, unlocking every door just when he needed it. He could do no wrong on this night. It was pure magic—and this was what he called being in the Zone.

Before the injury, he was in the Zone all the time. When he stepped onto the field, his opponents worried about him. Every game was a master performance. Back then he knew he had something special, a one-in-a-million talent. He wasn't arrogant about it, but he made a point of enjoying it.

After the injury, even when he knew the rehab was working and he was certain he could play again, he wondered if the old magic would still be there. Could he still get into the Zone with the Frankenstein joints? He'd been amazing in the past, but he hadn't seen any signs of it lately. He played well enough the first two preseason games, but he wasn't about to deem them amazing.

Before the third game, on the bus ride down, he decided it was time to find out, to cast aside all inhibitions and just let loose. He couldn't play like this all the time, worrying if the knee was going to fall apart again. That kind of fear could cost him dearly.

Greenwood took him out of the game at the start of the fourth quarter. That was a good sign, Reese knew; it meant the coach felt he had seen everything he needed to see. So he sat on the sidelines with a towel around his neck and watched his two rivals. He was surprised to see them struggling. Hamilton's mind was definitely somewhere else. He dropped three passes, was knocked on his ass twice, and missed a crucial block that gave one of Cleveland's DEs a direct route to the Giants' backup quarterback. They were picking turf out of the guy's face mask after that blunder. And Foster, although as quick and eager as ever, was finally starting to show his rookie colors, missing routes on some of the more complicated plays and getting pushed around by more experienced linemen and linebackers. Most of the weaker players had already been filtered out of Cleveland's roster. In spite of the fact that the Giants were losing the game by ten points with five minutes left, Reese felt like he'd had one hell of a night—and might have cemented his future.

On the sidelines, unnoticed by all three candidates, Jim O'Leary strode over to Dale Greenwood and said, "So, what do you think?"

Greenwood had his headphones down around his neck and a clipboard in hand, jutting out from his gut. "I think I was wrong."

"About what?"

"About telling Gray that none of those guys could take T. J.'s place." Greenwood turned and faced him. "That's what *I* think. How about you?"

O'Leary nodded. "I think you might be right."

26

They were dropping like flies.

Two more cuts immediately after the Cleveland loss, and another four earlier this morning. Mondays were the worst, everyone came to realize. The coaches had a chance to review the game film, make their notes, and cast their judgments. Then they'd get together for final discussions with Gray, and the axe would start to fall. One seemingly offhand comment by a position coach could decide someone's future. One comment, one observation, one mistake—your career hung by a thread every minute.

Jordan "Itchy" Fisher seemed to know this as well as anybody. From the day he came to camp, he was as nervous as a bee. He never sat still, which was why his teammates gave him the nickname. Itchy was a wide receiver in his fourth year in the league, a free-agent pickup from Green Bay. His record there had been mediocre at best.

When the team cut him at the end of his rookie contract, only two other teams seemed interested, and the Giants were closer to his home state of Pennsylvania. He wanted to do well, to get on the team at least, even if he wasn't going to be a starter. But he had such a negative outlook on the whole thing, it was almost as if he were condemning himself to a predetermined fate.

A few more cuts and it would be all over. The tension was so heavy it even made breathing difficult. Itchy was sitting on his cot thinking about how he would break the news to his wife when the inevitable occurred. Then he got to his feet, wringing his hands, and paced up and down between the two beds.

"She's gonna cry," he said. "I know she's gonna cry."

"You'll be fine," his roommate replied. Clarence Pittman had also been a free-agent pickup, in his fifth year in the league and a former victim of the salary cap. He'd done extremely well during his tenure with the Saints, but when it was time for a new contract, he and his agent discovered there was very little loot left in the New Orleans till, so they decided to try their luck elsewhere. Lying on his cot with one knee raised and the other leg propped over it, he flipped through a magazine and said, "You're going to give yourself a stroke."

"Yeah, sure, what the hell do you have to worry about? You're safe."

"Mmm—not necessarily. No one's safe until the end."

He was just trying to be humble. Inside, however, he believed Fisher to be correct—he would cruise past the final cut and coast into a nice fat contract. He'd had a great camp. Not his best ever, but pretty damn good. He'd studied his competition carefully and played just well enough to outdo them. It was the same theory motorists used to make sure they didn't get pulled over for speeding—as long as they were going slower than the Other Guy, how could they get in trouble? Pittman knew the training camp game; he'd played it before.

"Yeah, well . . . I made some mistakes out there," Itchy rambled on, taking his playbook off the dresser, fanning the pages absently, then throwing it back. "I know I did. They noticed, Pitt, I know they did. I don't even know why I'm here *now*."

"Because you've got heart," Pittman told him, scrutinizing a full-page ad for women's underwear. He believed this much, at least—for all of Fisher's shortcomings, he did have passion. It almost made up for his errors. Yes, he'd made a few. Pittman wasn't even an offensive player and he'd spotted them. But Itchy's enthusiasm and competitive fire were unmatched. Pittman felt sorry for him. They had become casual friends. He didn't want to see him disappointed, but. . . .

"Heart," Itchy snorted. "Who cares about heart when you drop the ball?"

"Nah," Pittman said, now tired of the conversation—so much like others they'd had. "You'll be fine."

They fell quiet for a while. Itchy sat down with his book and reviewed the plays they'd gone over that day. More study never hurt.

When the knock came on the plain wooden door, Fisher felt like a frozen hand had grabbed his heart. He looked over at Pittman, who casually returned the glance before going back to the magazine.

Itchy was about to say, *Who do you think that is?* Before he got the words out, someone on the other side said, "Fisher? Pittman? Are you in there?"

Fisher swallowed hard. He knew that voice. Everyone did by now. "Uh . . . yeah. We're in here."

The knob turned. This happened at a normal speed, but in Fisher's overdramatizing, hyperemotional mind it was much slower, like in a horror movie.

Then the Turk's grim figure filled the doorway. He was wearing a navy blue windbreaker and a Giants cap that seemed absurdly large in relation to the size of his head.

Pittman closed his eyes and asked God for the incident to be quick, and for Fisher to find another team as soon as possible. He didn't want to see the guy hurt any more than necessary.

". . . would you come with me, please?" he heard the Turk say colorlessly. "Coach wants to see you. And bring along your playbook." *Heartless sonofabitch*, Pittman thought. *How can anyone do this for a living?*

He had hoped he could get through the moment without becoming personally involved, but he was unable to control the desire to turn his head just enough to see the look on Fisher's face. It was, he supposed, the same macabre fascination that made people slow down at car accidents.

Knowing Fisher as he did, his primary expectation was that the guy would bawl like a child. Pittman had heard about one guy who had to be pried from his cot and carried to the elevator. Fisher wasn't of that stripe. He'd go peacefully, but he wouldn't be able to control himself.

There were several other scenarios Pittman had envisioned as well, but none had the expression that he eventually found on Itchy's face—slack-jawed astonishment. What was even more surprising, though, was that Fisher wasn't looking at Blumenthal.

He was looking at *him*.

"Pittman," the Turk repeated with a touch of impatience, "come on, let's *go*."

Clarence Pittman brought the magazine down slowly. He hadn't actually *seen* Blumenthal yet, and for the rest of his life he would remember the moment with exquisite clarity—as the magazine slid away and the image of his executioner was revealed.

"What . . . ?"

This came out with no force at all. He wanted it to sound angry. Instead it was feeble, almost pathetic. It was shock and disbelief and despair all jumbled together.

"Come on," Blumenthal said. "Get your playbook. The coach has a lot to do today."

Pittman turned again to Fisher, who looked utterly *terrified*.

The next twenty minutes would replay in Clarence Pittman's memory in a soft-edged blur. He would remember his hand reaching out to retrieve the playbook, remember being led down the echoey hallway into the elevator and then onto a floor he'd never been to. He would recall the brief conversation with Alan Gray (. . . *really thought you had a shot . . . felt some of the other guys did better . . .*) and then, finally, being escorted to his car by someone other than Don Blumenthal—someone he'd never seen before and, he was sure, would never see again. The guy said something ridiculous like "Take it easy," then walked away, leaving him there alone.

Just like that, it was over.

27

In the Matter of the Arbitration Between—

THOMAS JAMES BROOKMAN AND
THE NATIONAL FOOTBALL LEAGUE PLAYERS
ASSOCIATION

and

THE NEW YORK FOOTBALL GIANTS AND
THE NFL MANAGEMENT COUNCIL

Hearing held before William T. Serra, Esq.

APPEARANCES—

For the Management Council
- Craig Little, Esq.
- Walter Bartlett, Esq.

For the National Football League Players Association
- Matthew Blackman, Esq.
- Bill Chachkes, Esq.

Opinion

Before the start of the New York Giants' (hereinafter the "Club") training camp, the plaintiff, Thomas James Brookman (hereinafter the "Plaintiff"), requested that his present contract with the Club be terminated, and a new contract drawn up, this due to his above-average performance during the previous three seasons—particularly the latter two—in connection with the fact that said contract, having been offered during his rookie year, provided him only with league-minimum compensation.

When the Club declined his request, the Plaintiff, through his agent, Barry Matthias Sturtz (hereinafter the "Agent"), informed the Club that the Plaintiff would not be participating in any further Club activities until the issue was resolved to the Plaintiff's and Agent's satisfaction. When the Club insisted it would not alter its position on the matter, the Plaintiff then filed a formal grievance and request for independent arbitration, which was eventually granted.

Issues

1. Is the Plaintiff within his rights to temporarily set aside his responsibilities to the Club per his existing contract because he feels said contract is no longer representative of his best interests and reflective of his current skill level?

2. Should the Club be obligated to offer the Plaintiff a new contract commensurate with his improved skills and contributions to the Club? If not, should the contract then be terminated and the Plaintiff allowed to seek adequate employment with a different club?

Relevant Contract Provisions

Collective Bargaining Agreement
Article XIV: NFL Player Contract
Section 5: General
5(c): No Club shall pay or be obligated to pay any player or Player Affiliate (not including retired players) other than pursuant to the terms of a signed NFL Player Contract or a contract for non-football related services as described in Section 5(b). Nothing contained in the immediately preceding sentence shall interfere with a Club's obligation to pay a player deferred compensation earned under a prior Player Contract.

NFL Player Contract (generic)

Section 2, Employment and Services: Club employs Player as a skilled football player. Player accepts such employment. He agrees to give his best efforts and loyalty to the Club, and to conduct himself on and off the field with appropriate recognition of the fact that the success of professional football depends largely on public respect for and approval of those associated with the game. Player will report promptly for and participate fully in Club's official mandatory minicamp(s), official preseason training camp, all Club meetings and practice sessions, and all preseason, regular season, and postseason football games scheduled for or by Club.

Management/Club Position

The Club (and Management Council) maintains that the original contract awarded to the Plaintiff was made in good faith, with both parties understanding and agreeing to the terms therein. Furthermore, the Club maintains that the Plaintiff and his agent at the time (note: not the same individual as the "Agent" as referred to elsewhere in this document) were fully cognizant of the awards provided to the Plaintiff in the original and present contract, and that the Plaintiff was *expected* to make every reasonable effort to improve his skills so that his value to the Club would increase over time. Finally, the Club has made it clear that it has every intention of offering the Plaintiff a new contract once the original contract has come full term (i.e., at the end of the present season), or, in the event that a new agreement cannot be reached, the Plaintiff, who currently is not tagged as a franchise player (see Collective Bargaining

Agreement, Article XX), is then free to seek employment with a different Club. Thus, the Club believes that the Plaintiff is duty-bound to honor the terms of the contract and agreement into which he entered, regardless of his above-average performance.

NFLPA/Plaintiff Position

The Plaintiff (and NFLPA) maintains that his skill level and contribution to the Club has increased beyond even what would be considered "normal" and that he is now consistently performing at a level comparable to the top players in his position leaguewide. The Plaintiff further maintains that he is now a "key" element in the Club's success, and as such should be compensated appropriately. Aware that the Club is willing to offer a more lucrative deal at the end of the current contract, which is less than one season from its natural terminus, the Plaintiff sees no just cause for putting off the negotiation of the new agreement, as he wishes to continue contributing to the team's success as he has in the past, but feels that he cannot do so until such an agreement has been settled.

Analysis

There is little doubt that the contributions by the Plaintiff to the Club during his tenure thus far have been outstanding. While he had a modest rookie season due to the fact that a senior player was occupying the starting role at his position, the Plaintiff did an admirable job of handling those duties after the senior player sustained an injury and was forced to concede the position. From that day forward, the Plaintiff devoted himself wholly and fully to becoming one of the finest at this position among active players, and, from all accounts, succeeded tremendously.

There is also little doubt that the Plaintiff, due to his excellent abilities and consistency of performance, is likely, based on "market value" (this determined within the context of others playing his position combined with their salaries), worthy of increased financial consideration. There is little doubt that the Plaintiff, either with the Club or with another organization, will be receiving greater compensation in the future, barring a career-ending injury or other misfortune.

However, the facts given above do not, regardless of their merit, automatically grant the Plaintiff the right to a greater salary, or, more to the point, the right for the Plaintiff to, essentially, "blackmail" the Club into agreeing to a higher salary by refusing to fulfill the duties outlined in his original contract. Also, while it may be true that, colloquially, it is the opinion of this committee that the Plaintiff is, in fact, performing at a level deserving of greater rewards, the matter still must be resolved by the Plaintiff and the Club independent of this committee, i.e., the Club should not be the tool with which the Plaintiff forces the Club to submit to his wishes. Under alternative circumstances this might indeed be the case, e.g., if the Plaintiff was still early in his current contract and had several years of substandard salary ahead. But in this instance the original contract is nearing its end, so a premature termination would not be justified.

Furthermore, it is not the desire of the arbitrator to set forth a standard by which other players and their representatives will be eager to follow the same inappropriate actions that the Plaintiff has taken in this matter, e.g., refusing to fulfill his duties to his team as a means of leverage when a situation is not to his liking. There is a tremendous degree of flexibility within the interpretation of what entitles a player to a renegotiated contract, and the point should be made that improvement of one's skills is a natural, fully *expected* progression in the league, i.e., *all* players are expected to become more valuable to a team as time passes. But this does not automatically entitle them to greater compensation than that which has already been outlined—and agreed upon—in their existing contract. Due to this flexibility of interpretation, such matters are best handled on a case-by-case basis, again, between the players and organizations in question. Only in extreme cases is independent arbitration justified, and this does not appear to be one of those cases.

Thus, it is recommended that the Plaintiff continue his course of exemplary performance and improvement, and plan to negotiate a substantially more rewarding contract at the end of the current season.

Award

Grievance denied.

William T. Serra, Esq.
August 18, 2006

Less than two hours later, the rest of the world knew about it.

"That's correct, Tommy," Greg Bolton said on the screen. "The arbitrator has decided he cannot force the Giants to renegotiate T. J. Brookman's contract, regardless of Brookman's outstanding play these past two years." A tiny microphone was clipped to his maroon tie, and he stood in front of a blue fabric backdrop.

Spencer, back in ESPN studios in Connecticut, shook his head. "Boy, rough news for Brookman and his agent, Barry Sturtz. Probably not what they wanted to hear."

"No, I would think not."

You're damn right about that, Sturtz thought as he stood in his home office. He'd had the TV on all day in case ESPN knew about the decision before he did. It wasn't inconceivable, considering the depth with which they'd covered the story thus far.

In any event, he and his client did find out first, in the form of a fax that came out of the machine on Sturtz's desk about an hour ago. It now sat squarely on his blotter, isolated from all other paperwork. It was the only issue on his mind at the moment.

He hovered by the tall windows again, looking across the yard to where the deer had been. There were none out there now. No signs of life at all, which Sturtz found ironic since there weren't too many in here, either.

"I'm really sorry, T. J.," he said for the third time, the Bluetooth headset jutting from his ear like a *Star Trek* prop. He was dressed in gray slacks and a light blue shirt open at the neck. "Is there anything I can do?"

"No, not that I can think of." Brookman sounded exhausted. "So what do we do now?"

Sturtz took a deep breath. "Well, we've got two choices. You get in there and play, make the best of it, do a great job, pray you don't get injured, and try to land a solid new contract at the end of this season, either with New York or someone else. . . ."

"Or?" His tone made it clear this wasn't his preferred option.

"Or we can ask for a trade again."

"Can that really happen?"

"In theory. I've still got this one team interested," Sturtz said, thinking back to the James Bond–type meeting he'd had in the middle of Nowhere, USA. "They said they'd be willing to give up quite a bit."

"And who's that?"

"I can't tell you, I really can't."

"Not even now?"

"No. None of it is supposed to be happening in the first place, remember?"

"Right."

"So let me take care of it."

"Do you think the Giants will go for it?"

"They're going to want a lot. Remember—they don't really want to let you go."

Irritated, T. J. said, "They don't want to pay me, but they don't want to let me go. It's ridiculous."

"I know it is. So what do you want me to do? Do you think you can tough it out for one more season, or should I make a call?"

After a brief pause, Brookman said, "The coaches are going to treat me like shit if I go back."

"Not all of them," Sturtz replied. "Dale Greenwood and Jim O'Leary seem to know that this is part of the game. They're decent individuals."

"But Gray. . . ."

"Gray's going to be an asshole." Then, almost to himself, Sturtz added, "But he *is* an asshole, so what choice does he have?"

"What if he makes Greenwood sit me? What if he signs one of those other guys who's there now and I sit on the bench all year? Who'll want to take me then? And what about my stats?" Brookman's voice was rising.

"I'm not going to lie to you, I've seen it happen before. Some coaches can be very vindictive."

"And Gray is that type of guy."

"Yes, he is."

"Christ. . . . But if we insist on a trade, then we look bad, right?"

Sturtz turned away from the windows, finding no comfort there. "Well, it doesn't look *good*. You can get a reputation as a guy who isn't a team player."

"But people will know why I did it. They'll understand, right?"

"Oh, everyone will know *why*. Even Gray knows *why*. He knows damn well that we were justified in our demands. But that doesn't mean someone won't use it against you." He wandered without direction around the room, hands in his pockets. "This will be a tough, unpleasant negotiation. Everything will be on the table. If someone can use your . . . your *uncooperativeness* . . . as leverage, they will."

"Same with you, right?"

"Huh?"

"Trying to force a trade will make *you* look bad, won't it?"

"Yeah, a little. But not too much." He surprised himself by smiling. "Everyone thinks agents are scum anyway, so what's the difference?"

If nothing else, this got his client to laugh. "Shit . . . well, I'm sorry. This is causing a lot of trouble for you."

"No, pal," Sturtz replied, absently picking up a *Greatest Hits of the Seventies* CD that sat atop a pile of others by his stereo. He turned it over several times, then set it down again. "We made the decision to do this together. You have nothing to apologize for."

The conversation faded again. Sturtz moved away from the stereo and toward a collection of autographed photos framed and hanging on the wall over the minibar. "So what do you think?" he said finally. "What would you like to do?"

Now it was Brookman's turn to take a deep breath. He didn't hurry with his answer.

But when it came, Sturtz was pleased. "You got it," he said. Then he was on the phone again.

"I gotta tell you, Alan, I was nervous there for a while."

Palmer sat facing Gray, slumped in one of the two guest chairs on the other side of the coach's desk. He held a can of Coors in both hands, resting it on his stomach. He'd been nursing it for nearly thirty minutes, and it was warm now. He wasn't much of a drinker, but he was the only one around at this late hour, and Gray didn't want to celebrate alone. The coach had knocked down three in the same span and had just taken a fourth from the little fridge.

"*I* wasn't worried," Gray said, delivering the lie in the easy way a person when they knew there was no way of disproving it. "There was no angle from which the arbitrator could justify the grievance. No way. If they okayed Brookman, then they'd have to rubber-stamp every punk in the league who thinks he should be getting paid more just because he had a good season. We'd be dealing with this shit every damn day."

"I guess you're right," Palmer said, taking another tiny sip and trying not to wince. "So what happens now?"

"With Brookman?"

"With everyone. With everything. Guys have been flying out of here left and right lately."

Gray wiped his mouth with his hand. "Well, we've got to cut six more in total. Six more, and then we'll be at the magic number."

"No problem with that?"

"None at all. I have only one more cut to make on defense, and I'm pretty sure who that's gonna be—Loman."

Palmer nodded. "And on offense?"

"That's up to Greenwood."

"What about your mole? Any progress there?"

Gray cracked open the new can, took a long swig, then belched mightily. "We haven't found the fucker yet, but we will."

There had been two other interrogations, both similar to the one with Abraham. Like Abraham's, they were both dead ends. Blumenthal did check out Abraham's claim that he was only communicating with his father and discovered that the kid had been telling the truth. For the briefest moment, he thought about dropping in and issuing a brief apology. Then he heard that Gray cut the kid right in the middle of a practice, in front of everyone. Abraham fled before Blumenthal got the chance.

"And when Brookman returns, what do I do? Do I start putting together a new offer of some k—"

Gray was already shaking his head. He did this in a severe, self-important way that Palmer found irritating. "No new deal."

"But we promised him—"

"That's irrelevant. No new deal. We'll squeeze another year out of him cheap, then dump him. I'll need that money for defense. I'm not blowing it on one kid. He and his agent will get nothing from us."

He lifted the can and took another sip. Palmer watched this, fascinated not so much by the man's capacity for alcoholic intake as his unabashed nastiness. He realized Alan Gray wasn't so much hard-nosed or a taskmaster or any of the other names given to unflinching, ruthless people—he was just plain *mean*. A coldhearted sociopath with just enough charm to get ahead. Worst of all—he enjoyed it.

"So . . . what happens when he returns? Do we fine him for—"

"Fine him," Gray said quickly. "Keep fining the bastard as much as we're allowed to fine him. That'll make him even cheaper than he already is." He chuckled, pleased that the arbitration decision had essentially become a license to screw T. J. Brookman into the ground.

"And what about the three guys Greenwood brought in to replace him?"

"What about them?"

"Well, they've been doing pretty well, but we can't sign them all."

"Again, that's Greenwood's department. But you're right—we can't keep them. I'll tell him to cut 'em." Gray waved his hand. "They all have to go by Monday."

He leaned back in his chair, closed his eyes, and folded his hands across his chest. Palmer continued staring dead-eyed at this man whose nerve was not to be believed. He had manipulated the situation flawlessly, bringing in three eager hopefuls, all of whom had performed magnificently in the belief that they really had a shot. Now that Gray had what he wanted, they were to be tossed out like any other trash.

What Palmer didn't know was that someone else was even more amazed by Gray's audacity than he was—someone who had been standing outside the half-open door and had heard every word.

29

Jermaine Hamilton possessed the enviable gift of being able to fall asleep anywhere, at any time, in any position. No matter what the circumstances, if he was tired enough, he could simply close his eyes and drift away.

He lay sideways on his too-small cot, atop the messy sheets rather than under them, snoring generously. Just overhead, reared back like a cobra poised to strike, was the reading lamp he'd purchased at Wal-Mart on that first night with Freddie Turner. It was still on and shining into his face. Alongside his pillow, lying open, was his playbook. He'd gone through it so many times that he'd just about memorized everyone else's assignments, too—to the point where he occasionally (and with the requisite diplomacy) corrected some of his teammates, on both offense and defense, during practices. He could not remember a time in his career when he knew a playbook so well.

The door opened just minutes before one o'clock. Corey Reese crept through first, followed by Daimon Foster, both dressed in dark tracksuits. Foster closed the door quietly.

Reese knelt beside Hamilton and set a hand gingerly on his shoulder. This caused Hamilton's snoring to become louder and more erratic.

"Jermaine?" Reese whispered. "Hey, wake up." He gave him a gentle shake. "Jermaine, come on. . . ." He turned back to Foster briefly. "Maybe if I kicked him in the balls."

Foster didn't even crack a smile; the whole idea of this visit didn't sit well with him. Reese had woken him up less than an hour ago and spilled his story, so he knew it was inevitable. But he still didn't like it.

"Jermaine, come on. . . ."

Reese shook him hard once, and that did the trick. Hamilton came to in an instant, rolling over and croaking something unintelligible, his eyes wild with confusion.

"What? Huh? Hey, what are you—"

Reese put both hands up. "Take it easy, now, take it easy. I'm unarmed, see? Okay?"

Hamilton looked from him to Foster, and those red eyes narrowed. "What the fuck—what are you two doing here?"

"Shhh," Reese said, putting a finger to his lips. "You'll wake up the whole damn floor."

"What? Get the hell out of—"

"Jermaine, shut up," Foster said flatly. That seemed to have some magical effect, for Hamilton, stunned, fell silent. Nevertheless, he looked like he had murder on his mind. "You need to hear what Corey has to say."

Hamilton looked to Reese again, who managed a smile. Then he took the liberty of sitting on the empty bunk on the other side. It had been vacated five days earlier, when the Turk came to claim Turner. Hamilton hadn't been here when it happened, but he found a note on his pillow. Short, sweet, and a little sentimental, but the pain between the lines was unmistakable. Hamilton imagined Turner trying to keep a steady hand as he wrote it, then handing it to Blumenthal so he could review it for acceptable content before letting Turner set it down.

"Okay, look," Reese began, "you and me and Daimon here, we're all in some trouble. Big trouble."

"Trouble?"

"I was on my way to see Coach O'Leary a few hours ago, and as I was walking past Gray's door I heard him talking to someone. I think it was Chet Palmer."

Foster watched Hamilton closely, the way one cop standing in the darkened corner of an interrogation room watches a suspect while another fires the questions. "So?"

"So, I don't make a habit of eavesdropping, but I heard them talking about *us*." He motioned to the three of them with a quick sweep of his finger. "All of us."

Concern dawned on Hamilton's face, diminishing an equal part of his anger, and he slid up onto one elbow. "Yeah? So why is that—"

"We were set up," Reese said, and he said it with no pretense or emotion. Because of this, it carried even greater impact.

"I don't understand."

"We were brought here as leverage for Gray against T. J. Brookman." Reese's disgust was communicated through his emphasis on the word "leverage."

Hamilton's eyes shifted back and forth between them. "*What?*"

"We never had a shot at making the team," Reese added. "We were never supposed to make it."

"You're full of shit."

"No, he's not," Foster said. "I believe him. It all makes sense."

Reese was nodding. "Think about it—first the grievance, then the arbitration . . . and now that T. J.'s lost it, he has no choice but to stay here. Between him and Maxwell, what do they need any of us for?"

Hamilton held his stare with Reese, then turned his eyes downward as he considered everything. In those few seconds, his expression changed from angry to helpless. "My God. . . ."

"I know," Reese said. "I know."

"I thought Greenwood was—"

"He wasn't in on it," Foster cut in, not wanting Hamilton to start down this path of reasoning. "Neither was O'Leary."

"My agent has dealt with both of them in the past," Reese added. "I called him before I went to see Daimon, and he believes that. He says they've always been good guys. Totally above suspicion. It was Gray who knew. Gray and Palmer."

"It was part of a big plan," Foster said. "And so were we."

Hamilton kept going over it in his mind, gazing into empty space. Then he began shaking his head, his eyes reddened with renewed fury. "I needed this," he said. "I needed this bad. . . ."

"Hey, if it makes you feel any better," Reese continued, "I needed it, too. I'm so in debt I've got banks and creditors calling my house every day, scaring the shit out of my wife. If I don't make this team, we'll be living in our Escalade."

"And I wanted to get my mom and my girlfriend out of the shit-hole we've all lived in since I was born," Foster added, suddenly feeling sick to his stomach at the possibility that this dream would now be put on hold once again . . . maybe forever. A death sentence if ever there was one.

Hamilton, still within himself, didn't respond. He sat up, folded his hands together, and stared at the floor. Foster took the opportunity of this break in the conversation to glance back at the door, half expecting it to fly open and see the Turk standing there with his damn flashlight.

"So what happens now?" Hamilton asked.

Reese said, "Well, we've come up with an idea, and we wanted you to hear it. When I first found out about this, I was pissed, too. It took all the discipline I had to keep from running in there and killing those two assholes."

"That's what I'm going to do," Hamilton said. "What does it matter n—"

"No, you're not," Reese replied, and it came out like a military order.

Hamilton looked up quickly, meeting him eye to eye.

"We're not going to do it that way," Reese went on. "We've got a much better idea. *Much* better."

"Yeah?" Hamilton said after a few seconds. "What's that?"

Reese smiled. "Check this out. . . ."

Hamilton's room was empty when Weasel entered it two days later, but then he knew it would be. The first practice had ended, and everyone was in the dining hall, having lunch. He didn't have much time; he didn't need much. This would be a quick in-and-out. Quick, but supremely effective if successful.

He moved about silently, scanning everything as the rain spattered against the shade-covered window. The cot opposite Hamilton's was perfectly made up, its occupant long gone. Weasel went through the drawers in the student desk, then into Hamilton's bag. He even looked under both cots. No dice.

He stood, hands on hips, wondering if he had made a mistake. *No, I know what I heard.* Then where could it be? When his eyes fell upon the bathroom door, he laughed to himself. *Of course . . . you dumb shit.*

He went straight to the medicine cabinet. Same type as in every other dorm room, including his own—a tall steel box with a mirrored door. The glass on his had a diagonal crack running from one corner to another, whereas Reese's was perfect. The only other noticeable difference was that Reese's had a faded, rippled sticker along the bottom advertising an REM concert from eight years earlier.

Weasel pulled the door back and found what he was after; there was nothing else on the shelves. Just a plastic orange prescription bottle standing in the dead center. He took it out and read the label carefully to be sure.

Vicodin.

Beautiful.

"Let's see how well you do without these, hotshot," he mumbled through a grin. He cheerfully tossed the bottle once in the air, then stuffed it into the pocket of his tracksuit.

His heart thumped to a halt when he stepped back out—all three were waiting for him. In that instant he knew he'd been had.

There was some kind of distant fascination in the fact that he never suspected it, never even had a clue he was being set up. He considered himself a fairly intelligent individual, and he'd done this kind of thing plenty of times before, hadn't he? Yet he'd been masterfully outsmarted.

"You motherfucker," Hamilton said with a scowl that would've scared Satan. "You slimy motherfucker."

Glenn Maxwell, the team's quiet and cooperative "other" tight end, found himself unable to respond.

Reese, standing in front of Hamilton, was nodding. "I had a feeling it was you. I was hoping I was wrong, I really was." They'd talked it over, figured it out for themselves. Once they had convinced each other of their mutual innocence, they worked on puzzling out who the guilty party might be. At one point Hamilton thought it might be one of the coaches—he'd seen it before.

"Piece of shit," Foster chimed in. He stood at the back, near the half-open door.

It had been Reese's idea. He'd instructed Hamilton to make a point of talking about how much he needed the pills—how they were helping him cope with his back and he doubted he could play without them—to anyone who would listen. In practices, during meals, at meetings, everywhere. He focused on a handful of "prime suspects," guys who seemed to have the most to gain by the sabotage. Then they simply waited.

Maxwell decided to try the offensive and see what happened. "What the hell?" he said in a lame attempt at anger. "I was just going to borrow some for myself."

"Borrow some of what?" Reese said innocently. "We didn't know you took anything."

Maxwell opened his mouth. Then, almost on its own, it closed again.

Fuck.

"You sonofabitch," Hamilton said, starting forward. "I oughta break your neck right n—"

Maxwell took a fearful step back. Reese turned and held Hamilton at bay. "No, take it easy. We'll bring him to Coach Greenwood. We caught him, that's good enough."

"Yeah," Foster added. "I'm sure the coach will have something to say about this."

"Uh-huh," Hamilton cut in, "like go the fuck home."

"Maybe. Let's find out."

They took their prisoner by the arms and led him out of the room.

The Giants organization cleared out of Albany the Friday before the final preseason game. As much of a novelty as it was to have them there at the beginning, their hosts were happy to see them go at the end. During the first few weeks, students and other fans lined up along the chain-link fences around the practice fields to watch drills, get autographs, and, if they were lucky, have a conversation or two. Now those same fences stood empty.

Practices were held on Saturday in the bubble next to the home stadium in New Jersey's Meadowlands Sports Complex. Like most bubbles, it was basically two enormous layers of vinyl, with a thin layer of insulation between them, puffed up by air pumped from outside at a pressure of no more than .05 pounds per square inch and held in place by hundreds of criss-crossing cables. Like the college fields, it was surrounded by a chain-link fence, this one with the added privacy of dark green slatting.

After the first practice, while most of the team was having lunch, Hamilton, Reese, and Foster detoured to the weight room—a magnificent, state-of-the-art facility, recently renovated by the team's strength and conditioning coach. With bright fluorescent lighting and a cement floor painted Giants blue, it featured long rows of benches, racks, weight trees, lateral raises, and pullovers, plus leg presses, incline and decline combos, treadmills, and hundreds of dumbbells. A veritable playground of bodily health.

Hamilton lay on a bench doing three-hundred-pound presses while Reese spotted him. They were both dressed in shorts and nylon tops. Hamilton huffed and puffed, his face glistening with perspiration. Reese had a white towel around his neck and wore a filthy pair of fingerless lifting gloves. Nearby, Foster wore a navy tracksuit and had just passed his third treadmill mile. A heart monitor was wrapped around his right wrist.

Jim O'Leary came in through a far door, a clipboard in one hand and a whistle bouncing off his chest. Reese nodded to Hamilton, who set the bar into its cradle and sat up. Foster also saw him and stepped off the rolling rubber platform.

Surrounded by the shining equipment, the four men clustered together. O'Leary managed a small, forced smile.

"He said we're keeping him," the coach told them. Hamilton threw his hands up; Foster laughed and shook his head.

"Just like that?" Reese asked.

"Yeah. Dale said he wanted him to go, but Gray said no. He said he knew the playbook too well, and he was valuable at other positions. Which, I admit, is true."

"This is a *joke.*"

"I know," O'Leary replied. "I don't like it, either. It changes the whole dynamic of the team. It's going to cause havoc in the locker room. I don't think anyone was crazy about Maxwell before. Now they'll be looking over their shoulder every time he's around."

Word of Maxwell's clandestine activities had spread quickly, and his teammates began treating him like he had leprosy. In response, he'd been walking around with the wide-eyed look of a child who'd lost his parents in a department store.

"Doesn't the coach care?" Foster wondered. "Doesn't it bother him that this guy is like a poison now?"

O'Leary shrugged. "Apparently not."

"Unbelievable."

"Or," O'Leary added, lowering his voice, "maybe he *likes* it. Maybe this is the kind of thing he secretly admires." Such a clear condemnation from the normally neutral O'Leary was surprising.

Hamilton lowered his head so his face was hidden. Reese took his gloves off and stuffed them into his pockets. Foster, looking away in disgust, couldn't help but laugh.

"So that's it then," Reese said finally. "No openings for a tight end. We're *all* screwed."

"Well, yes and no."

"Huh?"

"Dale and I have been talking, and we've come up with an idea that might help." Another smile, this one sly. "In tomorrow's game, we're going to feature the three of you big-time. Lots of plays, lots of action. You're all going to get the ball, make key blocks, the works. It's going to be your final showcase."

"What difference will that m—" Foster began.

Hamilton cut him off. "So other teams can get a good look at us?"

O'Leary nodded. "You got it. You guys are gonna have the spotlight from start to finish."

"Oh, yeah," Reese said. "Yeah, definitely."

"Come Monday, when the final cuts are announced, your agents' phones will be ringing around the clock. You've got thirty-one other organizations to choose from. So your hard work probably *will* pay off in the end."

"That's great," Reese said.

"Almost makes me wish I had an agent," Foster added. He'd thought about getting one but wanted to wait until he made the team. That way, his business mind had decided, he'd have more leverage and could take his pick from the best people available. "I guess I'm still screwed."

"I can recommend a few," O'Leary told him. "It shouldn't be a problem."

Foster said, "Seriously?"

"Seriously."

"Wow, I really appreciate it."

"Sure. I'm sorry I can't do any better, but that's how it is right now. Your fate after the last preseason game will have to be *your* challenge, all of you. So get ready to play the best four quarters of your lives. It might not be important in terms of score, but it could be the key that unlocks your future. I certainly hope so."

O'Leary turned to leave. Just before he reached the door, Reese called out, "Coach?"

"Yeah?"

"Just curious—what about T. J.?"

"What about him?"

"He still has to play here, right?"

"Yes."

"For the same contract? The same money?"

O'Leary's smile faded a bit. "Yeah, same everything."

"That kind of sucks. I mean, for him."

"Yeah," Jim O'Leary said. "It sure does."

After a thorough and exhaustive search of the area during the first six months of his residency in North Carolina, Barry Sturtz managed to find just one restaurant that he really liked. It was called O'Mearas, in honor of the owner's wife (whom he eventually divorced, but by then the name had become ingrained in the public's mind, so he was stuck with it). It was a white-linen-and-crystal type of place, with soft lighting and cocktail-hour piano music. Not exactly what Sturtz had grown accustomed to during his wild youth back in Brooklyn, but it captured a certain New York ambience that, to his surprise, he missed quite a bit.

Sitting there now, in a darkened corner booth with a glass-globed candle flickering in the center of the table, he put his napkin in his lap as the waitress set down a plate of steaming veal francese, his favorite item on the menu. He'd decided this would be *his* night, a few hours all to himself, with no concern for his clients and their troubles. First his favorite restaurant, then a stop at his favorite bar. Have a few beers, shoot a little pool. He knew some of the guys there now, and none of them asked what he did for a living. (If someone did, he decided, he'd tell them he was in "career management." That was obscure enough, yet truthful enough.) He needed this release more than he'd needed one in a long time. He was going to savor every moment.

His cell phone vibrated during dessert (pistachio ice cream). In spite of his vow, he'd left the phone on in case of a true emergency—and his clients had already been warned that, should they call him under circumstances that were anything short of dire, he would remove their testicles with a dull knife.

He didn't recognize the number, nor could he even place the area code. He'd spent enough time on the phone over the years to know most of them, but this was a new one. *Maybe a misdial,* he thought. He doubted it, though. Odd how many wrong numbers landed on someone's home phone, but so few on a cell phone.

He stuck his headset into his ear and took the call.

It turned out that he did know the person after all. Knew him quite well, in fact. They had never spoken before, but he recognized the name instantly.

He asked about the purpose of the call. The caller told him.

His carefully constructed plans for the evening were quickly forgotten.

"Come on, let's go! Let's *go!*" Jermaine Hamilton bellowed from the sidelines, clapping and pacing. His helmet was off, his uniform filthy. His hands had been bandaged, a bloodstain colored his pants on the right thigh, and every joint and muscle was in agony. He hadn't felt so alive in ages.

This is what I remember, he thought. *This is it right here. This is what I've longed for.*

From the start of what Jim O'Leary called the Game of Their Lives, all three burst out of the gate and never stopped. Not once did it feel like a preseason game. It wasn't exactly the Super Bowl, but it could've been. Every play mattered. Their senses had never been so sharp, so focused. They watched and absorbed everything. The only disappointments came when the offense had to hand over possession, forcing them off the field.

With Maxwell keeping the bench warm, Greenwood made good on his promise and dazzled the Dallas Cowboys' defense—ranked eighteenth the previous season—with a variety of double tight end sets. On the second play from scrimmage, Reese caught a shovel pass in the backfield that he then tossed to Foster for a twenty-two-yard gain. Six plays later, Hamilton pulled the ball down over the middle, smashed his way through two safeties, and pounded into the end zone. Then Foster, in a special teams role, caught a Cowboys kickoff four minutes later and ran it back to his own forty-seven.

In the second quarter, with the Giants leading 17–3, Greenwood blew everyone away by putting all three in the same play—Hamilton on the right side, Foster on the left, and Reese as fullback. Hamilton went in motion, the ball was snapped, and it drifted past quarterback Mark Lockenmeyer directly into Reese's hands. He tucked it in and plowed forward. With Hamilton leading the way, Reese motored through a hole up the middle and added another eighteen running yards to his eventual total of seventy-one—unheard of for a tight end. With less than a minute remaining in the half, Foster caught a Lockenmeyer laser in the end zone after finding open space in the corner. That one was so easy he went into the locker room laughing.

Early in the third, with the score 27–6, Reese was the final recipient of a double reverse, with Hamilton again throwing key blocks along the left side for a gain of twenty-two. On the next play, Hamilton ran a slant pattern and stiff-armed two defenders simultaneously on his way to his second touchdown. Daimon Foster would push the crowd into a frenzy at the end of the period when he drove into the middle of the field on a screen play, leaned down for a low block, and inadvertently flipped the guy up and over his back. The defender, more amused than humiliated, slapped Foster on the helmet and said, "Thanks for the ride, kid," as he jogged away.

By the middle of the fourth quarter, with the score a comfortable 45–21, the media was running out of superlatives.

"I tell you, Jack," WNYN broadcaster Martin Cole said from the booth, "I have never, ever seen a performance like this from a group of tight ends in all my years. I am just speechless."

"And what's even more amazing," Jack Neuweiler said, "is that none of them will be here come Monday, as you know."

"Right. For those of you who *don't* know, the three young men who've been embarrassing the Dallas Cowboy defense all afternoon have been living on borrowed time since an independent arbitrator denied the grievance filed by star tight end T. J. Brookman in his quest for a more lucrative contract with the New York Giants. That decision effectively issued the death warrants for these three remarkable talents."

"But only as far as the Giants are concerned," Neuweiler added quickly. "They are free to sign with whoever else they wish."

"And you know, Jack, maybe that's exactly why we're seeing so much of them today. Maybe someone down there likes them."

"Maybe."

Cole and Neuweiler weren't the only announcers to make the connection; Dale Greenwood knew the media would eventually put the pieces together. The rest of his offensive guys figured it out, too. For that matter, so did the defense, special teams, the kids who carried the towels and the Gatorade bottles, the stadium security, the fans, and everyone else who watched the game.

Including Alan Gray.

Greenwood began feeling his icy stare starting around the middle of the second quarter. He made a point of putting as much distance between them as possible. He knew Gray was going to say something sooner or later. At halftime, he stayed at the far end of the locker room, but Gray finally caught up to him in the hallway as they approached the tunnel. Grabbing him by the sleeve, Gray said gruffly, "What will you be getting, a percentage of their new contracts?" When Greenwood didn't respond, Gray added, "Cool them off, Dale. And do it now." Seconds later they were enveloped by the deafening roar of the crowd.

Greenwood made no effort to heed Gray's command. If anything, he was more determined than ever to see that the three young men were put front and center. When Daimon Foster caught his second touchdown, the head coach stood with his arms folded and stone-faced. It was such an odd moment—a head coach unmoved by a score from his own team—that several broadcasters commented on it.

O'Leary walked over to Greenwood at one point and said, "We're going to have detention for a month," to which Greenwood gave no reply. *The hell with him,* he thought. *If I'm going to get fired, I'm doing it with a clear conscience.*

With less than five minutes remaining, Greenwood asked his magical trio if they wanted to sit out the rest of the way. They vigorously declined.

The Giants got the ball again with 4:14 to go. On the first play from scrimmage, at their own thirty-one, backup quarterback Blair Thompson—who was now making the calls on his own—threw an incomplete post route. On second down, an end run produced just two yards.

When they returned to the huddle, Reese said, "Blair, this guy on the right, number 67, is exhausted. I can put some space between us pretty quickly." Thompson agreed.

Following a short count, the offense executed the out pass perfectly. Reese started inside, 67 fell for it, and he cut out and took off like a bullet. When the ball came, he'd achieved a separation of almost five yards. He had to go up to get the throw, but not much. And he knew there was nothing but empty space ahead. One more score to cap off an unforgettable game.

Then it all went horribly wrong.

As he came down, he failed to notice the Dallas safety charging in his direction. This was Andre McKinney. Like Hamilton, McKinney was an aging veteran trying desperately to squeeze as much time as possible out of his career. Unlike Hamilton, he was failing miserably. Dallas still had eight cuts to make to get to the required fifty-three on Monday, and it was all but certain that he would be among those to go. He believed he still had a fighting chance today, but the stellar performances by New York's three tight ends dashed any remaining hopes. As a result, McKinney, his blood boiling, was waiting for the opportunity to get even.

His plan was not to injure Reese in any way, just to smash him good and hard. Ring his bell, as the saying goes. As he dove, he aimed for Reese's midsection. But that wasn't where his helmet—and, subsequently, the full weight of his 270-pound body—made impact.

There was perhaps a half second when Reese realized what was going to happen before it did. And just like the first time, everything unfolded in slow motion. As he came down with the pass, he saw McKinney in midair. He tried to turn away—or at least he thought he did (later he wouldn't be sure)—but quickly realized he'd never make it. He first felt the knee bend too far inward, then the dull snapping sensation—and then the fire, as if someone had doused it with gasoline and set it ablaze. In the next moment he was on the ground, his hands grasping either side of the ragged joint, struggling not to scream but screaming anyway. He pressed and prodded the muscles and ligaments in an attempt to switch off the agony, but the shock waves kept coming.

Hamilton and Foster rushed across the field just behind the physicians. Foster knelt down, unsure what to do. Hamilton, conversely, took a swing at the baffled McKinney and landed it squarely in his stomach. The latter went down like a shot buck, and a referee signaled for Hamilton to be ejected. He couldn't have cared less.

"Corey, is it the knee?" asked head physician Michael Grady. Grady was forty-six, still boyishly handsome, and in his fourth year with the team.

"Yeah . . . my God. . . ." Tears had begun streaming down his face.

"Let me have a look. Let go for a second."

Grady cut the pants up the side, revealing what he feared most—the area was already beginning to swell. *Not a good sign.*

"Okay," Grady said to his assistants, "get a brace for it right away, and get the stretcher and the cart out here. He's not going to be able to walk this off."

As they waited, Reese said through clenched teeth, "How bad, Mike?"

"I don't know yet. I'll have to—"

"Mike, *how bad*?"

"Well, sorry you boys lost," Gray said, "but that's the way it goes. You win some, you lose some."

He sat directly across from Barry Sturtz, in the same conference room, and in fact the same chair, as he had over a month ago. His fingers were laced behind his head, his feet up on the mirror-glossy mahogany table. All he needed was a big cigar and a diamond stickpin. Chet Palmer was next to him, going over the final paperwork. He was almost as giddy as Gray, but he worked hard not to show it. To the victors go the spoils . . . and the bragging rights . . . and the arrogance . . . and an open license to act like assholes. . . .

"Yeah, I agree with you," Sturtz said, a smile on his face and his leather shoulder bag in front of him. Both Gray and Palmer couldn't understand why he wasn't acting more . . . *defeated.* Denial? Smug defiance? Well, whatever the case, he could act however he wished. The cards had been played and the hand was over. Their puzzlement at this petty rebellion was a small price to pay. Still, it was *irritating*.

"You'll have to sign this," Palmer said matter-of-factly. He glanced at the sheet one last time, then slid it over. It bumped against Sturtz's bag before coming to a halt. He ignored it.

"It basically tells us you have read and understood the fines that are about to be levied on your client," Palmer plowed on. "If they were relatively minor, we could do it verbally, but considering the amount, there needs to be paperwork. You understand, of course."

"Of course," Sturtz said.

"And he is required to return to his duties immediately," Palmer added.

"Right."

An uneasy silence drifted between them, and the staring match went on. Palmer looked to Gray, whose cocky grin was fading fast.

"Don't you understand what's happening here?" Gray said finally, an edge to his voice for the first time. "Don't you know what's going to happen to your client going forward?"

"No, please enlighten me."

Gray pulled his feet from the table and moved into a sitting position so fast Palmer jumped. "I'm going to work the *shit* out of him. I'm going to make him pay for embarrassing me, and us, and this team. I'm going to teach him a lesson in humiliation that he won't forget for the rest of his life. Do you understand me?"

"I believe I do," Sturtz said, gently setting his fingers together and swiveling back and forth in the chair.

"Then what the hell is your problem?"

"No problem here, Coach." He picked up the paper Palmer had

passed over, lifted it about a foot off the table, then let it fall again. It seesawed twice before coming to rest somewhere in the middle. "But this is bullshit, and we're not going to do it."

Gray's neck started turning red. Palmer had identified this barometer of his temperament long ago—he was about a second away from a full eruption.

"What?"

"I said we're not doing it. No fines, no suffering, no nothing. T. J.'s still sitting out as far as I'm concerned."

Gray, to Palmer's amazement, did not blow—he just sat there, staring, for what seemed like a long time. In an oddly robotic way, he turned to face his general manager, then turned back. "Are you out of your fucking mind? Are you on drugs or something?"

"No, I'm quite clearheaded. I really appreciate your concern, though."

"You can't do this. You *can't!*"

The word "can't" came out in a grinding, spit-flying screech. A thousand pounds of rage delivered in one syllable.

"I beg to differ," Sturtz said politely. This caused Palmer to think, *My God, he's trying to give the guy a stroke.* "If you recall, the arbitration hearing was for the issue of a more generous contract, not the possibility of a trade. And if I recall, not only is a trade request part of T. J.'s contractual right, it was also on the table during our last discussion in here. You said yourself, 'It'll be expensive.' You did not say, 'It's out of the question.' We are within our rights to make such a request."

Again the stare and the brief check back to Palmer, who looked helpless.

Then Gray actually smiled. "I lied," he said with a chuckle.

"Okay? I *lied*. Your client is going nowhere." His voice was so calm that, somehow, it was even more unsettling than when it was raised. "He'll be right here, on our field, in our stadium, playing his heart out for *me*." Gray tapped himself in the chest with his forefinger. "And you," he went on, turning that same finger outward, "you slimy little pile of Brooklyn shit, are going to be *standing on the unemployment line before this season is over!*"

This last line launched the inevitable explosion. Gray jumped out of his seat and leaned forward, the redness from his neck having spread to his entire face.

But Sturtz, with an inner peace that Palmer couldn't help but admire, simply said, "No, I'm sorry. That's not how it's going to be." Finally, he unzipped his bag, and from inside he took out a single sheet of paper of his own.

"This is a tender offer from the San Francisco 49ers for T. J.'s services. As you will see"—he produced another copy and tossed one to each of them—"it is quite generous in terms of compensation. Draft picks, established players, even some cash to cover your losses." Sturtz waited just long enough to add, "But, as you'll see, the latter isn't much since . . . well, since he's not being paid very much in the first place."

Palmer waited for Gray to pick up his copy. When it became obvious he had no intention of doing so, the GM took his own and began reading. It took all of about thirty seconds to realize the 49ers wanted Brookman very badly and were willing to do damn near anything to get him.

"Until we get this issue resolved," Sturtz said, purposely choosing a phrase from their original meeting, "I'm afraid I'm going to have to insist that T. J. sit out."

Gray was impossible to read at this point. There was murder in his eyes, but no other signs of what lay under the surface. The silence returned to the room. A few seconds passed, then a few more. It stretched into a minute, then the next.

"If you continue to do this," Gray said at last, "I will sit your boy and take one of the others. I will sit him *all year and take one of the others!*"

"Oh, I doubt that."

"What?"

"You don't *have* any of the others. You ordered Dale Greenwood to cut them this morning. Or don't you remember? Jermaine Hamilton, Corey Reese, Daimon Foster—they all received their walking papers bright and early. You remember those guys, right? The ones you used to try to screw me and my client? They're gone. *Gone.* The moment you sent them packing, they were free to do whatever they wished." Sturtz checked his watch. "By my calculations, Foster should be inking his deal with Kansas City right about now. Hamilton is in discussions with Washington. And Reese— well. . . ."

The redness in Gray's face faded temporarily and was replaced by a distinct lack of coloration. Pale and ashen, he looked sick, drained out. He realized he'd been beaten. Sturtz had waited in the bushes, patiently, to spring this trap. It had been planned all along. He had effectively calculated the coach's own plan and, figuring that information into the equation, formed one of his own. He sat in the shadows until Gray removed all of his own options, then used that as the noose with which to hang him.

When the redness returned, it did so in accompaniment to the greatest explosion of temper Palmer or Sturtz had ever witnessed.

It made George Brett's famous pine-tar outburst look like a pleasant conversation between friends. For the next ninety seconds, Gray covered the entire catalog of English expletives and profanities (if a censor had been there, he would've simply held down the bleep-out button for the duration) and threw out enough spittle to polish an off-road vehicle after a muddy day in the woods.

"Hey, take it easy, Alan," Palmer said. "You're going to give yourself a—"

"I'm going to finish you," Gray said at the end, snarling and pointing as his chest heaved from exhaustion. "I'm going to break you like a goddamn—"

Then a fourth voice entered the conversation. "You are going to do no such thing, Alan." It was just as measured as Barry Sturtz's, but it had a bit more impact on the recipient.

All heads turned to Dorland Kenner, standing in the doorway.

No one said anything. No one knew *what* to say. The three men at the table were frozen in space and time, as if in a photograph that had been pasted into a scrapbook with the caption "Tense Times at Team Headquarters."

"Dorland?" Gray said, "What the f— What are you doing here?"

Kenner came into the room and held his hand out to Sturtz. "Barry, always a pleasure to see you."

Sturtz stood and, almost subconsciously, buttoned and smoothed his blazer. "Hello, Mr. Kenner. How are you?"

"Fine, Barry. Please call me Dorland."

"Oh, sure."

Then, to Gray, Kenner said, "So what's happening here? A bit of a disagreement, it seems."

Gray put on his best ass-kisser's smile. "A little bit, but we're working it out."

"Are you? It doesn't sound that way to me. From what I've heard, you are threatening, not compromising."

Gray laughed. "Well, this is the way these things are done, Dorland. Sometimes you need to—"

"No, Alan," Kenner said flatly, his voice never rising a decibel, "this is not the way these things are done. Not here."

"Uh, excuse me, sir, but I might know a little bit more about this than you, if you don't mind my saying so. I have been—"

"I appreciate your concern for my feelings," Kenner said, "but I *do* mind. I mind very much. In fact, I mind many things that you've been doing to this team lately."

"What?" Gray replied, and Palmer couldn't help notice that a bit of the anger was creeping back into his voice. *Uh-oh.*

"Alan, my father was a shrewd businessman. He knew how to get things done. He studied a situation, considered all angles, and made decisions. They didn't always make everyone happy, but they were fair decisions, and people understood why he made them. He did not manipulate, he did not coerce, and he did not *threaten*."

"I wasn't exactly threat—"

"Don't insult me. That's exactly what you were doing."

"Well, that's how I operate," Gray said, and this time he didn't bother candy-coating the delivery.

"Fine. Then you are welcome to operate elsewhere."

Gray's eyes narrowed. "Excuse me?"

"You're fired."

Another frozen-in-time moment, and even Sturtz looked stunned.

"You may clear out your office at once."

"You're joking, right?"

"I am not."

"This is fucking ridiculous."

"What was that?"

"No one fires a head coach right before the regular season starts. It's insane."

"No, here's what's insane—we've had nothing but failure since you came here. Complete and utter failure. Now, allowing you to run this team for another season—that would be insane. The way I see it, I can leave you in your current position purely for the sake of observing tradition, and that would all but guarantee another losing season. Or I could give someone else your job, and maybe he'd do better. Maybe he wouldn't, but with you I *know* what's going to happen. So, is making a change now really insane? I don't see it that way at all. Maybe it is unprecedented—but it's still smart. Keeping you here another minute, *that's* insane."

Gray scanned the room, realized he was surrounded by enemies, and said, "You can go to hell. I'm not taking one step out of this—"

Without hesitation, Kenner turned toward the open doorway and said, "Don?"

The Turk appeared, grim as ever. "Yes?"

"Would you be kind enough to show Coach Gray to his office, watch him pack up his things, then escort him to his car?"

"You bet." Don Blumenthal looked to Alan Gray—the man who had treated him like a dog, had insulted him in every way and as publicly as possible—and managed his first smile in a long time.

For an instant, Gray looked terrified. Then, as Blumenthal came around the table, Gray said, "You've got big problems here, junior. Problems that you won't be able to handle without me."

Kenner, setting his hands into his pockets, said wearily, "I'm sure we'll manage, Alan."

On his way out of the room, the Turk holding him by the arm, Gray continued with "Do you know you have a mole? Someone is leaking everything you do to the press! I would've found the sonofabitch, but now I'm glad I didn't!"

"We'll take care of it."

"Have a good time dealing with the Barry Sturtzes of the world!" Gray went on, even though his voice was dying in the hallway. "You'll get nowhere without me! Nowhere!"

Kenner took a deep breath and rubbed his temples. "That didn't go particularly well."

"No, you had to do it," Chet Palmer said swiftly. "He's been a loose cannon around here for years. You should've seen—"

"You, too," Kenner cut him off. "Get your things and go."

Palmer seemed genuinely bewildered. "Me? But—"

"I'm not arguing the point, Chet. You have put us deep into a hole with the salary cap. Unbelievably deep." Kenner went on to quote figures and structures from contracts that Palmer didn't think he even knew about. It was like the guy had been living inside his head. *But I thought he didn't know any of this.*

"And you lied to me, too," Kenner went on, "on many, many occasions. You covered for Gray"—he said this in a way that sounded as though Gray had already been gone for years, which Palmer found chilling—"and you made mistakes you tried to hide. You damaged this organization with no thought for anyone but yourself. I don't tolerate that with any of my people. Now go."

Palmer paused for a few more seconds, thought about trying to rally to defend his position, then realized it was hopeless.

Without another word, he rose, leaving all his paperwork exactly where it was, and walked out.

Now it was just the two of them.

The room had become eerily still. The hanging blinds were half turned, so a fair amount of sunlight was slanting in. A few birds were chirping outside, happily oblivious in the way that nature's creatures are to the boundless idiocy of men.

With Sturtz as his riveted audience, Kenner pulled out a chair and sat down next to him. "First of all, I want to apologize to you and your client on behalf of myself, my family, and all the good people in this organization for the way the two of you have been treated."

Was this really happening? Barry Sturtz wondered. Being understandably gun-shy, he thought for a moment this might be a ploy of some kind, where the higher echelon takes control of the out-of-hand situation and masterfully brings it back to the boundaries of reality.

But such fears were quickly assuaged when Kenner said, "I have been studying your client's contract. I have studied it thoroughly, and I have also been studying his performance since he joined this team, and it seems to me he is a remarkable young man."

Sturtz, feeling like he was caught in an episode of *The Twilight Zone,* said, "Yes, he is."

"I am deeply appreciative of his devotion, his effort, his discipline, and his passion. He has carried himself beautifully, both on and off the field."

"I agree."

"He is an asset to this organization, and I think it's about time we made that clear in some substantial way."

"Such as?"

"Such as a new contract. One that you and I will forge together, here and now."

Again Sturtz was unable to find his vocabulary. This was bordering on the surreal. Somewhere in his mind he thought about how he was going to report this to T. J., then dismissed the idea because there was simply no believable way to do it.

"I am—we are very grateful."

Kenner waved this off. "It never should have happened in the first place." He rose again and put his hands back into his pockets. "I blame myself as much as I do Alan Gray and Chet Palmer. Gray was at least partially correct—I didn't know enough about how this whole thing worked. When my father passed away, I was entrusted with the task of running this club. He believed in me, and I have let him down so far. I've been trying to juggle ten balls at once. I thought I could do it, with my highbrow education and my family name." He began walking around the room as if taking a stroll on a nice day. "But the truth is, I wasn't ready for it. Too much too fast. A man in my position has to have people under him he can trust. I thought I could trust Gray and Palmer, but I was naive. I see now what type of men they really are. It all comes down to the quality of the individual. I let down the people of this organization, I let down my father, and I let down the fans."

"Well . . . it happens," Sturtz said, amazed that he was part of this remarkable epiphany. "No one is immune."

Staring out the window, Kenner replied, "I know that, and I

know that mistakes are only valuable if you learn from them." He turned back. "And so, as of today, I'm putting this team back on the road to success."

"That's going to be kind of tough, isn't it? You don't even have a head coach or a general manager anymore."

"Yes, I do. Not long after you leave this room, you will learn not only of Alan Gray and Chet Palmer's dismissals, but also of Dale Greenwood's promotion."

"Dale Gr— Wow."

"He's been a faithful contributor from the start. I should've hired him into the position before, and I thought about it. In spite of our lukewarm record these past few years, do you know how fantastic his statistics have been?"

"Yes, I do. T. J. loves him."

Kenner was nodding. "Many people do, and that's what we need—good, quality people."

"So what about the offensive coordinator position?"

"O'Leary."

"Really?"

"Yes. I learned just last week that many of Dale's best plays were designed, either in part or in whole, by Jim. He is more than capable of handling the job. He has the smarts, he has the years. He's the man."

"That's great," Sturtz said. "T. J. thinks the world of him, too." Then, thinking of his client's future with the team, he added, "But then who'll be coaching the tight ends?"

Kenner smiled. "I was hoping you'd ask that."

He sat down at the big table, opposite Sturtz—in the same chair Gray had occupied earlier, which Sturtz found comically symbolic—and tapped the intercom button on the asterisk-shaped conference phone.

"Jodi?"

"Yes?"

"Do you have Mr. Nolan on the line?"

"Yes, he's here."

"Kindly forward the call now."

"Just a sec."

There was a pause, during which Sturtz was trying to figure out what Nolan, a fellow agent located in the Midwest, had to do with this whole thing.

"Hello?" came Nolan's voice.

"Matt?"

"Yes."

"It's Dorland Kenner."

"Yes, hello."

"Is Jermaine with you?"

"Yes, sir, he's right here."

"Very good. Tell me, have you been successful in finding a team?"

"Er, no. No, we haven't."

"I'm very sorry to hear that."

"So are we."

"I'm going to ask a question, Matt, and I'd like an honest answer from you."

"Sure."

"Do you feel you will be successful in finding one eventually?"

Another pause, and then, "Well, it doesn't look good. We'll keep trying, but the age issue, as you know. . . ."

"Again, I'm very sorry. Jermaine?"

"Yes?"

"I want you to know that, whatever happens, you've had a superb career on the field, and you should be very proud of yourself."

"Thanks . . . thank you."

Kenner looked at Sturtz and smiled again. "I know how hard it is to accept change, how tough it can be to get used to new things."

"Uh, yes. Yes, it is."

"But sometimes change can be good."

"Sure, sure." Hamilton, Sturtz thought, must be wondering, *Where the hell is this going?*

"Well, I want to make you an offer, and I'd like you to think about it very carefully."

"An offer?"

"Yes."

"To play?"

"Not exactly."

"Oh. Okay. . . ."

"Should you be unsuccessful in your search for a spot on someone's roster, I'd like you to come back to the Giants and be our new tight ends coach."

"Are you serious?"

Kenner smiled. "Yes, of course. You know we've had some changes around here today."

"Yeah, I heard."

"Today was the final cut, and . . . well, I did some cutting of my own. Some cutting that needed to be done a long time ago."

"It sounds like it."

"Yes, and now we've got some room on our coaching staff—room for someone with experience, a passion for the game, and a desire to be out there, every day, in the thick of it. What do you say? Wanna come help us out?"

There was another pause, and Sturtz thought he heard a faint "Holy shit" on the other end.

"Well, yeah. Sure. I'd love that."

"Are you certain?"

"Yes, I am."

"Great. Okay, let me know by the end of the week."

"I will."

"Thanks. And thank you, Matt."

"You're welcome."

Kenner ended the call with a tap of the button and pushed the phone away, as if being close to it for too long might give him the flu.

"What about the others?" Sturtz asked. "Reese and Foster?"

"I am already negotiating a contract with Foster's agent. A three-year deal, I hope."

"Really?"

"Really."

"But don't you already have two tight ends? T. J. and Maxw—"

"Glenn Maxwell has been released," Kenner told him. "I don't want that kind of nonsense here. His behavior. . . ."

"I heard about it. Bad stuff."

"It is. And as for Corey Reese, I'm sure you know about that situation as well."

Everyone did by now—courtesy, as usual, of Greg Bolton and ESPN. As they feared, Reese's knee was shredded for a second time. Multiple MRIs revealed damage far too extensive to repair through conventional means. Several surgeries would be required, plus at least another year of rehabilitation. He would walk again, the doctors said—but his playing days were over. One more injury like that and he'd be in a wheelchair for the rest of his life.

"A real tragedy," Kenner added. "A shame."

"It is."

"But let's focus on T. J. for now. Let's get to work."

Kenner hit the intercom one more time.

"Jodi?"

"Yes?"

"Can you bring in the paperwork I put together for the Brookman deal?"

"Right away."

"Thanks."

Kenner rose and took off his jacket, hanging it on the back of his chair. Then he loosened his tie. "Okay, Barry," he said with a chuckle, "get your boxing gloves on."

33

Six satisfied men sat around a big table at Gossen's Fishhouse, one of the trendiest new restaurants on Manhattan's Upper West Side. It was going on midnight, and three of them had to be up early the next day to prepare for the first match of the year, an away game against the Colts. But the food was too good, the drink too plentiful, and the mood too high to stop now.

"Here's to Daimon Foster," Freddie Friedman said to his newest client, raising his glass. Foster had been awarded a three-year, $1.7 million contract, almost half of which was guaranteed and included a signing bonus of a quarter of a million. His girlfriend had screamed into the phone, and his mother cried for half an hour. The search for a new home would begin the Tuesday following the game.

"Thanks," Foster said, holding a champagne flute for the first time in his life. "Thanks for everything."

"And to us," Sturtz said with a more pedestrian bottle of Heineken.

Brookman, who'd been sitting next to Foster all night, getting to know the young man who would be standing opposite him on the line many times in the years ahead, grabbed his own beer and did likewise. "To us," Brookman said, "proving once again that he who has the biggest set of nuts always gets the job done."

There was a round of laughter, including a few snickers from other diners who weren't so tight-assed that they couldn't appreciate a little schoolboy vulgarity.

Matt Nolan, Jermaine Hamilton's agent, said, "And kudos to Dorland Kenner for doing the right thing." Nolan was dressed in what Sturtz had already called "the ugliest damn sportsjacket I've ever seen in my life," a black-and-blue plaid.

Hamilton was still reeling from the shock of it all. It wasn't so much from the opportunity that had been dropped into his lap as from the realization that he'd never even thought of a coaching position as a way of staying involved. He felt like an idiot, although he had the good sense not to say as much.

"You know, it almost makes you believe in the future," Brookman observed.

"It does," Nolan said, nodding. "I think this team will finally get back on track."

"What about Gray?" Foster asked. "Anyone know what's going to happen to him?" He had surprised himself by feeling a little bit sorry for the guy. Not so much because he'd been fired, but because he'd reached the point where he felt comfortable doing the things he did in the first place. A sad story.

"He's interviewing at a few Division II colleges," Sturtz said. "He knows a lot of people. A master politician like him will find a home. Guys like him always do." The others grumbled. They felt he should be tarred, feathered, and hung from a lamppost.

"And what about Corey? Has anyone heard from him?"

"Not in two days," Friedman said. "In fact, I'm glad you reminded me, because I had something for him." He reached back and retrieved his cell phone from a small leather holster.

The others picked at their food and waited. Friedman let it ring more than a dozen times, then gave up. No answering machine, either.

"Oh, well," he said, closing the phone and setting it back in its case. "I'll try him later."

"A toast to him, then," Sturtz said.

"Good idea," Friedman agreed. "To Corey Reese."

They drank up, and then it was time for dessert. Friedman announced that he'd be picking up the tab, but Nolan and Sturtz insisted that no, *they'd* get it.

A halfhearted argument ensued.

In the end, the mole was never caught. He simply disappeared.

Greg Bolton was sad to see him go. He wasn't about to complain—the guy had given him the kind of insider information a reporter only dreams about. Still, it was a bitter pill to swallow.

Sitting in front of his laptop in a hotel room in San Diego, Bolton saw his IM screen pop up while he was getting his butt kicked in an online poker tournmanent.

CMC88: Are you there, Greg?

He dropped his pizza onto its plate, which was lying on the bed next to him.

GEB@ESPN: Yes, I'm here. What's going on?

CMC88: Nothing new. Just wanted to say thank you and let you know that I'm signing off now.

Signing off?

GEB@ESPN: What do you mean?

CMC88: I mean we're all done here. I don't have anything left to report.

GEB@ESPN: So that's it? No more information?

CMC88: I'm afraid not.

GEB@ESPN: But wait—what about future stuff? What about the regular season? And the draft?

CMC88: Sorry, Greg. Maybe someday, but not now. Not for a while. Take care.

GEB@ESPN: No, please—don't do this.

No response.

GEB@ESPN: Hey, are you still there?

No response.

Bolton waited a few more minutes, then accepted that he was sending messages into dead space. He'd had a feeling this was going to happen soon. It really did suck out loud, but hell. . . . He'd been lucky. He just wished he could've found out *why*. Why him? Why then? And what kind of axe did this guy have to grind? He'd single-handedly brought down the most dysfunctional, degenerate, corrupt coaches in the league, which was a remarkable thing when you thought about it. Bolton supposed he would never know who it was. All there was left to do was laugh, so he did. *What a strange, strange time we live in,* he thought.

Then he went back to his pizza and his poker.

Roughly twenty-eight hundred miles away, in an elegant town house not far from where the three tight ends and their agents were having their dinner, Greg Bolton's informant went through the steps necessary to eradicate his Instant Messenger account from existence, then erase all traces of his Internet presence. He had learned how to do this, ironically enough, from a hacker's Web site. His tech skills had always been limited, but since this was important, he took the time to figure out what needed to be done. Now he'd made a clean getaway. Most important—his objective had been attained.

Satisfied, Dorland Kenner turned off the laptop, closed the lid, and went to bed.

34

He'd been refusing all calls, all e-mails, and all visitors. He went into a cocoon and stayed there. Nothing mattered in the outside world. For Corey Reese, it was time to feel sorry for himself—sorry and angry. He was tired of the fight against shitty luck. Tired of being defeated, of being on the wrong side of the odds. He had come to realize that he'd been swimming against the current all his life. Nothing had ever come easy. Even when he did manage to chalk up a victory, it came at such a heavy price that it was impossible to enjoy. It had all been an illusion. He saw that now—saw that he had a destiny, and, ultimately, it was one of failure. He'd done what was required of him. He played the game and took the shots, and when he was down and out the first time, he said courageously, "I'll be back." That had become his mantra after the first injury—*I'll be back.*

But he wouldn't be back this time. Whatever forces of cruelty controlled the universe, Reese had clearly angered them by having the temerity to beat them before. He was being defiant, and that wouldn't do. People like that needed to be punished. They needed to be forced back into the box that had been built for them. That's what the plan had been for him all along—frustration, anger, bitterness. He finally understood that. No matter how hard he worked and how much he sacrificed, he would never have the things he truly wanted. It didn't matter that they were noble things, decent and honorable and selfless things. It didn't matter that he wanted to hand his family the world, provide for his children in ways that his own parents had never been able to. It didn't matter that he never took performance-enhancing drugs or that he never once cheated on his wife. He knew guys who did both—and plenty more—and they were living the Dream. Not him. The verdict was in, and he was out. Simply being a good man, once again, had produced nothing.

Inevitably, the idea of suicide surfaced. From a purely logical standpoint, it would work—the payout would guarantee Jeanine and the kids more than twenty million. There was no mention of it in the policy, no out-clause for the rich insurance company and their lawyers to use against her. Dead was dead. In one stroke, they would be out of debt and able to live well for years to come. She would learn from their past financial mistakes. Their money managers would invest well. Hell, she might even meet somebody else in the league and work her way into some *serious* money. She'd be fine. The kids would be fine. They'd have the life they deserved.

And in the end, I would win. Finally, I would win.

But could he bring himself to do it?

Jeanine Reese came through the door with the kids a few hours later. Their son fled to the rec room to play Xbox. Their daughter plopped down on the couch to watch Nickelodeon. She called out to her husband several times but received no answer. She'd been worried about him, but at the same time she'd been trying to give him some space. She'd stopped at the supermarket on the way back, and the cold stuff had to be stored in the fridge. Once that was done, she went on a house-hunt to find him.

She started in the gym in their basement, then the rec room. "Is Daddy down here with you?" she asked her son, who, controller in both hands, only shook his head. Then throughout the first floor. It was odd—she didn't even get a sense of his presence, yet his car was in the driveway. *He's here somewhere.*

On the second floor, the door to the main bathroom was open, as was the door to each of the kids' rooms. The only one closed led to their bedroom. Maybe he was sleeping.

Not wanting to wake him, she opened the door slowly. It was very dark, and unusually cold for early September. Corey had never liked the cold. She had a sudden feeling in her gut that something was not right. She tried to find him in the darkness, but her eyes weren't adjusting fast enough. Just a roomful of shapes and shadows.

She flicked on the light, and that was when she found him—lying on his side.

She shook him once, and he didn't move. Then she spotted the pill bottle on the nightstand. Her heart started pounding. She shook him again . . . and again.

Trembling, she turned to go back out. There was a phone in the hallway.

Then her husband called out groggily, "Hey."

She stopped in the doorway and spun around. He was trying to get up on his elbows.

"Sorry, I was out like a light. This pain medication is unbelievable."

Jeanine Reese laughed once, and a tear rolled down her face.

"By the way, Freddie called before," he went on, unable to see her clearly. "What do you think about the idea of me in a broadcasting job?"

She thought it was a great idea. So did he.

And life went on.